Sidney Chambers
and
The Persistence of Love

The GRANTCHESTER MYSTERIES
SIDNEY CHAMBERS
AND
The Persistence of Love

JAMES RUNCIE

BLOOMSBURY

LONDON · OXFORD · NEW YORK · NEW DELHI · SYDNEY

Bloomsbury Publishing
An imprint of Bloomsbury Publishing Plc

50 Bedford Square
London
WC1B 3DP
UK

1385 Broadway
New York
NY 10018
USA

www.bloomsbury.com

First published in Great Britain 2017

This is a work of fiction. Names and characters are the product of the
author's imagination and any resemblance to actual persons,
living or dead, is entirely coincidental.

British Library Cataloguing-in-Publication Data
A catalogue record for this book is available from the British Library.

ISBN: HB: 978-1-4088-7902-3
          ePub: 978-1-4088-7903-0

2 4 6 8 10 9 7 5 3

Typeset by Integra Software Services Pvt. Ltd.
Printed and bound in Great Britain by CPI Group (UK) Ltd, Croydon CR0 4YY

MIX
Paper from
responsible sources
FSC
www.fsc.org
FSC® C020471

For Marilyn

And in memory of my mother and father

Dem Leben sind Grenzen gesetzt,
die Liebe ist grenzenlos.

Life has limits, but
love has no bounds.

Contents

The Bluebell Wood

Saturday 8 May, 1971

M AY WAS SIDNEY'S BEST-LOVED month. After an overture of daffodils and tulips, the summer orchestra tuned to the sound of blackbirds, wood pigeons and the returning swifts. Each day outpaced its predecessor with new provision: an acceleration of green, a stretching light. The smell of wild garlic rose up in the hedgebanks. Warmth returned, and Hildegard served up the first asparagus of the year, with salmon, early peas, mint and new potatoes, followed by Sidney's favourite fruit: rhubarb, poached with ginger and honey.

Now aged seven and a half, Anna was just finishing her first year of Junior School and she was in the middle of a wild-flower project inspired by W. Keble Martin's *Concise British Flora in Colour*. Two years before, she had written to the author for advice, and the ninety-year-old priest had replied on a postcard to say that the natural world offered endless discovery, infinite possibilities. If she learned to appreciate the landscape around her then she would never be bored or lonely. Curiosity would keep her young.

Father and daughter were out walking through Nine Acre Wood by the River Ouse with Byron, their beloved

Labrador, alongside them. They ambled past the oak and ash trees, tall by a stream edged with swathes of ramsons and marsh marigolds, then went on through high cow parsley and flowering crab apple until they reached a sunlit clearing filled with early wood violets, herb Robert, meadow buttercups and sanicle.

This was a time for simple pleasures; a father, a lively young daughter and their dog out together in the countryside. A fringe had just been cut into Anna's short blonde hair and she was dressed tomboyishly, in dungarees over a long-sleeved yellow T-shirt. She put the flowers she had gathered in a hessian shopping bag: pink campion, ragged Robin, shepherd's-purse and germander speedwell. She liked getting home and making arrangements in glasses of water and painting them before putting them in her new press. Sometimes she was hesitant about doing so. She didn't like the flowers dying sooner than they needed to.

They stopped to rest, taking in the next vista and removing the sticky willy that had attached itself to their legs. They laughed when Byron attempted to chase a squirrel up a tree. He was so busy looking up that he ran straight into the trunk.

It was only when they were checking and consoling him that they noticed a strange shape under a group of silver birch ahead. By the stream, and next to a clump of monkshood and a swathe of bluebells that had yet to come into full flower, was the body of a man. He was not lying in the comfortable arrangement of someone asleep or at rest but the skewed position of a person who had either suffered a heart attack or been felled by an assailant. He lay on his front, the bulk of his face hidden by an Australian bush hat, and he was wearing a well-worn anorak, jeans and hiking boots. A long grey ponytail, tied with an elastic band, stretched across his right shoulder and by his gloved hands (*Gloves*, Sidney thought, *in May?*) lay a basket of wild flowers.

'Is he dead, Daddy?'

'He might be sleeping.'

'I think he's dead.'

'Stay back, darling.'

'I want to see him.'

Sidney knelt down and checked for signs of life. There were none.

'What are we going to do?' Anna asked.

'The first thing is to pray for him.'

'So he is dead?'

'I am afraid so.'

'I'm scared.'

'Don't be.'

'Is he in heaven?'

'I don't know.'

'Aren't you supposed to know?'

Any words spoken in the silence seemed an affront to the dead.

Sidney stretched out his left arm and gathered his daughter to him. She knelt down beside him, put her hands together and closed her eyes.

Her father prayed: 'Go forth upon thy journey from this world, O Christian soul, in the name of God the Father Almighty who created thee; in the name of Jesus Christ who suffered for thee; in the name of the Holy Spirit who

3

strengthened thee; in communion with the blessed saints, and aided by angels and archangels, and all the armies of the heavenly host. May thy portion this day be in peace, and thy dwelling in the heavenly Jerusalem. Amen.'

Sidney turned to his daughter. 'We need to fetch help. Let's see if we can go back to the road and find a phone box.'

'Do you know who he is, Daddy?'

The man seemed familiar but Sidney couldn't quite place him. Just before he walked away, he remembered the gloves and looked at the basket the man had been carrying. It contained blue drifts of wolfsbane interspersed with old man's beard, sun spurge, racemes of yellow laburnum, black bryony, corncockle, foxgloves and cuckoo pint. There was a small bunch of creamy yellow euphonium-shaped flowers with deep purple-netted veins and broad leaves with white sticky hairs. Sidney realised it must be henbane, part of the deadly nightshade family, and asked himself one perplexing question: why were all the plants the man had been gathering poisonous?

His old friend and colleague, Inspector Keating, arrived within the hour. 'Take Anna and the dog home,' he said. 'This is no place for a child.'

Sidney had tried to distract his daughter by collecting more wild flowers as they waited near the roadside, but it was hard to think of anything other than the drama of the dead man. He wondered how often she would ask him about the discovery of the body and whether he could downplay the situation, concentrating on other matters, pretending nothing unusual had happened in the hope that Anna was still so young that she might one day think the whole thing had been a dream.

When they got home and told Hildegard, all in a rush so that it was hard to take in, Anna asked again if the man would go to heaven and what it was like.

'It's a place without fear, my darling,' said Sidney, 'where people who have worried so much in life find a happiness that they had never been able to imagine.'

'Why can't they? If they *could* imagine it, wouldn't more people want to go there?'

Although it was possible the man had died from natural causes, and there was probably a good enough reason for the plants he had been gathering, Sidney could not help but brood on the nature of fate, the chance of discovery and the possible sequence of events that had led up to that moment. He went to his study where he began to pray, seeking some kind of guidance, the beginning of understanding. Was it a sin to be so suspicious so frequently, or was he using the natural intuition that God had given him? Was his role as an accidental detective making him less loving and less effective as a priest?

Byron slept under the kitchen table as Hildegard tried to distract their daughter from what she had seen with cooking and baking. She taught Anna how to bake *Leipziger Lerche*, the family's favourite German cupcake. Sidney referred to them as 'posh Bakewell tarts' and they cooked them in the same way Hildegard's mother had always done, roasting the almonds in the oven before wrapping them in a towel and bashing them to bits with a rolling pin. Anna helped to fold, knead and roll out the pastry before cutting it out and lining the special moulds they had brought back from their last trip to Germany. She placed a little slip of marzipan and a dollop of apricot jam in the bottom of each case and her mother let her ladle in scoops of the filling. Hildegard then re-rolled the remaining pastry and cut it into narrow lengths. Anna laid two strips into a cross on the top of each filled case, creating a partial lid, before they were put in the oven for twenty minutes. As the buns baked, Hildegard went over to the piano in the drawing room and made up songs with her daughter. Sidney smiled as he watched how lovingly and cleverly his wife distracted Anna from the memory of the dead body under a tree.

That night he tucked his daughter in. He sat on the edge of the bed, finding room amidst the dolls, teddies and knitted animals. Anna sniffed at her special little rabbit as her father read from *Tom's Midnight Garden*. They had reached that part of the story where the hero can no longer find his dream garden and his friend Hatty has disappeared. What is real and who are the ghosts? Anna asked. Was the man they had found today already a ghost?

Outside it began to rain. Sidney could not help but feel responsible for bringing Anna's childhood closer to an end with the first sight of a dead body. When they reached the closing of the chapter, and Anna was about to snuggle down to sleep, she stopped to listen to the rain against the hard dark glass.

'Look, Daddy,' she said, 'the windows are crying.'

Two days later Inspector Keating came up to Ely for a couple of pints in the Prince Albert. The dead man had been identified as Lenny Goddard, a local folk-singer, poet, forager, painter, decorator, real-ale drinker, knife sharpener and odd-job man. He lived on a houseboat on the Great Ouse, and he was married to one of Sidney's former parishioners.

'Stella Goddard. She says you know her.'

'I do, now you come to mention it. I think she's his third wife. She must be quite a bit younger than Lenny. She used to be a folk-singer too. I must have heard them sing together at some point, but it was in pubs or at summer parties when I was probably concentrating on something else. I thought I'd seen him before but I just didn't recognise him. He's aged quite badly.'

'Well, now he's died quite badly. I didn't know you were such a folkie. You're normally more of a jazz man.'

'I don't mind the odd ballad. I just think you need to watch out when they put their fingers over one ear.'

'Or poison in each other's stomachs.'

'You are suspicious?'

'I know *you* are. You mentioned the flowers he was gathering. We've had them checked and you're right. There's enough there to kill a whole village.'

'So I suppose you'd like me to ask a few questions, Geordie?'

'Word will get round. People will come and express their sympathy. It's been a horrible thing for Anna, a shocking discovery. You must be perplexed.'

'I am.'

'You can't understand it. You'll have to go and see the widow, and perhaps some of the people closest to Lenny.

7

They'll be upset. You'll be upset. Things will come out. You know the drill.'

Sidney went first to Anna's school to tell them what had happened and ask them to make allowances if she behaved a little oddly in the coming days. Her form teacher, Tom Tranton, was a small and portly botanist who had instigated the annual tradition of the Junior School wild-flower project and he affectionately referred to his pupils as 'the seedlings'. He sported a pair of dark-green corduroy trousers and a mustard-coloured pullover that looked as if it hadn't been taken off since 1954. This was worn under an old tweed jacket with so many rips and tears that he often joked that he slept outdoors. ('I've just come from the hedge! Woke up next to a lovely little grasshopper. We had quite a conversation. They do love a natter.')

Like a primary-school Keble Martin, Tom Tranton was famous amongst his former pupils for meticulous botanical drawings on the blackboard that displayed plant life and the process of photosynthesis. Everyone thought it a shame when he wiped the board clean.

'That is nature for you, boys and girls. So much of life disappears in the winter. But it all comes back in the spring. Remember that. There may be death, but there is also life. Always.'

As a not-so-secret atheist, Tranton held his prayer book upside down in chapel as a tribute to Darwin, and was keen to tell his pupils that all human beings, no matter what their status, were made up of the same constituent elements.

'Even the Archbishop of Canterbury,' he insisted, 'is sixty per cent water.'

Born in 1910, he was now teaching the grandchildren of his first pupils and he had introduced Lenny Goddard to botany in the late 1930s.

'I showed him how to dig up horseradish; even though it used to be illegal to do that round here. That boy was a natural chemist.'

Sidney asked how easy it would be to make poison from the flowers Lenny had been collecting.

'I thought you were here to talk about Anna?'

'I might as well kill two birds with one stone.'

'You know that's not technically possible, don't you?'

'Could you answer my question?'

Tranton was unperturbed. 'Monkshood is one of the most poisonous plants in the country. Henbane contains toxic tropane alkaloids that can dampen the nervous system and cause paralysis. It's quite easy to cause a lot of damage if you know your chemistry. But it takes a bit of work to kill someone.'

'And would Lenny Goddard be capable of that?'

'I should say so. But it's not in his nature. He was a gentle soul. Popular too. I can't imagine him having any enemies, if you're thinking along those lines. His only vice was that he was too easily led astray.'

'Might he have been gathering them for someone else to make the poison on his behalf ?'

'You are ascribing very malign intentions to the man, Mr Chambers. Perhaps the flowers were intended as decoration, or for something entirely different?'

'It seems an odd selection.'

'Lenny Goddard was not the type of man to go round poisoning people. He was a folk-singer and a bit of a hippy. I can't imagine anyone wanting to harm him, or him wanting to hurt anyone else for that matter.'

'Then why those flowers?'

'Perhaps you'd better ask his wife.'

'Do you know something I don't, Tom?'

'Rather a lot, probably. Is there anything specific you have in mind?'

The Goddards' houseboat was moored south of Ely, on the edge of Wicken Fen, at Pope's Corner. Lenny had taken it out of the water to re-blacken the hull after an eel had wrapped itself around the bow's thruster tube. Removed from the river, the boat looked as if it too was in the middle of a post-mortem.

Sidney wondered if the sense of absence could spread through a boat as quickly as it could fill a house. He told Lenny's widow that he had come to listen and to offer any support he could. He spoke to her about the pain of loss; that no matter how much we might fear or anticipate death, its finality always silenced us and reminded us of our own mortality. Grief could not be rushed. Attention had to be paid.

As Stella Goddard made him a cup of tea, Sidney surveyed the possessions that must have belonged to the dead man – guitars, books, sheet music, clothes hanging out to dry, a display of wild flowers, a half-finished painting of a sunset, Tupperware boxes filled with herbs, and a hookah pipe on the table. There was a dog bowl and three cans of Pedigree Chum, but no sign of an animal on deck.

Stella was smaller than he had remembered, slighter, with paler skin and darker hair, and brown eyes that could soon spark up into argument. She wore a floral blouse with a long denim skirt. It was functional clothing meant for a life on the water, her only concession to fashion being the brown woven-leather espadrille wedges, chosen to give her extra height.

'I've often wondered what it might be like to live on a boat,' said Sidney.

'It's harder work than anyone thinks it is. But once you're used to it you can't imagine living any other way. I'm sorry that you and your daughter discovered the body. I was on a trip downriver. Is she all right?'

'That's kind of you to think of her at a time like this. It's hard to tell. I'm never quite sure what's going on in her head, even though she's only seven.'

'Little girls like their secrets.'

'Have you thought about the funeral? Is there anything I can do?'

'We want a private cremation, and then the ashes scattered in the bluebell wood where he was found. It was his favourite place. I've been thinking a little bit about it. It's almost ironic. Perhaps Lenny had an instinctive fear that he was going to die and went there on purpose?'

'Was he worried about his health?'

'It was bad enough without him worrying about it,' Stella replied. 'Still, it's strange . . .'

'I'm sorry. It's impossible to define a loss at first. I suppose that's why we use the word.'

11

'Lost to decide what to think or do? Lost for something to say? There doesn't seem much point in anything any more. I like to think of him with a smile on his face amidst the wild flowers. Sometimes we used to go out at dawn with the dew on the grass and dance barefoot. Lenny always said that he liked the way I moved. When I was little I wanted to be a ballet dancer.'

'But you didn't become one?'

'My feet grew too big. I've got over it now. Lenny didn't think it mattered – not being what you originally wanted to be. You had to discover what you *could* be instead and be content with that. Anyway, he was never that good a dancer himself. He could never find the right balance. He kept you so tight and close that you could hardly move and then when he loosened up, he let you whirl away from him. That sums him up, I suppose. Never could hold on to him.'

'Perhaps he liked his freedom. Is that why he didn't join you on your trip?'

'He wanted to stay behind and work on the boat. We were going to go on our own adventure in September; just the two of us. I shouldn't have left him alone. He must have gone on the walk for a change of air. I still can't take it in. You kiss your husband goodbye, you don't really think about it at the time, you're too busy with everything else you have to worry about, and then when you come back he's gone and you remember all the things you should have said and all the different ways in which you would have said goodbye if you had known it was going to be for the last time. I can't even remember if I told him that I loved him. "See you!" – I think those were my last words – and he said,

"You're all right, love." Then he smiled. I think I was the first to turn away and look back at the river ahead. The journey. I wish I'd watched him for longer now; waited until he was a speck.'

Stella had been travelling up to the Norfolk Broads on Linda and Tony Clarke's narrowboat while Lenny stayed and did the repairs to his own. They had made their way up the River Ouse to Denver Sluice, past Downham Market and on to King's Lynn.

'We were going to return via the old course of the River Nene, but it's getting a bit shallow there and besides we'd heard the news by then.'

'How did you find out?'

'My sister phoned all the lock-keepers. We were at Salters Lode.'

'So not far?'

'About eighteen miles. It's half an hour in the car but four by boat.'

'Did she come and get you?'

'Linda came with me. Tony took their boat back. She showed the shock more than I did. I think I was too numb. We went to see the body together. He'd always had a lot of colour to his face had Lenny, first from health and then through drink, but that day it was paler than I had ever seen it. I couldn't decide if he was an old man or a little boy. He didn't seem to be anything any more, this body lying in front of me – the figure of a man who had been all that I had ever loved and, at the same time, that infuriating husband I was still learning how to understand. I knew Dr Robinson had told Lenny off about his health often enough – the high blood pressure and the drinking – but I didn't think he'd drop dead like that. There was no warning.'

Well there was, Sidney thought, but now was not the time to talk about the doctor. He realised he should be getting going. Byron had fallen asleep and began to make his little dreaming noises, thinking of all the squirrels that had got away.

'I like your dog,' said Stella.

'He's slowing up a bit, I'm afraid. Arthritis.'

'Labradors can be prone to it. You have to watch their weight.'

'As we all must do, I suppose.' Sidney finished his tea. 'Could I just ask why your husband was out gathering wild flowers? Was that something he did regularly?'

Stella poured out another cup. 'He liked to forage. He went out every day, rain or shine. We ate off the land and the river, fishing and shooting, poaching, snaring and netting. Lenny could get you anything: larks, plovers, game birds, you name it. We tried to live as naturally and as cheaply as possible, just like our grandparents did. As you can probably tell, we don't have much money.'

'Your husband's selection of flowers still seems a bit odd, don't you think? Henbane in particular has a terrible smell. I can't imagine what he would use it for.'

'Do you want me to spell it out?'

At last, Sidney thought. 'If you don't mind . . .'

'You know you can use all those plants for recreational purposes?'

'But they're poisonous.'

'Not if you know what to do with them. Lenny harvested the seeds and the leaves for his special recipes. You'd be

14

surprised what you can do with deadly nightshade just by rubbing it on your skin. I once thought I could fly. We had the police round thinking we had marijuana, but we showed them that we were just mucking around with sage leaves, magic mushrooms and the roots we'd gathered. There was nothing they could do about it. You know that you can get a version of cocaine from scurvy grass? And there's nothing like a cup of tea made from angel's trumpet. That's one of Tony's specialities.'

'Mr Clarke?'

'We make all kinds of stuff. I'd let you try some but I wouldn't like to lead you astray.'

'I think I must have misread the situation, Mrs Goddard.'

'We make our own alcohol too. Linda's an expert on sloe gin, carrot wine and strawberry wheat beer. Perhaps you'd like to try some of that instead?'

Sidney continued. 'Wolfsbane and laburnum, the plants that your husband was gathering, are particularly poisonous. I presume Lenny knew that? I still wonder if he had other intentions?'

'I can't imagine that he did.'

'And those plants aren't stimulants.'

'What are you imagining? You don't think he was planning to do me in, do you? We loved each other.'

Sidney and Geordie took their pints out to the back garden of the Prince Albert and discussed the results of Lenny Goddard's post-mortem. The coroner had found traces of aconitine, a neurotoxin commonly found in monkshood. So strong it was once used as an arrow-tip

15

poison, it had almost certainly been mixed with alcohol, probably a sloe gin.

'The questions are if he was aware he had taken it,' said Geordie, 'whether there's any of it left and who gave it to him.'

'The wife and the best friends are expert distillers.'

'We'll have to ask them.'

'I suppose it could have been a rogue batch.'

'They overdid the stimulants, you mean; an accident?'

'It's possible.'

'I can't imagine Lenny swallowed it all deliberately and then went out for a walk as if nothing was wrong.'

'So I think we can rule out suicide,' said Sidney.

'But surely he would have known something was up?'

'Unless it was a gradual process; a succession of small doses. That's how the Victorian poisoners did it.'

'Still. He must have felt ill. And if he was aware that he had taken poison, then wouldn't he have gone to hospital or made himself sick?' Geordie asked.

'Perhaps he realised what had happened but knew that he still had time to take revenge on whoever did it?'

'How's the wife?'

'She says she loved him and I believe her. But I can't understand why Lenny remained behind; why didn't he go on the boat trip with the rest of them?'

'Perhaps he didn't love his wife as much as she thinks he did? Perhaps there's someone else? I'll make some enquiries.'

'I suppose,' Sidney continued, 'that she still could have killed him if she'd found out about an infidelity?'

'"Love to hatred turned" . . .'

16

'But it could, also, just as easily, have been any one of the others.'

'Or all three of them acting together. Or someone entirely different,' said Geordie. 'Have you spoken to the Clarke couple yet?'

'I have less of an excuse to visit them.'

'I'm sure you can think of something to occupy their time. Rather convenient, don't you think, that the widow and the two best friends are all away from the scene of the crime; a joint alibi if ever there was one?'

'Or a coincidence.'

'I don't believe in them, Sidney. It looks to me like they're trying too hard. Have a word.'

Tony Clarke had lived on or near the water for all his life. His father had been one of the last eel trappers. He used to take his young son out in the early mornings. They set off on a long shallow punt through the fenland mists, moored and then waded through the water, pulling out the old baited wicker traps before submerging the new; each one marked with a willow stake. Tony said he knew every bend in the River Ouse, and his boat was filled with nests, rods, traps and fishing equipment, as well as bottles of home-made alcohol, dried herbs, framed fish, a small aquarium and a pet toad in a tank.

His wife was out walking. 'I think she's gone to the wood where you found Lenny. She's always doing it. She likes to have her thoughts.'

'Leaving you alone.'

'It was how I was brought up, on my own, by the water, paring the willow, waiting for the fish.'

'And did Lenny Goddard like to be alone too? I don't quite understand why he didn't come with you on the trip up to the Wash.'

'He said he wanted to work on his own boat.'

'But couldn't he have done that when he got back?'

'I don't know. He had his moods. Linda said we shouldn't make a fuss but leave him be. Besides, we like Stella. She's company enough.'

'And you didn't offer to stay and help?'

'Lenny liked to do things his way. He wasn't even prepared to share a lock, he was that stubborn. I said it was a bit hypocritical for a communist who believed that everything should be held in common, but he just laughed. In a way, I admired him for it. He was his own man. You didn't ever argue with Lenny.'

'And did people want to?'

'Sometimes; but never on the river. He knew his way around the tides and currents. After my old man died, Lenny was the only person who came close to knowing as much as me. You wouldn't catch him banging his head on a low tunnel, or snagging his boat in a sluice or doing something daft like fall in and drown.'

'So he was a careful man?'

'On the water, yes. He wasn't so good on land.'

'What do you mean?'

'Oh, I don't know.'

'Were you surprised by his death?'

'His health was never that good. Weak heart. Drink. Other stuff you don't need to know about.'

'I think I already do. Your special tea. Some sloe gin, perhaps?'

18

'That's all gone now. Like most of my friends. Most of them are dying off these days. That's why I keep myself to myself. If you practise solitude then you're ready for it when you're the last to go.'

'But, still, you went on the boat trip and Lenny didn't. It seems the wrong way round. I would have thought that you were the one most likely to stay at home.'

'Perhaps I felt like the company?'

'And were the three of you together all the time as you travelled downriver?'

'Not all the time. Sometimes the girls went exploring.'

'Would they ever have had time to get back to Ely without you noticing?'

'Only if they had a car. Why are you asking? I'm not sure why either of them would have wanted to do that.'

'And would you – if you got fed up?'

'There was no need to go off anywhere at any time. The river's all home. We went down the River Lark and moored there so Stella and Linda could look at the meadow near Prickwillow. They liked to give the dog some proper exercise. I think they even did a bit of skinny-dipping.'

'I wasn't sure Mrs Goddard had a dog.'

'Whisky. He was a black retriever. The name must have seemed like a good idea at the time. People in pubs always thought it was funny when they first heard it – *you don't want to let him out on the rocks* – but Lenny soon got bored of the joke.'

'You say he "was" a black retriever.'

'He disappeared. I thought he'd drowned, but Stella said he was an excellent swimmer and someone must have stolen

19

him. God knows who would want to do that. We last saw him at Eau Brink. Annoying he was, always pestering, wanting food, getting in the way. I'm surprised it took them so long to notice he'd gone. So they reported him missing.'

'And never found him?'

'I don't think so.'

'You wouldn't know?'

'Well, I haven't seen him. We looked everywhere; asked all the lock-keepers. I can't imagine anyone stealing him. Perhaps he got run over.'

'So Stella Goddard has lost both her dog and her husband in the space of a few days?'

'That's right.'

'It's strange,' said Sidney, 'that she didn't say anything about the dog. We even talked about them; how Labradors are prone to arthritis. She could have mentioned it then.'

'Perhaps she was too upset?'

'Perhaps she was. But still, it's strange.'

A week later Lenny Goddard's body was released to the crematorium. On the coffin was a spray of white roses and lilies on a bed of trailing ivy, Timothy and rye grass. Anna had brought wild flowers too: comfrey and corncockle, harebells and forget-me-nots. Hildegard had doubts about her daughter attending Lenny Goddard's funeral, but Sidney thought it might be good for her. Younger children are often more resilient than people think, he said. It would help her make sense of what she had seen.

The ceremony was appropriately personal (English folk songs, an American–Indian lament, a reading of the

'Desiderata', a recording of 'Light My Fire' which was not as amusing as everyone had thought it was going to be). There were men in denim suits and cowboy boots, women with daisy chains in their hair and dressed in Indian blouses or tie-dyed summer smocks, all looking as if they had stopped off on their way to a festival on the Isle of Wight. If this was the secular future of funerals, Sidney wondered how far the Church of England was going to have to stretch its traditions to keep up.

He tried to add a note of sober dignity by presiding in a dark suit and dog-collar, offering a welcome, prayers and a short address. He took his text from 'The Song of Songs', and spoke about the divine harmony, how both nature and life itself could be seen as a piece of music. It all depended upon the pace, the rhythm and the interpretation. The singer was as important as the song, and what a song Lenny had sung.

When he finished he admitted to himself that he had not preached at his best. During one paragraph he had looked up and seen Tom Tranton in the congregation, and Sidney couldn't work out if the smile given back to him was one of encouragement or quiet amusement, as if to say, 'Come on, we both know you can do better than this.' Before his next funeral, Sidney decided, he would devote more time to a properly researched and thoughtful tribute, one from the heart that was less distracted by suspicion and investigation.

Nigel Martin, the funeral director, told Lenny's widow that the ashes would be ready the next day. Then she could scatter them in the bluebell wood where Lenny had been found. Linda Clarke said she'd go with her for support and company. She was a small woman with a blonde bob, as slight as an English Edith Piaf, wearing a pink gingham dress that made her look like a child who had never grown up.

'It's all right,' said Stella. 'I think I'd best be on my own.'

'No, we'll both come with you,' said Linda. 'Won't we, Tony?'

'If you need the company . . .'

'I'll be OK on my own,' their friend replied. 'But if you want to say your own goodbye . . .'

'We insist,' said Linda. 'Four friends still together. Lenny can't be confined to a box. He belongs to the elements. He's had the fire, now let's give him back to the earth and the wind and the water.'

Afterwards, when told of the plans to scatter the ashes back in the bluebell wood, Geordie was perplexed. 'If they've flung them all over the place, doesn't that make it difficult when the Lord comes calling at the Resurrection? He's got a bit of an assembly job on his hands, hasn't he?'

'Geordie, I have warned you before about applying human parameters to the divine mystery.'

'I know it's "beyond human understanding". But you might think he'd give the clergy some extra help so they can at least explain it on a Sunday.'

'You don't have to come to church.'

'You know I do. I like to be respectable.'

'And it's perfectly all right to "dwell in mystery".'

'Well, in that case we're making a decent fist of the situation.'

Instead of attending the wake, the two men went off to the pub.

'Best leave them to it,' said Geordie.

It started to rain. On the way, they sheltered for a while outside a dressmaker's run by identical twins. A card in the window read: 'Hems taken up. Bridalwear. Mourning.'

'Just about covers everything,' said Geordie. 'While we're stuck here I might as well let you know that the coroner confirms poor old Lenny had so much inside him and such a weak heart that it's hard to tell what's what. It may have been nature taking its course. It may have been deliberate. All we know is that his life stopped. But I want us to have a proper think. It doesn't feel right, does it? They've all got the same story. Do you think we've missed anything, Sidney?'

'If it was murder, then one of those nearest and dearest to him surely has to be responsible. They all had easy access and any one of them could have done the poisoning. But what's the motive?'

'I don't know. Suppose Lenny Goddard was having an affair with Linda Clarke, or they were planning to run off together?' Geordie mused. 'His wife finds out and she kills him. Or, he decides to stay with said wife, and lover Linda kills him for staying.'

'Or the husband, Tony Clarke, finds out his best friend is sleeping with his wife and does the necessary.'

'Yet all three of them were away at the same time. If it wasn't a slow-acting poison administered in advance then how could one of them have got back without the others noticing?'

'Unless all three of them did it?'

'That's possible too. But why would all three of them have wanted to get rid of Lenny Goddard? What could he have had on them?'

'And why was he collecting the poisonous flowers?' Sidney asked. 'We still don't know about that. And I'm sure there's something going on with the dog.'

'Perhaps he's been poisoned as well? He's not turned up.'

'But they reported him missing. Was that just to give themselves an alibi?'

'It's certainly worked. I've had that checked. King's Lynn. All three of them were there.'

'One of them could have come back on the train.'

'They seem very keen to cover for each other. We can't even be sure they had the dog with them in the first place.'

'Do you think it could be something to do with money, Geordie?'

'They didn't have very much.'

'Or drugs?'

'They made their own. But perhaps they sold them? It could be some kind of revenge from other people selling drugs in the area. I've put the word out.'

'It goes round and round in your head if you let it,' said Sidney. 'I don't suppose they could all just be thoroughly nice and decent people?'

'Not a chance. There's even the possibility that our man could have killed himself in order to frame the others; or perhaps he just miscalculated on one of his chemical adventures?'

'An accidental overdose? Tranton will know about that.'

'I don't suppose the teacher could be a suspect?' Geordie asked.

'Why would he want to kill an old pupil? He's a lovely man.'

'Everyone's lovely when they like you, Sidney. I think we need to go back to the wood and have a think there. I'll pick you up at three tomorrow afternoon. You can bring Byron. He might find something.'

'I should collect Anna from school.'

'Can't Hildegard do it?'

'She's teaching. She's got pupils in for some exam at the Royal Academy of Music. I'm on childcare duties. If I forget, then I'll be the next dead body you find.'

'I'll come at half-one then. If we take up too much time I'll put on the blue light and we can fetch Anna in the police car. She'll like that.'

'She almost certainly won't.'

It had rained again the next morning, but a swift wind blew the clouds to the east and the day had improved so much that by the afternoon it was hard to remember its gloomy start. Then, when they parked the car and started off on the walk to the bluebell wood, Sidney confessed that his mood was not so variable. He was still feeling guilty about exposing his daughter to suffering and for being preoccupied with the world of crime.

'Imagine how I feel,' said Geordie.

'And how do your children cope? They seem to have done all right.'

'We have just about survived each other. There's been nothing dramatic so far. They all have quite boring girl-friends and boyfriends.'

'Some people would consider that a relief.'

'I don't know, Sidney. You can't legislate for your children.'

25

'Have you got any tips?'

'Not really. You can't learn from other people because they don't have your kids and they haven't made your mistakes. Perhaps the secret of parenting is to be as kind as you can, plough on and hope for the best. Then there comes a moment when your children no longer need you and you get your freedom back. The only thing is that by then you don't want so much liberty because you're too knackered to know what to do with it. You discover that you're in the world of Shakespeare's seven ages of man or in the middle of the last reel of a film that you didn't even know you'd been starring in. Then, soon enough, it's all over. What's wrong? Are you listening to me?'

Sidney was not.

'Look,' he said.

Half submerged in the waters below the bluebell wood was the dead body of a woman dressed in black. It was Stella Goddard. An empty box of ashes lay abandoned on the riverbank.

Sidney and Geordie made their way to the Clarke boat. Linda couldn't believe the news. She said she had only just left Stella in the woodland. Now she had to be told several times about her death.

'It's not possible. You're lying. It can't be true. You're making this up.'

Her husband came up on the deck. 'What's going on?' he asked. He looked as if he had just woken up.

Stella had asked for a few moments alone after they had scattered the ashes, just so that she could take in the moment.

26

She had told Linda and Tony to go on ahead. After an hour or two they had started to worry but knew that their friend might like more time. How could she now be dead?

'Did you see anyone else in the wood?' Sidney asked.

'There was a family with children. No one we knew. We had to wait for a bit. We didn't want anyone to see us. It had to be private.'

'And afterwards,' Geordie wanted to know, 'you didn't hear or see anything suspicious?'

'Nothing.'

'And did you come straight home?'

'I did,' said Tony. 'I had to see the man from Mason's. The engine needs servicing. Linda went for a walk.'

'I went downriver,' his wife continued. 'I wanted to remember Lenny in my own way. We had so many walks together in the past few years. I wanted to imagine him by my side.'

'They were childhood sweethearts,' said Tony.

'We didn't know that,' said Keating.

'It doesn't make any difference now.'

'And you didn't mind, Mr Clarke?'

'It was a long time ago. We've all got a past.'

'It's good to stay friends,' said Linda. 'And that's what we all were. The four of us made our own family. And now, look, it's just the two of us, me and Tony. I can't believe it.'

'But you weren't together after you had scattered the ashes?' Sidney checked.

'Tony wanted to get on. He doesn't like to dwell on things. It upsets him.'

Sidney asked about Stella's state of mind.

'What do you think?' Tony asked. 'You're the clergyman. You must have seen grief before.'

'I think,' Geordie cut in, 'we'd both like to know if Mrs Goddard had ever had suicidal feelings.'

'Is that what it looks like?' Tony asked.

'I don't think her death can be that,' said Linda. 'Stella was strong. She was determined to do her husband justice; to have a last goodbye. She wouldn't have given up straight away like that.'

'Sometimes it's hard to tell what people are thinking,' said Geordie.

'Not with Stella. She had always known Lenny's health was frail. She had been half expecting him to die soon and she'd already done most of her mourning in advance. That's what you try to do when you know. We'd talked about a longer river trip next year and Lenny had said: "Don't mind me. I'll probably be gone by then. You have a good time without me." And do you know what Stella replied? "We will, you old bastard." And then we all laughed.'

'And were you planning on taking this river trip as well, Mr Clarke?'

'He was my best mate.'

'Even though he once loved your wife?'

'That doesn't matter. As I said, all that is in the past. I love her. She loves me.'

'I can't understand how Stella's gone,' said Linda. 'We went swimming together just about every day and if she'd meant to go in the river she wouldn't have been wearing any clothes. She preferred skinny-dipping. Stella wouldn't have swum in a dress.'

'Even if she had wanted to kill herself?'

'Especially then,' said Linda. 'She loved the feeling of the water against her skin.'

'She wouldn't have minded the embarrassment?'

'She wouldn't have cared. But it's not that. It can't be that. It must have been an accident. She was in mourning. But she still had us. We loved her. She knew that. We'd just told her so.'

'And you didn't think it was a mistake to leave her on her own?'

'She asked to be by herself. I think we've all wanted a bit of solitude at one time or another in the past few days – just to take it all in. It's all been so shocking. And now it's even worse.'

Linda hesitated and then asked: 'Can I see her? I don't think I can believe anything unless I do.'

'We can arrange that. You could come too, Mr Clarke?'

'I'll stay here if you don't mind,' he said. 'I've seen enough death for one lifetime.'

Sidney was desperate for a return to the routine of his regular religious duties and the distraction of a day off. He suggested a family picnic by the river. He would prepare it himself, he said: cucumber sandwiches, hard-boiled eggs, a pork pie, new young tomatoes, lemonade and the last of the *Leipziger Lerche* that Anna had made with her mother. They could have ice cream on the way home. It was time to do something good to make up for the bad, he said. Simple pleasures.

'After all, what else can go wrong?' he asked.

Anna brought her new camera, an Instamatic, and asked if they could stop by the ponies in the field. She hadn't forgotten her mother's promise of a present to make up for her horrible experience and she was now asking what kind of pony she might have – Fell or Dale, Exmoor, Welsh Mountain, Highland or Shetland – rather than whether she could have one at all.

Impressed by his daughter's negotiating skills, Sidney changed the subject by pointing to a narrow grass slope in the distance. 'Let's play roly-poly,' he said. 'Last one there's a nincompoop.'

The three of them ran towards the little hillock, got to the top and rolled over and over down the slope, laughing and becoming dizzy and all ending up in a heap. At only one point did Sidney fear that they might come across yet another dead body. Was this now his life, he wondered, always to have such dread in prospect?

Byron seldom barked but he did now, confused by this onset of high spirits, and worried that the family might have hurt themselves. He went up to each one to check that they were still alive. Then they laid out the food and began to eat, careful to ration the amount they handed over to Byron, never forgetting that time in younger life when he had run across Grantchester Meadows and destroyed a chocolate cake that had been carefully placed at the centre of a picnic rug.

'You know, Sidney, you can be quite good at family life when you want to be,' said Hildegard.

'This is what I want it to be like all the time,' her husband replied. 'Sometimes I wish it wouldn't stop.' He cupped his hands. 'That we could hold it all here like this. A summer's day, you and me, a young daughter who never grows up and never knows suffering. If we could hold on to it all for just a bit longer.'

'Enjoy the moment,' said Hildegard, taking his hand. 'It is precious because it is rare.'

'Lord, behold our family here assembled,' said Sidney, offering up a quiet grace before they ate. He was quoting the prayer Robert Louis Stevenson said every day. 'We thank thee for this place in which we dwell; for the love that unites us; for the peace accorded us this day; for the hope with which we expect the morrow; for the health, the work, the food and the bright skies that make our lives delightful . . .'

Anna's teacher, Tom Tranton, passed by on his bicycle. He gave a merry wave and then doubled back, circling round them, pretending for a moment that his bicycle had a mind of its own and that he could not control it. Then he asked Sidney if he could have a quiet word. He had just heard about Stella Goddard's death and had been thinking.

'I know that you and your daughter discovered Lenny was collecting a particularly suspicious group of wild flowers, including digitalis,' he began, 'but I still cannot believe he had any malice in him. I wondered if you might consider a different theory; that the poor man did not intend to do any evil but to stop it?'

'How?'

'Suppose he suspected that he had been poisoned and was trying to find an antidote? One way of fighting aconitine poisoning is to administer a combination of atropine with either digitalis or strophanthin at maximum strength to act on the heart. You can't get strophanthin so easily, but if you know your way around your henbane and your foxgloves you can use their poison to reverse the dose. Perhaps that's why he was gathering those flowers?'

'Why didn't he just telephone the doctor?'

'Lenny always thought he knew best. And, if he suspected that someone he loved was trying to poison him, then perhaps he didn't want to say so in order to save them from suspicion?'

'So he knew?' Sidney asked.

'I think he did.'

'And you suspect his wife?'

'Or a lover. Or a lover's husband. Or an enemy hitherto unknown. But somebody he loved enough to forgive – and perhaps even to prevent them being incriminated. You could think of it as a last act of love.'

'That sounds too good to be true.'

'Have you found out if Stella Goddard had been drugged before she was drowned – either by herself or others?'

'We don't know that yet. I am not the police.'

'Yet you police our morals, Sidney, and if the Bible is to be believed, God's judgement is more lasting than that of any man.'

'I know you don't believe in such things.'

'Oh, I believe in judgement, but not for all eternity. There's no need to scare people with stories they can't imagine or, more likely, with something that doesn't exist. Sometimes I think I'm quite looking forward to oblivion: somewhere there's no trouble.'

'I think that's what Tony Clarke's after.'

'I don't think he'll get much of that with the wife he's got. I remember her as a little girl. Such concentration in biology lessons. The way she dissected a frog . . . she knows her chemistry too. They all do. Where she is now?'

'Seeing the dead body.'

'Leaving Mr Clarke on his own?'

'He just wants a quiet life.'

'Unfortunately, Sidney, there is no such thing as a quiet life. Even the smallest atom has to keep in a state of flux. It's impossible for any life form to discover a state of constant equilibrium. Take the haemoglobin molecule and its violent oscillations . . .'

'I'm not so sure I need to know about that, Tom . . .'

'Life exists only in so far as it evolves in time as a never-ending stream of events. The story never concludes. Nature has no morality. That's why we need you, Sidney. But I'm afraid I must take my leave. You need your family and I need my life. Embrace the chaos. Adieu!'

As soon as he got home, Sidney decided to telephone Geordie and ask if Linda Clarke had returned to her boat. It might be an idea, he suggested, to follow her and keep a watch on her husband.

'Don't worry,' his friend replied. 'That's all in hand.'

'Only, I was thinking of popping in.'

'Oh you were, were you?'

'I just had a few more questions.'

'Then it promises to be quite a party. I was just out the door myself.'

'I'm going to call on Tom Tranton first,' said Sidney. 'There's just one more thing I want to ask him.'

'Is it about the dog?'

'How did you guess?'

'Because I'm the one that's the detective.'

It was a warm summer evening and people were sitting out on the decks of their boats, drinking beer or mugs of tea, playing guitars, waiting for the stars to come out on a three-quarter moon. Sidney and Geordie passed a half-hearted game of French cricket being played in the last of the light and a pair of lovers lay on the long grass, beside a weeping willow, stroking each other's hair.

The Clarke boat was moored further away on a darker stretch past a bend in the river. There were lanterns on board, a table laid out for supper, drinks on deck and the unmistakable aroma of a barbecue.

Music was playing – easy listening, perhaps a bit of Radio 2 – and, as they approached, Sidney and Geordie could hear laughter. For a moment they wondered whether they had made a mistake. This, perhaps, was a couple trying to return to normal after the death of their best friends. Linda emerged wearing the longest chiffon scarf Sidney had ever seen. 'I saw a natterjack this afternoon,' she was saying. 'They're quite rare. They have this beautiful yellow stripe down the spine. It's the same colour as my scarf. Would you like another drink?'

Her husband was tending the barbecue. 'I don't mind. I feel a bit funny.'

'I hope it's not one of your turns.'

'You can talk . . .'

34

'Can we be of assistance?' Geordie asked, as he and Sidney arrived on the quay.

'What do you want now?' Tony answered, moving the meat to one side.

'I hope we haven't interrupted anything.'

'What does it look like?'

'Is there any news?' said Linda.

'I think we'd like another of our chats.'

Sidney announced that he wanted to talk about friendship. Could Linda and Tony remind them how long they had all known each other?

'Lenny, Linda and I were at school together,' said Tony. 'You know that. All taught by Tranton.'

'And why do you volunteer that now?'

'Because he's been poking his nose in.'

'How do you know that?'

'He came to see us,' said Linda. 'And he was at the funeral.'

'What did he want to know?'

'How we were keeping. But I think he really came to snoop.' She turned to Geordie. 'Did you send him?'

'No, I didn't,' said Geordie.

'Did he talk about frogs?' Sidney asked.

'Why would he do that?'

'Because he remembered you, Mrs Clarke, dissecting one at school.'

'I don't see what that's got to do with anything . . .' Tony cut in before his wife could answer.

'Bufotenine,' said Sidney.

'I don't think I know it,' Linda replied.

'I think you do.'

Her husband was perplexed. 'What are you talking about?'

'You extract it from amanita mushrooms and from the skin and venom of toads. According to Tranton you were something of a zoologist at school, Mrs Clarke, and then, when you went to university, you became an expert in herpetology . . .'

'The study of amphibians,' Geordie continued, 'frogs, newts, salamanders and . . .'

'Toads. Yes, I know what herpetology is.'

'And now,' the inspector concluded, 'so do we. It's how the dog died, isn't it? All he had to do was play with a toad, lick it or catch it in his mouth, and that's it. Cardiac arrest. More common at night, apparently, when everyone else is asleep. Easier to get rid of the body.'

'The dog died by accident,' said Linda. 'I didn't know he was going to try and eat a toad.'

'And you didn't tell the others because reporting him missing would give you an alibi.'

'I didn't say anything to the others because I didn't want to upset them. It was a horrible death. I thought if we just assumed he had run away it would be kinder.'

'You wanted to be kind?' Geordie asked.

'I hope so, Inspector.'

Sidney turned to Tony Clarke. 'Did you know about this?'

'No, I did not. But I don't like asking too many questions. Then you don't have to worry about the answers.'

'So you've never asked your wife about her feelings for Lenny Goddard?'

36

'I don't need to.'

Linda spoke out. 'This is none of your business,' she said. 'A woman can love someone else without it getting in the way of her marriage. You don't always have to bring everything out into the open, Mr Chambers. I'm sure you must have friendships with women yourself.'

'I do.'

'And your wife doesn't mind?'

'She doesn't say anything.'

'Well, then,' said Tony Clarke. 'Neither do I.'

'As long as no one wants anything more . . .' Geordie added.

'Sometimes,' said Linda, 'love can be beyond the physical. People don't understand that but it's true. You go past the body to find something deeper. Truer.'

'And you had that with Lenny?' Sidney asked.

'I wouldn't want to attempt to describe it.'

'But you did want your relationship to be exclusive?'

'It already was.'

'He was married.'

'We understood each other. We had a past together. We were more than married.'

Sidney pressed on. 'I don't think you were, Mrs Clarke. I think you were having a relationship and Lenny stopped it. That's why he didn't join you downriver. He wanted to be on his own.'

'That's not true.'

Geordie was losing patience. 'Perhaps he wanted to be shot of the lot of you.'

'Never.'

'We think you poisoned him. If you couldn't have him, no one else could – not least his wife.'

Tony Clarke had had enough. 'Linda is not the type of woman to poison her friends. She loved them.'

'We're not saying she didn't,' Sidney continued. 'Lenny Goddard guessed what had been happening – that you had been poisoning him slowly, over several weeks – and tried to find the antidote because he still loved you enough to protect you, Mrs Clarke. Perhaps he felt guilty? Then Stella drowned herself in grief. Unless, of course, you poisoned her too? We're still waiting for the post-mortem. I'm not sure about the dog. That may not have been an accident either.'

'This is a lot of supposition,' said Linda.

'But once we find the bufotenine, everything will follow.'

Tony turned to his wife. 'Is this true?' Linda Clarke remained silent, but he continued to focus on her alone. 'I don't know why you needed to do all that. Everything was fine. We could have just carried on. Didn't I love you enough?'

'Perhaps I've always wanted too much,' she said at last. 'I don't know. Perhaps I wanted everything.'

'I thought you loved me.'

'I do.'

'But not enough.'

'Differently,' said Linda. 'Lenny said he was going to go away. He said it was too stifling. He couldn't cope. He was going to leave and go as far away as he could and he was just going to be with Stella. They were planning to start again. He said he couldn't bear to live with me being so close. We loved each other too much. He couldn't breathe, he said. And I told him I couldn't live without him.'

'But that's what you've done,' said Sidney. 'You've made that come true.'

'You should have told me,' said Tony. 'Why did you keep this from me? I could have helped you. I could have understood.'

Linda looked out over the night water and spoke to no one but herself. 'Now Lenny's gone I can love him without any fear of losing him. A dead man can't reject you. I can love as I have always wanted. No one can stop me and he can't ignore me or leave me. Stella can't provoke me. She's gone. There's no widow to claim his memory. I can have Lenny to myself. And that love won't end. And I won't ever doubt it. Even in prison. Even in death.'

Sidney and Geordie drove back into Ely together. 'You'd think we'd get better at this, wouldn't you?' the inspector began. 'But it could have been any of them. Do you think Tranton knew all along?'

'He told me about the poison. It was up to us to prove it.'

'I'm not sure we have yet.'

'Do you know if we will?'

'I hope so. By the way, I wonder if, in time, Linda Clarke would have poisoned her husband as well?'

'I do think that's possible, Geordie.'

'So at least we've stopped one thing. I don't suppose you fancy a quick pint before last orders? Hildegard won't mind, will she?'

'She's had ten years of this already. She'll probably be asleep by now.'

'By the time I get back to Cambridge, Cathy will definitely be out for the count. She's been so tired recently. So why break the habit of a lifetime? We could even fit in a game of backgammon . . .'

'I can't believe we're still doing all this,' Sidney replied.

'What's wrong with you, man, what else would you be doing?'

The next night Sidney and Anna read a Tintin story and were amused to find their namesake, an Inspector Chambers, in *The Seven Crystal Balls*. The inspector shot the intruder who put Professor Tarragon into a coma and called police head-quarters when Professor Calculus was kidnapped. He was a dark, angry man with a toothbrush moustache who appeared in only two or three frames, dressed in a traditional trench coat and looking nothing like Sidney or his father. Still, it could have been worse. The only clergyman they had spotted in the series so far was the Reverend Peacock in *Cigars of the Pharaoh*, a bemused and elderly hanger-on who turned out to be a member of an international gang of drug traffickers.

It was light behind the curtains and the room had a dusky air. Sidney prayed with his daughter, tucked her in and kissed her goodnight. Then he left the door slightly ajar so that she would not be afraid if she woke up later, when darkness was at the full.

'Does a story always have to be true?' she asked, just as he was leaving. Anna was always good at delaying tactics to pro-long bedtime.

'I think it has to be truthful even if it didn't really happen,' said Sidney from the doorway. 'You have to care

40

about the story you are telling and then make people believe it.'

'But can you sometimes make it *become* true if you work hard enough? Is that why people pray? To force their stories to come true?'

'Or to make them better.'

'Even if they're not true?'

'They can be true in spirit if not in fact.'

'What's the difference?'

'That might take a long time to explain; a whole life . . .'

'Can you come and read me something else – a story with a happy ending? Then I don't mind if it's true or not.'

She finished her wild-flower collection just before the end of term, filling her scrapbook with the blues of periwinkle and lady's-smock, the yellows of celandine and marsh marigolds, the pinks of cuckoo pint and rosebay willowherb, each with little descriptions. 'Gorse is too spiky,' she wrote, together with 'My mum's favourite' next to the sweet violet, and even a little picture of a skull and crossbones by a foxglove: 'Warning: poison'.

Linda Clarke was arrested and charged. Yes, poison, she said. She had wanted Lenny for herself, but he had refused to leave his wife. Love had turned to hate, then to vengeance and on to despair, murder, fantasy and illusion. Her husband had known and loved her through it all, but she had been too determined to accept what he had to offer, pursuing an idealised vision of a past with someone else; what she thought had been, and always would be, a better love, even if it was one that was entirely without a future.

41

All that devotion or passion or shame or humiliation or obsession – whatever it was – made Sidney think about the waste of misdirected adoration and the persistence of desire; and how important it was, perhaps, to recognise the quieter, humbler, lasting love of a marriage like his own, one that took its place beside his and Hildegard's side so often that it came and survived almost without them noticing, waiting patiently for acknowledgement.

The bluebells were long gone now, replaced by the wild flowers of June and July: figwort and field roses, giant hogweed, musk-mallow and montbretia, tansy, vervain and sweetbriar; the height of summer, the fullness of light.

Authenticity

SIDNEY HAD BEEN READING a book about the presentation of the self in everyday life; how we behave differently depending on who we are talking to and how sometimes we can be several people at the same time, all contained in the one body, just as so many different people could all be housed in the same Christian Church. How could so many constituent parts be reduced to a single definition of faith and identity; and what was the authentic self? How can we ever find out who we truly are?

It was one of those mornings when he couldn't quite work out what he wanted to say in his next sermon and, at the same time, he was troubled by the nagging feeling that he had forgotten something. He knew that he was having lunch with his old friend Amanda, that his former housekeeper, Mrs Maguire, needed a visit and that he still had to find a priest for a vacant parish in the north of the diocese, but none of these things were particularly troubling. Then, as he was shaving and a shaft of sunlight hit the edge of the tin mirror, Sidney remembered. It was his wedding anniversary.

Ten years. That was why Hildegard had kept saying the word 'tin' recently; and Anna had kept pointing out tin toys – frogs, elephants, fish, cars and carousels – laughing when they were reading their Tintin stories as if they contained some great secret. His wife and daughter had dropped so many hints it was a wonder he had forgotten.

Even though he rather disapproved of spurious commercialism, he decided to research the significance of tin as a symbol of marital wellbeing. He discovered that its flexibility was supposed to represent the tractability of a good relationship; the give and take that makes a marriage strong. Perhaps he could preach about that?

Tin. What on earth was he going to buy? A tray? A bangle? He couldn't give Hildegard earrings again. He remembered Amanda talking to him recently about Goya's series of fantasy and invention painted on tin (perhaps she was even in on the joke): bullfighting scenes, strolling players, a marionette seller, a yard filled with lunatics. She had just returned from a short holiday in Madrid and was excited about one of his other paintings, but Sidney hadn't been concentrating because he was still thinking about the Goddard murders and Linda Clarke's obsessive love. Wasn't there also a paint called 'tin yellow'? Perhaps he could get an artist to undertake Hildegard's portrait? If he did so, he reminded himself, he wouldn't forget a former friend's bid to do the same, telling his wife that he wanted the painting done 'before you lose your looks'.

He couldn't imagine Hildegard ever desiring such a thing. It was bad enough attempting to take her photograph, an activity that was now forbidden in bright sunlight lest it illuminate the telltale signs of her middle age. Some kind of tin picture frame would not be the answer either. Her present would have to be jewellery, carefully chosen, something that didn't look too cheap or tinny but represented the authentic heart of their marriage.

It was at moments like this, wondering what on earth he could get that might please her, that Sidney began to question how well he knew his wife. Hildegard certainly still liked to retain an air of mystery and keep part of her personality private. This, she insisted, was a deliberate attempt to retain Sidney's interest because he was, apparently, 'so easily distracted'.

As he finished shaving, scraped the last of the lather and splashed his face in all-too-bracing cold water, he thought about the ideal marriage and what it might mean. Did Sidney and Hildegard really need to know everything about each other to be complete as a couple?

He wondered if a lack of self-knowledge was sometimes not a bad thing; that if we acted instinctively and almost without awareness it could perhaps be a better way of thinking than being self-conscious all the time. And were there some things that were best kept hidden, even from our own selves? Was it dangerous to have an all-consuming marriage in which both members were overly dependent upon the other? What if we gave away so much of ourselves to our partner that we were no longer defined individually but by our married state? Did Hildegard now own a part of him that he would never get back; and did he own a part of her?

He could hear her voice. *It is not a question of ownership.*

Now, in thinking about such things and in remembering that he had forgotten to buy his wife anything at all, not even a card, he was filled with fear, particularly as he could hear Hildegard's footsteps on the stairs and knew she would wonder why he was shaving so late in the morning and what was keeping him in the bathroom.

'How much longer are you going to be?' she asked.

'I'm just coming, my darling.'

'What are you doing?'

'Shaving.'

'It can't take that much time. Are you all right?'

Sidney opened the door. 'I do love you,' he said.

'You've forgotten, haven't you?'

'Our wedding anniversary? Of course not.'

'Have you booked a restaurant for tonight?'

'I'll get us a table at the Old Fire Station.'

'Won't they be full?'

'Not if I ask them nicely.'

'You're very sure of yourself for a man who has forgotten all about it.'

'I haven't forgotten.'

'For a man who has only just remembered, then. It's just as well you're getting a new secretary. Next year she can remind you.'

'I won't need reminding, my darling. I promise.'

'I did put it in your diary; just as it tells me that you are supposed to be meeting her at the Deanery before your lunch with Amanda.'

'Now?'

'Five minutes ago. I thought you'd gone.'

'Oh dear.'

'She's called Miss Morgan. I hope you like her. Perhaps she can babysit?'

'I very much doubt it.'

46

'Then I'd better find someone who can. You still want to go out?'

'There's nothing I'd like more.'

'You haven't forgotten anything else?'

'Of course not.'

'And Geordie won't telephone with another crisis?'

'When has that ever happened?'

'You do know that you're impossible, Sidney?'

'I do. And I hope it's why you love me.'

'You'd better get on. You're late already.'

Hildegard turned to go back downstairs but Sidney just managed to stop her. 'What about a little anniversary kiss?' he asked.

His wife closed her eyes and opened out her arms. Their lips touched softly.

'I love you,' he said.

'You're still impossible.'

A few weeks beforehand Sidney had complained, quite gently, to the dean about the amount of paperwork that he had to deal with, and they had come to the decision that the new diocesan secretary would be able to help out on a part-time basis. He was therefore due to meet the most likely candidate for coffee and biscuits in order to see how the arrangement might work in practice.

Vanessa Morgan was a petite and precise woman, who might have passed for a French *assistante* at a local school, with fine features and long dark hair that had been tied up in an Audrey Hepburn bun. Sidney imagined that she must be used to rejecting flirtatious advances from unsuitable men, and that such attentions probably irritated her a great deal, but, having attempted to disguise his initial intrigue and met his future secretary's challenging stare with what he hoped was a graceful politeness, he told himself that he really must try and stop judging people, particularly women, by their appearance alone.

Miss Morgan had been recommended by an accountancy firm where she had worked for the last five years, only leaving because, it was rumoured, she had plans to enter the Church as a deaconess. Part of the attraction of her new employment, therefore, was to get a feel for the Church of England at first hand and understand the ways in which it worked. At the same time she could bring some of her financial training to bear on the Diocesan Board of Finance, as the firm she had come from was well known for its attempts to cure 'the British disease' of industrial malaise by streamlining management and implementing efficiencies.

If she was to be truly effective, she told Sidney, she would have to know his every movement: where he was, who he was talking to and how long he planned to spend at each meeting. A proper schedule was essential, with routine consultations, daily catch-ups, and access to Hildegard's diary. She would need the telephone numbers both of his family and of all the people he met regularly, and she would also like to know his attitude to key theological issues so that she could help prepare his response to any general enquiry. Meetings would run to set lengths. Coffee, lunch and tea would be at the same time each day and she would be available in the evening for emergencies. Nothing would be left to chance.

Since chance was Sidney's main modus operandi, this seemed an ambition too far, but he reluctantly agreed to try out a suggested new regime in which he was assured that he would be able to 'worry less and get more done'.

He thought that he was 'doing' quite enough already, but Miss Morgan was particularly firm on this point. 'A great many priests waste so much time that they have none left for prayer. We need to make sure that the monastic tradition of religious discipline is preserved.'

'I don't think anyone would argue with that.'

'I should hope not, Mr Archdeacon. It is, of course, a paradox.'

'Is it, Miss Morgan?'

'It is. In order to discover the regular rhythms of medieval life we have to embrace modern management techniques. The Church has been stuck in the Victorian era for too long.'

Each day that someone told Sidney about the need to move with the times, he thought of a church in London that had recently installed a lavatory next to the chancel. Members of the congregation were given pieces of toilet paper on which they were told to write down their sins. Then, after a moment of prayer and penitence, and through the mercy of Christ's forgiveness, the vicar would push down the handle and flush those sins away.

It seemed extreme but now, perhaps, was not the moment to engage in a debate about the tension between tradition and modernity.

After they had established that Miss Morgan would run Sidney's diary from her office, take dictation and organise his correspondence (letters would need to be signed by 4.30 p.m.

49

ready for the last post), the conversation turned to the cathedral itself.

Her first suggestion was that the vergers take on more cleaning duties. Sidney had anticipated something altogether different; that she might question the number of clergy or raise the possibility of charging admission for entry. There was a precedent for this. In the nineteenth century many cathedrals kept their Naves free to visit but charged sixpence for admission to the Choir, Lady Chapel, Chapter House and Tower.

Instead, Miss Morgan seemed to be picking on the vergers.

'Why can't they take on the cleaning as well?' she asked. 'You know that they are already doing this at Winchester. We need younger, fresher staff who can get more done and in a tighter time frame. The Church has to embrace the modern age.'

'But some of the men have been here for years. Loyalty and tradition are important.'

'Not if the finances are impractical and the size of the congregation is on the decline.'

'It's not that bad.'

'We have to act before it's too late.'

'What do you mean by that, Miss Morgan?'

'Bankruptcy.'

'I don't think the Church is in any danger of that.'

'And yet without radical new ideas it may wither on the vine.'

'But what other radical new ideas do you have in mind?'

'As you can no doubt imagine, I am in favour of a contemporary, inclusive ministry.'

'I had heard that you plan to enter the Church yourself.'

'As a deaconess, yes. To begin with.'

'You have further ambitions?'

'I do hope that one day there will be women priests. I would have thought that a modern man like you might approve of such a thing.'

Sidney tried to follow the current liberal Anglican line that although he didn't disapprove of women in principle, unlike some of his colleagues who argued that Christ's choice of twelve men as his apostles should be preserved in the priesthood, he did not feel that the Anglican communion was ready for such an historic change.

Miss Morgan was not convinced. 'The Church of England has to take a lead. If Jesus were living in an age with a greater appreciation of women's dignity and gifts, he would have chosen female disciples and ordained women priests.'

'That may well be the case, but he didn't. Although he lives now.'

'And we should reflect his life in us by ordaining women.'

'We don't all have to do the same job. Even if they are not priests, women still have a unique role in the ministry, Miss Morgan. The fact that the Blessed Virgin Mary, Mother of God and Mother of the Church, received neither the mission proper to the apostles nor the ministerial priesthood clearly shows that the non-admission of women to priestly ordination cannot mean that they are of lesser dignity, nor can it be construed as a discrimination against them.'

'But it *is* discrimination against them, Archdeacon. Tradition preserves the misogyny of exclusion.'

'I wouldn't put it as strongly as that.'

'Remember St Paul writing in 1 Corinthians 14:33–35? He states: "As in all the churches of the holy one, women should keep silent in the churches, for they are not allowed to speak, but should be subordinate even as the law says."'

'But Paul also wrote to Phoebe as a deaconess, Priscilla as a missionary partner, and Junia as an apostle. It was another age, and we all have different ways of following Christ's example. Everyone can't do everything.'

'Why not?'

'Because it's not possible, Miss Morgan. I can't give birth to a child. I may want to, but I can't.'

'That is a biological rather than a theological problem. If it were physically possible, you should not be excluded from childbirth solely on the grounds of gender.'

'That is quite an extreme position, if you don't mind my saying so.'

Miss Morgan was almost amused. 'I do mind you saying so, as a matter of fact.'

'Then I apologise. I can see we are going to have a lively old time together.'

'Even more so if I become a priest myself.'

'I don't think we're likely to see that, however much you may want it,' Sidney replied. 'At least not in our life-time.'

'You know,' Miss Morgan countered, 'the Edwardians probably thought the same thing about votes for women.'

Bloody *hell*, Sidney thought, after the conversation had been interrupted by Amanda's fortuitous arrival. Hildegard sent her round to the Deanery to fetch her husband for lunch and after a brief introduction the two friends found themselves walking home alone.

'Well, there's a surprise,' Amanda began. She was wearing a dark-purple trouser suit that was more King's Road than King's School, Ely.

'What do you mean?'

'Your "secretary"?'

'Why do you stress the word? That's what she is.'

'I hope you don't find her distracting. I presume you have spotted that she is rather beautiful.'

'She's not attractive at all. She's terrifying. She might even be ghastly. She wants to be a priest.'

'I don't think you need to worry about that. There aren't any women priests.'

'I think her plan is to make sure that there are.'

'It'll never catch on. I can't imagine a woman giving me communion.'

'When was the last time you went to church, Amanda?'

'Now then, Sidney, don't be a bully.'

'I'm not.'

'All I will say is that Miss Morgan doesn't have much return of serve.'

'She does with me, I can tell you. She has made it perfectly clear she has no time for triviality.'

'Seems a bit of a waste.'

'What are you saying, Amanda?'

'For God to make a woman who wants to be a priest so attractive . . .'

'Her personality is decidedly spiky.'

Sidney had an involuntary flashback to their conversation and remembered another thing that had irritated him: the way Miss Morgan nodded at the end of sentences she thought significant, as if impressed by the precision of her own intelligence.

'I think that's deliberate,' Amanda replied. 'Protection. She won't want unnecessary attention.'

'I thought you were all in favour of attention?'

'Not the wolf-whistling; although at my age things have certainly calmed down. I can't turn heads as much as I used to. You remember when the balls started up again after the war?'

'You were radiant. Always the belle. You could have married any man you wanted.'

Sidney had already fixed one of his earliest memories of his friend: dancing the foxtrot in a deep-emerald-green silk taffeta gown that had been extremely fitted to her tiny waist. She was wearing long white gloves, her dark hair was swept up, her shoulders were bare, her eyes bright, her face flushed, her smile never faded.

'What a mess I made of everything.'

'You're still radiant. When I look at you now, I can picture you at twenty-five.'

'You're too kind. But I have to acknowledge that I am entering my more dignified years.'

'I wouldn't call them that. How's your work?'

'Rather exciting, if you must know. I've brought you a catalogue to have a look at: a country-house auction at West Riding Hall, just outside Leeds. Have you ever been to one? I thought we could all go together and make a day of it. You might pick up something nice; something made out of tin, perhaps?'

'Don't you start. I don't think Hildegard and I can afford anything antique at the moment. Why are you going? Do they have something you can't find in London?'

'There's a very interesting painting in the sale; easy to miss, not particularly attractive, but quite extraordinary. It's advertised as a Spanish, early-nineteenth-century picture by José de Madrazo y Agudo, but I think it's a Goya.'

'And that would make a difference?'

'You could say that.'

'And what makes you so sure?'

Amanda hesitated, assessing whether or not to convey doubt, reluctant to give her friend ammunition. 'I'm not, but part of the iconography matches an engraving we have in the British Museum. The provenance is uncanny. The painting has been in the Fairley family at West Riding for over a hundred years.'

'Do you know them?'

'Unfortunately not. The grandfather bought it from the Marquess of Worcester, who had been Wellington's aide-de-camp in the Peninsular War. The marquess married the duke's favourite niece, Georgina. After she died there was a bit of a hoo-ha, as he then married his former wife's half-sister. Wellington threw a hissy fit, cut off relations and, so the story goes, asked for the painting back. Unfortunately, the marquess had already sold it to the Fairleys to raise cash. You know that Goya painted Wellington?'

'Wasn't that the portrait that was stolen from the National Gallery a few years ago?'

'Very good, Sidney. A man called Kempton Bunton left the window of the Gents open and came back later and climbed through it . . .'

'It was as easy as that?'

'There were some building works at the back.'

'But shouldn't the security guards have checked from the inside?'

'Well, they didn't and Bunton then asked for a ransom of £140,000 to set up a charity to provide free television licences to the elderly and the poor.'

'Really?'

'Yes, Sidney, really. He said that the affluent society neglected their needs.'

'Television licences?'

'The BBC inflicts a tax on everyone regardless of income, as you know. The case gives you an idea of how much a Goya might be worth these days – £140,000 was the same amount the National Gallery had paid for it in 1965.'

'So this could be another of your "sleepers"?'

'I am pretty sure it's a Goya. During the Peninsular War, in August 1812, Wellington was in Madrid following the Battle of Salamanca. Goya painted at least two portraits of him – one just of his bust with all his most recent medals . . .'

'The one in the National Gallery?'

'Correct, and an equestrian portrait that was put on display in September in the galleries of the Academia.'

'Quick work.'

'Well, originally, it wasn't Wellington on the horse. Goya just changed the head and a bit of drapery on the body of a

Spanish commander he'd already been working on. You have to think fast in wartime . . .'

'To the victor, the spoils.'

'Exactly. Wellington left Madrid in March 1813 with more than two hundred paintings seized from the palaces, convents and churches of Spain. He also brought several canvases of his own back to England: two portraits of himself, one of which he gave away to the Duchess of Leeds, and another two that remained rolled and unhung until the middle of the last century. One of these was of the Marquesa de Santa Cruz, but the authenticity of that painting has been disputed, so could he not have brought the one I've just found instead? Might the painting have been kept rolled up in Stratfield Saye and then sent on to West Riding Hall by a subsequent duke who found the subject matter too gloomy?'

'And is it gloomy?'

'The image is of a female nude looking at herself in the mirror. But instead of her reflection she sees the head of a donkey. Through a window to the right is a battlefield scene reminiscent of one of the Disasters of War, *Infame Provecho: Infamous Gain*. Behind, and to her left, an artist with an easel is painting her. I think this must be a self-portrait, because the pose is similar to one found in an earlier Goya painting, the family of the Infante Don Luis. The title, written on the back, is *Nadie se Canoce: nobody knows himself*. This is a reference to each part of the image; that the lack of self-knowledge applies to every subject: the female model, the painter, and the war. That same inscription, in similar handwriting, is found on one of Goya's engravings.'

'You've done your homework.'

'The engraving is one of the Caprichos and it's perfectly possible that the duke was given a set, because the series the family owns comes with explanations in Goya's handwriting.'

Sidney tried to stick to the key facts as he remembered them. 'Is the painting signed?' he asked.

A fleeting look that managed to contain anger, disappointment and the fear of being caught out ran across Amanda's eyes and forehead. 'Unfortunately not. But I think the paperwork backs up my theory.'

Sidney persisted. He was determined to retain interest without being annoying. 'It doesn't mention the painting by name?'

'It doesn't, but I think there's enough to go on. We also have to make sure this isn't a pastiche or a later copy.'

'And you are doing that?'

'I'm going half and half with a friend of Daddy's: Charles Beauvoir. He works in fine art and he's already got one of his men on to it; X-rays and everything. I've been seeing him a bit and he's on his uppers.'

'"Seeing him a bit"?'

'Nothing you need to worry about, Sidney. He may adore me, but you're still top dog.'

'On his uppers?'

'Debt. He might even lose his estate. But he knows West Riding Hall and has had a bit of a sniff around, so he's asked me to take a look. If they know Charles is interested they might cotton on to the fact that something's up and revise their estimate. That would be a disaster. So I'm going to check up for him.'

'Won't they recognise you?'

'In Leeds? I don't think so. Besides, Charles is a bit short of the readies. So I'm going to buy the painting and we'll split the proceeds later.'

Sidney never quite trusted his friend when she talked at speed. It was her way of heading off any alternative point of view. Perhaps she thought that the faster she spoke the more difficult it would be to contradict her. Sidney's simplest tactic was therefore to wait until she exhausted herself.

'So you're taking the financial risk. Does your boss have anything to say about this, Amanda?'

'Roland Russell? Why should he?'

'Have you told him what you're planning to do?'

'Not specifically.'

'But will he find out that you have been offering your services to art dealers? And what will he say if he does?'

'I don't think he'll mind. He does it all the time. I'm only buying a painting. I don't have to seek his permission.'

'But you are using your reputation to increase its value.'

'That's true.'

'By how much?'

'If it's a real Goya then it will sell for thirty or forty times as much as a painting by José de Madrazo y Agudo. At the moment, minor paintings by Florentine and Spanish School artists are going for two or three thousand pounds. If you can reattribute and add a distinguished name then you can resell for over £100,000.'

'And a Goya?'

'I've checked. Between 1951 and 1969 his prices have increased nineteenfold. The last set of *La Touromaquia*, his thirty-three bullfighting scenes, went for £11,000 last year, and those were prints. An undiscovered Goya painting could solve all of Charles's problems at a stroke. The estimate is only £1,500.'

'So it's in his interest to buy it and get it reauthenticated. Would that be by you, by any chance?'

'And one other.'

'And who might that be?'

'Xavier Morata. He's the world expert on Goya.'

'Does he know about any of this?'

'Don't be daft, Sidney. If he knew he'd be on to it and want to buy it too. This whole business depends on the utmost secrecy.'

'But what if this Morata fellow refuses to help you or doesn't agree with the reauthentication?'

'He won't.'

'How do you know?'

'Never you mind, Sidney. There are ways and means. The art world is sometimes quite complicated.'

'You mean that every man has his price. It sounds dubious. I don't understand how you can reauthenticate your own painting.'

'It's not illegal. People do it all the time.'

'Then why can't you keep all the money? Why do you have to have this Charles person?'

'Because he spotted the painting first and I am a decent woman.'

'And why does he need you? Why can't your man just go straight to Morata?'

'Because he can't trust Morata, he doesn't have the cash and I've already done half the detective work for him.'

'I wish we could make sure that you are not taking any undue risk . . .'

'I'm not.'

'. . . with both your money and your reputation. I can see that it's in your interest to make the authentication stick; but can you trust yourself to behave objectively as an art historian?'

'I think, Sidney, you'd be just as squeamish if I asked you to behave equally objectively as a priest. I stand to make a mint on this.'

That Sunday it was Sidney's turn to take the Harvest Festival service, a celebration of East Anglian bounty where apples, plums and pears, marrows, pumpkins, kale and cabbage were brought forward to be blessed along with tinned ham, salmon, baked beans, bottles of cider and home-made carrot wine. Sprinkled around the main display were harvest loaves, jam and treacle tarts, and unwanted cans of peaches, pineapple chunks and condensed milk.

Anna joined a parade of Brownies and Girl Guides, each carrying a corn dolly as they processed around the Nave of Ely Cathedral to a heartfelt rendition of 'We Plough the Fields and Scatter'. Sidney preached on a text by Robert Louis Stevenson – 'Judge each day not by the harvest you reap but the seeds you plant' – offered prayers of gratitude and compassion, celebrated communion and sent the congregation on its way with the admonition to 'Let All the World in Every Corner Sing'.

Sidney's good mood after the service was lowered when the dean asked him for a quiet word over a pre-lunch drink.

He had told his archdeacon to be particularly vigilant in counting the money donated during the offertory hymn, because several of the clergy had recently noticed discrepancies between the total entered into the account book and the amount subsequently banked by the head verger.

'It's like the Mrs Price Ridley situation in *Murder at the Vicarage*.' (Felix Carpenter was an Agatha Christie aficionado.)

'I don't know if I recall it.'

'She was convinced that she had put a pound in the collection, but when the total amount was posted she was pained to observe that one ten-shilling note was the highest amount mentioned. The vicar brushes it off, she complains to Colonel Protheroe, he creates a stink, the vicar wishes he was dead and the next thing we know the colonel is murdered.'

'I think that's where fiction departs from fact, Felix.'

'And the vicar is a suspect! It's a tricky situation. These things can get out of hand, Sidney. We all know Ted's never been that good with numbers, so we have to establish whether this is a series of mistakes or if he really has been cooking the books.'

'Or if it's not him at all.'

The dean was not impressed by such a suggestion. 'That would make one of the clergy culpable.'

'I know that.'

The dean poured out Sidney's glass of white wine, remembering, at last, that his guest couldn't stand sherry. 'I don't think it's likely. The recent decimalisation has, of course, confused matters. We are used to setting aside the old currency and people pretending they are still contributing by throwing in their old pennies and threepenny bits, but this has been going on for over a year now. The amount deposited in the bank is never quite what anyone remembers it being and because we do the vestry accounts in pencil, it's easy enough to amend.'

'So I imagine Miss Morgan is now suggesting we change to ink?'

'Then, if you make a mistake you can Tipp-Ex over it, but an auditor can still spot if there have been alterations.'

'How much has gone missing?'

The dean sank into his armchair and crossed his long legs. 'None of us can be sure. It's half a crown one week, but it might be as much as ten bob the next.'

'I think we're supposed to say fifty pence these days.'

'Out of a total of twenty pounds it soon mounts up. Why do you think he's doing it?'

'We don't know that he is, Felix. His sister's been ill. And he does the pools. But Ted doesn't look like a spendthrift.'

'Although we probably don't pay him very well. We need to be more vigilant, Sidney, that's the thing.'

'If we don't suspect Ted then it has to be one of the canons, or the precentor.'

'Anyone who celebrates and has time in the vestry.'

The dean put down his wine glass and leant forward in his chair. 'I've delegated the investigation to Miss Morgan. She's going over the accounts for the last three years and is planning to put a new system in place.'

'And what is that?'

'Envelopes. Everyone on the electoral roll will have them, and then they can put the money inside every Sunday. No one else can see how much other people give and there will be no more cash temptingly out in the open to steal. She's also going to set up regular donations by standing order so the congregation can pay from their bank accounts.'

Sidney thought momentarily about the economics of the situation. The whole process of collecting money on open platters was a delicate exercise that alternated between the pride of the generous and the humiliation of the poor. Perhaps anonymity might help, and a standing order from the bank might make contributions more regular, particularly during the holiday season. But there were also disadvantages.

'Do you think people will agree?' he asked. 'It means that during the offertory they will have to pass the plate on as if they aren't giving anything at all.'

'No. They put in their envelopes.'

'Not if they are paying by standing order. They won't want the embarrassment of seeming to give nothing.'

'We could provide them with special badges.'

'I don't think so, Felix.'

'Well, Miss Morgan is convinced that we need a new system and she will set it all up so we don't have to worry. Isn't that wonderful?'

'Providing we can trust her.'

'We do. And it's one less thing for us. You know we've never been very good at all this.'

'Money?'

'We like to imagine we have our minds on higher things, but sometimes I think it's just that none of us can be bothered,' the dean admitted.

'I suppose it is because the money is not our own.'

'Perhaps if our salaries were dependent on the amount the congregation gave we'd be a bit more beady about it.'

'They are.'

'But not directly.' Felix Carpenter stood up and made his way back to the bottle of white wine on the side-table. All this talk was giving him a headache. Like many clergy, he left the tedious business of domestic finance to his wife. 'Anyway. Thank goodness for Miss Morgan. You know her last job was with an accountancy firm?'

'That doesn't make her an accountant.'

'It gives her a start. And I don't want the police involved just yet.'

'The police?'

'You know what I mean.'

Now Sidney realised why he was being drawn into the drama. There was no such thing as a free secretary. 'So that's why you are telling me all this?'

'I am sure we can clear the matter up on our own, Sidney; especially if I let on at the next meeting of the Chapter that you might be involved.'

'Please don't do that.'

The dean pointed a finger at his archdeacon in mock suspicion. 'Unless you are the culprit yourself?'

'Felix . . .'

'I am teasing you, Sidney.'

'I have learned to be wary of any jokes involving crime. The situation always comes back to bite you . . .'

'Very well. But you will keep an eye out, won't you? Are you sure you won't stay for lunch? Cordelia is experimenting with a new dish: *Veal sine nomine*.'

'That could be anything.'

'I think it's a type of lucky-dip casserole with cheese on top. I haven't dared enquire too closely. One can't have one's fingers in every pie.'

Sidney was intrigued. 'I wonder about the origins of that expression, Felix. How many people eat with their hands these days? And what if the pie is hot?'

'Doesn't Shakespeare use the phrase? He seems to say most things. Isn't it about people going secretly into kitchens and tasting all the pies before they are served? I think it's Cardinal Wolsey in *Henry VIII*. "The devil speed him! No man's pie is freed from his ambitious finger!" You will need to be careful, Sidney.'

'Wasn't Cardinal Wolsey beheaded?'

'Exactly. We don't want people saying the same thing about you.'

Sidney wondered whether to tell Geordie about the problem with the collection money the next time they met in the Prince Albert but decided that police attention would only exacerbate the situation. Instead, he asked how much his friend knew of fraud in the art world.

'Is this about Amanda?'

'It might be.'

66

'You mean you won't tell me until I have given you a general answer to a hypothetical question?'

After a well-edited briefing, Geordie did not seem to think that Amanda was guilty of any wrongdoing. 'It's like getting good information on the horses and refusing to share it so the odds don't drop. She's betting on her own expertise.'

'She says she's also unearthed the documentation that proves it.'

'As long as that hasn't been faked or stolen then she should be all right. But I don't know that much about it, Sidney. The art world has its own rules, just like the university.'

'And the Church.'

'Why don't you ask that friend of your old curate – Simon Hackford? He knows a thing or two about the business.'

'He's more of a furniture man.'

'But he deals in art. He'll know. Then you could see Leonard at the same time. I've always thought it's a pity he's not a priest any more.'

'He was better in the parish than he thought he was. You know, he was the kindest man I've ever worked with.'

'Those who think they are good "people persons" are often the worst. His successor, for example . . .'

'Malcolm? He's not too bad.'

'The thing is, Sidney, I never trust people who are relentlessly cheerful. They've always got something to hide.'

'Or they're heading for a deep depression in old age. But Malcolm means well. He has a good, honest faith.'

'It's a difficult business, sincerity. People go on about it as if it's a good thing, but murderers are sincere when you think about it. Even Hitler was sincere. It didn't do Germany much good. Not that I'd say any such thing to Hildegard.'

'Please don't. You know she doesn't have much of a sense of humour.'

'German.'

'Stop it, Geordie. You know that sets her off.'

'She's stronger than you think.'

Sidney resisted the temptation to say that he probably knew his wife better than his friend did, and returned to the subject. 'I'm still worried about Amanda.'

'The art malarkey? Some of it doesn't sound right, I'll give you that. I don't understand why the aristocracy would be so careless about a masterpiece. If it is a Goya, and they got it direct from the artist, they wouldn't just give it away to a relative.'

'Amanda says his paintings weren't fashionable in the nineteenth century. His work took a while to catch on.'

'Didn't I read somewhere that the last time they had an exhibition in London they had to hide all the pictures in a container lorry filled with tomatoes? You wouldn't want that crashing.'

'It's remarkable how often lost masterpieces turn up, though, isn't it?'

'Yes, Sidney. But it's not so extraordinary when a family needs a lot of cash at the same time. You're sure they haven't hinted at all this to Amanda so that she overbids on a painting that's not a Goya at all? I don't want her to be the victim of a sting.'

'You think she could be being set up?'

'If something seems too good to be true, Sidney, then it generally is.'

'I trust Amanda.'

'So do I, but when money's involved, trust and judgement tend to go out the window.'

Sidney had wanted to ask Leonard and Simon Hackford over for lunch for a few months now and Amanda's intrigue provided a useful excuse. Hildegard prepared a golden harvest casserole, with chicken marinated in cider, honey and soy sauce with sliced peaches added towards the end.

'You wouldn't think it would work, but it does,' she said. 'A bit like our relationship, my darling.'

'Careful,' Leonard warned as Sidney opened his mouth to reply.

Hildegard smiled. 'My husband has been on very shaky ground recently.'

'Another case?'

'Not yet,' said Sidney. 'It's Amanda. She thinks she has discovered a masterpiece that no one else knows about.'

'Didn't she once uncover a Holbein?'

'This time it's a Goya.'

'Not her period,' Simon warned. 'She'll have to be careful who to trust.'

'I suppose it's best not to trust anyone at all. But that's not very Christian.'

'What's Beauvoir like?'

'Almost bankrupt.'

'And therefore desperate. Has Amanda told you much about the painting itself? Has it ever been restored or "improved"? How much of the original is intact?'

Sidney thought for a moment. 'I've always wondered if, once they start retouching, you can still refer to the painting as having been executed by the hand of the master; especially if we can no longer tell what is original and what has been restored. When does restoration become an act of deception? Is the subsequent appreciation of the art any less real?'

'When a woman wears make-up is she still the same woman?' Hildegard asked. 'Or is she, perhaps, even more of herself – herself perfected?'

'It is a complex area,' Leonard began, 'the question of originality in an age of reproduction. A photograph has less value than an engraving and an engraving has less than a painting. But if the engraving was done first . . .'

'Amanda says that is unlikely.'

'But *if it was*, then the block for the engraving would be the original work of art and should therefore be worth more than the painting.'

'The first work is not always the most valuable,' said Simon. 'Think of studies for paintings, preparatory drawings. You could argue that those works were the true originals, the beginning of the act of creation.'

'But the finished work requires so much more effort,' Sidney observed. 'Surely labour, skill, time and application have their price?'

'Isn't the question of apprentices and assistants relevant?' Hildegard asked. 'If other people have helped, can the work of art still be called original?'

'It depends on the execution,' said Simon.

'What if it is a great painting in its own right but doesn't happen to be by Goya? How much does the name "Goya" add value, even though the painting without its attribution should already be valuable and might even be better?'

Sidney took up his wife's argument. 'How much does the context within an artist's oeuvre add value? Can a work of art have an independent value, freed of its original setting and outside the biography of the creator?'

'Of course.'

'Then why do people concern themselves so much with authenticity?'

'I think it is all to do with the hand of the master,' said Simon. 'You are one step away from the flick of the artist's brush. If you touch the surface of the painting it is as close as you can get to the indefinable spirit of the creator. It's almost religious.'

'And that's just how the priesthood works,' said Sidney. 'You could argue, Leonard, that even though you have resigned the priesthood, you still retain your status because you have been ordained. You took part in a ceremony of blessing that goes back to Christ himself. Hands were laid upon you. That cannot be reversed. Other people may be able to dress up as priests, they may even be able to behave as priests, but they *are not priests*, just as a Goya painting by another artist *is not a Goya*.'

Driving up towards Yorkshire, Sidney wondered what else he might have been doing instead of gallivanting off to an auction with Charles Beauvoir and his oldest friend. A couple of years ago he could have gone with Hildegard to hear Radu Lupu win the Leeds Piano Competition; in Lent he could have attended a retreat with the monks at Mirfield;

71

or that very Saturday he could have taken his father to see Don Revie's mighty Leeds United play Everton.

It was a glorious day for a trip on the road. The leaves on the trees were at that brittle yellow stage before they transformed themselves into the full autumn glory of russet, gold and burnt toffee. A gentle wind pushed the clouds so steadily that the flow of light across the hills was in constant flux. A murder of crows started up out of the fields.

Amanda explained how vital it was to retain an air of detachment during the auction. She didn't want people to guess that they were going to target the one painting. 'You're my cover, Sidney. No one will think that a priest can afford any of this stuff.'

'But once the bidding starts it'll be obvious you're interested.'

'Never forget the art of surprise. I'll come in as late as I dare. We should watch for the competition.'

'I'll be keeping a very low profile,' said Charles, although Sidney found it hard to see how a tall, bulky aristocrat in a windowpane-checked coat and trilby could carry that off.

Charles explained about family tradition and the fear of forfeiting a country estate that had been theirs for generations. It made him who he was to such an extent that if he lost his home he would lose all sense of himself.

Sidney was about to ask how he had managed to accumulate such debts, if it was through gambling or incompetence, but Amanda headed off any further questions. 'Death duties are so terrible,' she said. 'It's almost impossible to pay them.'

'I should have kept all my investments in property and antiques. But I'd always been taught to diversify,' said Charles.

'Have you had to sell up?' Sidney asked.

'I should say so.'

'Only I once heard a man say that you should never convert a paper loss into a real loss. You wait for the market to come right.'

'I'd expect a Christian to say that,' Charles replied. 'It's your whole philosophy: waiting. Some people can't and if you are forced to sell and unable to choose the moment then you are as stuffed as the proverbial turkey.'

West Riding Hall was a smaller version of Harewood House, built in the eighteenth century by the same architect, with a large Italianate terrace, a series of cottage, rose and fruit gardens and a ha-ha that separated the grounds from the nearby farmland, stables and tenanted houses. The Fairley family were selling off as many of their possessions as they could. They too had been hit by death duties.

The auction was divided into the contents of the rooms – hall, drawing room, study, gun-room, stairs, bedrooms and library – with plenty of furniture, carpets, stags' heads and curios. Selling alongside the Old Master paintings was a series of fine French and Continental silver, extensive sets of porcelain dinner plates, Japanese bronze vases, model ships, barographs, barometers, clocks, guns, and the head of a water buffalo that had been shot in East Africa. There was a random assortment of Persian rugs, antique books and furniture; a Louis XV tulipwood and marquetry commode, three Italian *cassones*, a collection of taxidermy (including a bizarre display of frogs at a boxing match) and some Dutch blue-and-white delftware. There were also lacquer cabinets, walnut hall chairs, an Etruscan satyr, two fine Egyptian cats and an ancient terracotta figure of a woman playing knucklebones.

Sidney was intrigued to see one of his old sparring partners, the journalist Helena Mitchell (née Randall), in attendance. 'I thought you normally covered crime?' he asked.

'I could say the same about you, my old friend. Perhaps it's both of our days off?'

'Do you think if the two of us are here then the chances of anything going wrong are doubled?'

'I'm writing a special "state-of-the-nation" piece. It's with a photographer. We're going to show contrasting Britain. You know the kind of thing: a stately-home auction and a struggling coal mine slap bang next to each other.'

'Not exactly subtle.'

'There's not much about contemporary journalism that is.'

'And the photographer?'

'Frank Downing. I've known him for years. He's mainly done war stuff – you'll have seen his Biafran photos – but he wants a rest from being shot at. He's doing a book: *England Through the Lens*.'

Downing was on the other side of the room framing up an image; a handsome man with 'colourful past' written all over him. He carried a Billingham bag and wore a gilet packed full of lenses, filters and light meters. Sidney remembered another photographer, Daniel Morden, planning a similar venture over ten years previously. It was odd to think how the old ideas came round again.

'How's Malcolm?' he asked.

'He doesn't like me going away, especially at weekends, but it's overtime and we need the money. You know how it is.'

'Hildegard is often telling me how we need to economise.'

'No one joins the Church of England for the money, Sidney. But now you're here I feel right at home. Something unusual is bound to happen. You must have been out of trouble for, what is it, *weeks*? It would probably be easier if the paper made me their Sidney Chambers correspondent. It would save so much time.'

'You'd soon get bored of me.'

'That's one thing I know for sure will never happen. I will never tire of you, Sidney. I'm just amazed how you've got away with it all for so long. But we should take a good look at what's on sale before the bidding starts. God knows who all these people are and what will turn up.'

Plump women with sharp elbows and an advanced air of entitlement were shown to their chairs by weary men who would probably rather have been on a Mediterranean cruise than stuck in a damp environment that smelled of dying lilies and old school dinners.

Sidney, Charles and Amanda sat next to a few young would-be connoisseurs who dressed like their parents. Also in attendance was the owner of a group of Chinese restaurants, a tweedy hotelier after some 'classy tat', and an aristocratic couple who would never buy anything but were there simply to check the prices and revalue their possessions accordingly. There were journalists from the *Yorkshire Post* and the *West Riding Gazette*, a local estate agent, a woman

Amanda recognised from the Courtauld Institute speaking in Spanish to a friend with a notebook (how much did they know? she wondered) and a mustachioed man in a sheepskin coat who had just won the pools and was looking for 'some proper swank' for his new country house outside Ripon.

The auctioneer was a suave, thin, silver-haired man with a slight stutter that might have been an affectation in order to prolong the bidding. He was wearing a three-piece brown tweed suit and a yellow polka-dot bow-tie. His quiet demeanour was perhaps a counter-intuitive attempt to persuade people that it was perfectly natural to spend vast sums of money on objects that might not merit the financial outlay.

Sidney was surprised how deceptively low some of the estimates were and was informed that the 'punchy prices' had been set to lure people into bidding. It was easy to get carried away by thinking 'it's only another twenty pounds', as if the amount people had already offered no longer counted.

The heavy old furniture, some of it in poor condition, sold cheaply while the porcelain, the paintings and the taxidermy exceeded expectations. The bidding for the José de Madrazo y Agudo, Amanda's alleged Goya, started at £1,000, with the auctioneer announcing that it was a handsome curio that 'should clean up nicely'. There appeared to be two rival bidders and the price reached Amanda's intended price of £4,000 in under a minute.

Sidney wondered whether she would continue, but every time he tried to give her one of his quizzical 'Are you sure?' looks she brushed him aside to concentrate as the auctioneer kept up the interest.

'I'm at £5,000. Do I have £5,100? Thank you, sir. £5,200. Madam? £5,300, £5,400, £5,600, £5,700. Was that a nod or a bid? Thank you. £5,800, £5,900, SIX THOUSAND POUNDS. It's with YOU at the back, sir . . .'

Who were these rival bidders and did they suspect as much as Amanda? Might one of them be a plant to push the other two up? Sidney knew that as long as there were three people bidding, the price was likely to rise, but he didn't expect them to reach £10,000 in the next minute and a half. This was double the amount that Amanda had said she would bid and the battle showed no sign of abating. By the time the price hit £15,000, one of the bidders dropped out but that still left what appeared to be an American gentleman in the race to acquisition.

'Now at £16,800, £16,900, SEVENTEEN THOU-SAND POUNDS. It's with you, madam. Seventeen thousand pounds. £17,100, £17,200, £17,300, £17,400, £17,500, £17,600, £17,700, £17,800, £17,900. EIGH-TEEN THOUSAND POUNDS. At eighteen thousand pounds, do I hear £18,100? Thank you, sir. £18,100, £18,200, £18,300, £18,400, £18,500 – with you now, madam. £18,500. Sir?'

The rival bidder shook his head.

'Last chance at £18,500. All done? No more? No one? Going once, going twice, at £18,500 . . .'

The hammer came down.

'Sold to the lady in the red coat at £18,500.'

There was applause. Charles Beauvoir asked Amanda what the hell she thought she had been doing. With the auction house adding their charges to the hammer price and the cost of transport, insurance, cleaning and restoration, the total was likely to touch £25,000.

'I thought we agreed that we wouldn't go above £4,000; £5,000 in an emergency: how are you going to cover it?'

'With the profit.'

'But what if you're wrong?'

'I'm not.'

'It's £25,000, Amanda,' said Sidney. 'Isn't that the cost of your house?'

'How did you know?'

'You told me.'

'Well, risk is exciting, don't you think? Provided all goes well after the reauthentication, we are still going to make around £180,000 profit at the next sale.'

'And if you've made an error of judgement?' Sidney asked.

'I haven't.'

'But *if* you have?'

'Then I'm ruined.'

Back in Ely, Sidney's mind turned to lesser expenditure and the curious case of the offertory collection. Vanessa Morgan had tightened her net of suspicion.

'It's either Ted Burgess or Canon Jocelyn Smith.'

'How do you know?'

'Because they were the only two people present when the money banked does not match the money raised.'

'I find it hard to imagine either of them stealing from the cathedral. Why would Jocelyn want to do such a thing? Doesn't he have everything he needs?'

'That may be the case, Archdeacon. But does he have everything he *wants*? Perhaps there's a bit of devilry in him?'

It was true that Jocelyn had recently read a newspaper article which argued that men became more attractive as they get older, and he had been vain enough to think this applied to him, but that, as far as Sidney was concerned, was the limit of his sin.

Miss Morgan was not so sure. 'What about the lure of disobedience and the thrill of the theft? Canon Smith may be compensating for the mundanity of his surname. As for Ted, well, you just have to look at him.'

'You cannot judge people by appearances, Miss Morgan. I know that you wouldn't approve of that.'

'But it's obvious he has very little money. Have you seen his shoes?'

'Perhaps we should buy him a new pair?'

'Not until we get to the bottom of this, Archdeacon. Charity has to be earned.'

'I'm not sure the quality of mercy should ever be *strained*.'

'There's a difference between drama on a stage and the reality of life itself. We can't all be in a Shakespeare play and, before you say anything more, I would ask you not to tell me which character I most remind you of.'

'I wouldn't dare do such a thing,' said Sidney. 'You are beyond comparison: quite unique.'

'I'm not sure you intend that as a compliment, Archdeacon, but I'll take it all the same.'

A week later Amanda travelled with Charles Beauvoir to have their painting examined by the appropriate Goya expert. Under a swooping black seventeenth-century cloak Xavier Morata was dressed entirely in red. He was a thin but fit man with long dark hair streaked with grey, a waxed moustache and a pointed beard that made him look like a cross between Salvador Dalí and a Manchester United footballer.

He shone a light across the surface of the painting, took out his magnifying glass and scraped a tiny sample of paint from the edge of the canvas where it would have been hidden under the frame. He then asked to see the paperwork and pointed out that the picture was not named specifically and the inventory could refer to almost any painting.

'The watermark on the documentation is genuine; D and C BLAUW, which occurs in at least two of Goya's drawings, dated 1810, and now in the Prado,' said Amanda.

'And you think the handwriting is Goya's?'

'It is a fair match with other documents in Wellington's possession.'

'People were taught to write very similarly in those days. It is not necessarily Goya's handwriting . . .'

'The title also matches one of his Caprichos.'

Xavier Morata completed his examination, took off his glasses and, after an overdramatic pause, announced: 'I think this is a pastiche at best; and a contemporary forgery at worst. Goya wouldn't reuse his subject matter three times like this. The composition is too crowded. He preferred the simple strong image rather than a portmanteau. The lack of a signature is also a problem. He liked to sign. I need only remind you of the 1797 portrait of the Duchess of Alba, pointing to his autograph on the ground beneath her feet: *Solo Goya.*'

'But she was his mistress.'

'Are you suggesting the reclining figure here could also be her?'

'No,' said Amanda. 'I think it is Pepita Tudó, the Spanish Prime Minister's lover; the same woman that is in the celebrated Maja paintings.'

'Why would he want to ridicule her with an ass's head in the mirror?'

'This is a vanity painting. Goya is the young immortal painter; any model, no matter how beautiful, will grow old and die.'

'And the war in the background?'

'A sign of the times in which they live. The painting is a nude, a memento mori and a vanity painting all in one.'

'Goya always tells one story; never three. I cannot authenticate on this evidence.'

'Could you say that it is *possibly* by Goya?'

'No. You should have come to me before you bought the picture.'

'But then you would have bought it for yourself.'

'You think I can afford that kind of money, Mrs Richmond?'

'I don't think I can.'

'Then you should have thought about that before you bid.'

'But if it *is* a Goya . . .' said Charles.

'It is not.'

Charles had begun to sweat around the neck. 'And what if we made it worth your while to say that it was?' he asked.

'That would be most improper. I have my reputation to consider.'

'No one need know.'

'You might have enough to convince an auction house to take it on. But without my word, I don't think you will get very far. Both Christie's and Sotheby's will ask me.'

'We'll give you £10,000,' said Charles.

'Please do not insult me.'

Amanda was surprised by such resistance. 'You want more than that?'

'I can't be bought. If anyone found out, I'd never work again. Thirty years of ignominy? You can't put a price on that.'

'Try me,' said Charles.

At Canonry House, Anna was watching *Look: Mike Yarwood* on television with her mother. They were laughing at the impressions of Harold Wilson, Denis Healey and Edward Heath. Sidney wondered how much Anna understood and how much the joke fell flat if you didn't know whom he was impersonating. The entertainer ended his show with a song prefaced by the words 'And this is me . . .' but, Sidney thought, was it really Mike Yarwood or was he performing a showbiz version of himself? When was 'Mike Yarwood' really Mike Yarwood? When are we ever ourselves?

Amanda telephoned and attempted a breezy tone to assure her friend that the situation was under control, but Sidney knew her well enough to recognise that she feared she had made a colossal mistake.

Later that night he raised the question of authenticity in literature, art and music and the differences between an original, a fake and a pastiche. He asked Hildegard what, for example, made a Bach piece better than anything by his pupils or his imitators?

'I think there has to be an authority of expression; a sense of control that is also combined with effortlessness – what the Italians call *sprezzatura*. It never shows how hard it is. It seems easy, right, natural, even if it is hard to play.'

'With music it needs interpretation and performance. It cannot just exist on the page.'

'It can. But it is meant for more than that. It also needs an audience to become itself; just as we always need other people to help us realise who we are.'

'Perhaps, then, there is no such thing as the authentic self? We are defined by our parents, our children, our friends and those we love. We are dependent on how other people see us and change us; and how we change them.'

There was, however, no alteration in the formal authentication of the Goya painting and, in a second telephone call, Amanda confessed that she was starting to panic. The auction house was requesting immediate payment (bailiffs had been mentioned) and Roland Russell, her boss at the British Museum, had heard what he referred to as 'unsavoury stories'. If it were true that she and Charles Beauvoir had tried to bribe Xavier Morata to say that a certain painting was a Goya when it plainly was not, then she would have to look elsewhere for employment.

'Bribery, Amanda! Whatever possessed you?'

'It wasn't me. It was Charles.'

'Were you in the room at the time?'

'Yes.'

'And you didn't stop him or retract?'

'It's only Morata's word against ours. Nothing happened. He said no and then reported us.'

'And you're denying it.'

'I can't really admit it, can I?'

'But you could be ruined. Morata might try to do that.'

'But if he does then that will prove the painting is a Goya.'

'Has he offered to buy it from you?'

'Not yet. But I think he is waiting until we are desperate.'

'And the Fairley family won't take it back?'

'The deal is binding.'

'Why can't you put it up for sale? What about the under-bidder? The man who stopped at £18,400? Can you find out who he is?'

'The auctioneer won't say, but I suspect Morata knows. He may even have been in on it. This is jealousy and envy. It is his revenge on us for preventing his own little adventure.'

'It was your adventure too.'

'I will not let him beat me.'

'Can't your parents help?'

'I don't want to tell them too much. They've hardly recovered from my divorce. And then if I lose my job as well . . .'

'There's no chance of that, surely?'

'There's *every* chance, Sidney.'

'So what are you going to do?'

'I'm taking the painting to Spain. There's a man in the Prado. He'll authenticate it for me.'

'You think so?'

'I'm going to make him do it by any means I know how.'

Vanessa Morgan's investigations into clergy finances settled on the head verger and she insisted that Sidney question him. This was straightforward but awkward; Ted Burgess was an uncomplicated character without guile or malice who had served Sidney well ever since he had arrived in Ely.

'Am I in trouble?' the verger asked.

'That depends on your answers,' Miss Morgan replied.

'I don't know what to say.'

'You need to tell us if you feel you've done anything wrong,' said Sidney, 'even if you didn't intend to do so. It may be a misunderstanding.'

He mentioned the discrepancies in the accounting of collection money. In many cases there had been shortfalls between the money they thought had been donated and the amount that was finally banked. But in one case, rather surprisingly, there had been a surplus. Did Ted know anything about that?

'I've always been honest.'

'We're not saying that you're not. Have you, yourself, been short recently?'

'It's always tight, Archdeacon.'

'So you've been taking money from us?' Miss Morgan asked.

Sidney placed a restraining hand on her arm. It was the first time he had touched her and he was sure she flinched at the intimacy. 'Let's not call it that,' he said. 'Perhaps we should see it in terms of borrowing. Is that what you've been doing, Ted? Taking a little money to tide you over and then paying it back when you can. Is that what accounts for that surplus payment?'

'It's not stealing. I haven't done that.'

'We're not saying it is, Ted, because I know you. You always planned to give the money back. Perhaps it was easier than borrowing money from the bank?'

'They wouldn't give me a loan.'

'So you thought of this as some kind of informal loan system that you were too embarrassed to tell anyone about?'

'Or rather,' Miss Morgan cut in, 'it was one that you felt you could get away with.'

Ted was on the verge of tears. It appalled Sidney that this decent, slightly lost man on the verge of retirement, who had fought bravely in France at the end of the First World War, should be subjected to unnecessary humiliation.

'I just needed the cash to help out,' he said. 'I'm going to pay it all back, I promise. It will work out about even in the end.'

Miss Morgan resisted the need for compassion. 'About?'

'I didn't keep accounts. I was more "back of a fag packet" in my calculations.'

'Perhaps if you gave up smoking you'd be better off?'

'We all have our weaknesses, Miss Morgan.'

'Tell us what's been troubling you,' said Sidney.

'I don't like to talk about it. It's a frightening thing, debt. There's only so much you can do on twenty-seven pounds a week and with retirement only a few years away. I got a bit scared, I suppose. I don't have savings and the thought of living on a pension that's less than a tenner, well, I don't really know what that's about. Nine pounds and seventy pence for a married couple? I can't work out how we're going to live on that, what with inflation and the cost of electric and the dogs.'

'We all have to make sacrifices,' said Vanessa.

'But some of these things are necessities.'

'If you can't afford to keep your dogs . . .'

'You think I'm supposed to give up their company?'

'You have to cut your cloth.'

'It depends on how much cloth you've got in the first place. It's like the politicians telling the people to tighten their belts. Some of us are down to the last notch.'

Vanessa turned to Sidney as if she wanted nothing more to do with this man. He wondered whether she had been in a situation like this, or ever known poverty. 'What were you spending the money on, Ted?' he asked.

'Nothing fancy. The vet, mainly.'

'You mean the dogs have been ill?'

'I love them so much. I won't see them harmed.'

'No one's asking you to let them suffer.'

'*She* was.'

'I didn't mean that,' Miss Morgan replied. 'But you could give up smoking.'

'I suppose you want me to give up eating and drinking as well. It would probably be better for you all if I just got on with it and died.'

'Now you're being dramatic.'

'What do you expect me to be?'

'Look, Ted,' said Sidney. 'I am sure we can help if you are on the breadline.'

'It's not that. I'm just above it. I'm not skint. I'm poor. There's a difference. Being broke and being poor are different things, Archdeacon. I can't see how I will ever have enough. It's going to be cold this winter.'

'We will make sure you have enough blankets. I will talk to the dean about a pay rise.'

'The vergers in Winchester are about to be sacked.'

'We don't know that.'

'Yes, we do, unless they agree to do the cleaning too, which puts those cleaners, who are already employed, out of a job. Why can't people treat others properly? Even in a cathedral things go wrong.'

'It's an expensive place to run. The Church isn't as well-off as it used to be.'

'You can't put a price on people, Archdeacon.'

'That's very true.'

'But,' Miss Morgan interrupted, 'neither can you run a deficit for ever.'

Sidney tried to calm the situation down. It seemed ridiculous that in the same month Amanda had paid nearly £25,000 for a painting, a cathedral verger was worried about a pint of beer and a packet of cigarettes that cost twenty-one pence.

'You know we have a charitable foundation for the needy, Ted. Almshouses. Perhaps you could move in there?'

'I'm not old enough for them.'

'Better to go too early than too late.'

'I don't know about that. Some people say that about life. Besides, I didn't like to ask.'

'You were too proud?'

'I don't like to depend on charity. I just needed a bit of help to see me through. I'll stop now. Honest.'

'I will help you make an application to the charity.'

'There's no need for that.'

'There is, Ted. You've been here thirty years. Let us help you.'

'What's going to happen to me?'

'There may well be consequences,' Miss Morgan warned, before picking up her files and heading off to her next meeting.

Sidney stayed on. 'Don't worry. I'll talk to the dean. And I promise you, Ted, I'll make sure there are *no* consequences. Come and have a drink.'

While Amanda was away in Spain, Sidney returned to his duties, his wife and his child. He was so grateful for the latitude Hildegard allowed him in their marriage but wondered why she did it. Was she granting him the freedom to be himself or was she happier to be rid of him so that she could get on with her own life? He couldn't work it out and decided not to spend too much time thinking about it lest it make him feel even more guilty or selfish than he already did.

It was easiest to feel most himself when he could tick off what he knew was right: preaching a good sermon, visiting the sick, walking Byron, giving people the time they needed. What he had to do now, he decided, even if she might not properly appreciate it, was visit Mrs Maguire, his former housekeeper, who was now in a Cambridge care home and suffering from dementia.

As he bicycled from the station he wondered how much of her identity was dependent on self-awareness. Was she still 'Sylvia Maguire' even if she was no longer aware of who she was?

She was sitting in an armchair with her feet up and a rug over her legs. She was trying to pin her favourite brooch back on her blouse but could not remember how to do it.

'Have we met before?' she asked.

'It's Sidney. Let me help you . . .'

'I can manage, thank you. Are you my father? Did you let me have this brooch?'

It was eleven cultured pearls on a sprig of silver leaves. Her husband Ronnie had given it to her before he went off to fight in the First World War.

'No, that was from your husband.'

'I'm too young to have a husband.'

'I'm your priest. We are friends.'

'Am I dying?'

'Not yet.'

'It feels like I am. Or I've already done it. Am I dead? Is this heaven? Where is everyone? They told me it would be different. Did you tell me? Who was it? It's so hard to think. Is this a dream? Who am I?'

'You're Sylvia.'

'That's a nice name.'

'Sylvia Maguire.'

'I don't think that's right.'

'You used to be Sylvia Reynolds. Then you married Ronnie.'

'Married. Am I married now?'

'He died.'

'How did he die? Did they tell me?'

'I took his funeral. We were there together.'

'I don't think I was. I don't even know who he is. Why would I go to the funeral of someone I don't know?'

'You were very good to him.'

'Was he good to me?'

'In the end he was.'

'Are you good to me?'

'I hope so. I try my best.'

'Can't you do any better?'

'I'll try, Sylvia.'

'Who is Sylvia? And who are you?'

'I'm Sidney.'

'And we are friends. Did you say that? Does it mean I have to be kind to you?'

'No, the other way round.'

'What other way round? I don't know any other way round. Don't you know the right way round? Do you know right from wrong? Why don't you tell me? Who are you again?'

'I'm Sidney.'

He bumped into the dean on the way home, who said that he had let Ted off with a warning. Vanessa Morgan had been 'unimpressed' by the behaviour of the clergy. 'I think she expected us to take a tougher line on petty theft.'

'I'm not sure she's in the right job, Felix.'

'That is what I have suggested. I think she's going to come and have a word with you in the pub.'

'How does she know I'm going to be there?'

'Thursdays. That's your night with Inspector Keating. Everyone knows that.'

'As long as she doesn't get him involved.'

'She may have a go.'

'I think he's not in the mood for petty theft. He has bigger fish to fry.'

'Our Miss Morgan doesn't consider herself one of life's minnows.'

'Indeed not, Felix. I must confess to being rather scared of her.'

'She's quite harmless when you get to know her.'

'I'd rather not take the risk.'

That night, having told the men that she had expected to find them in the pub, her tone managing to combine the disappointed, the patronising and the aggressive, Miss Morgan announced she was leaving.

'Already?' Sidney asked.

'I haven't enjoyed working here.'

'Oh, really?' Geordie answered. He was already on his third pint. 'And why is that?'

'If you have to ask, Inspector . . .'

'Is it the fact that they are all men?'

'It is not only that.'

'Or is it their complacency, absent-mindedness, vanity, disguised selfishness, laziness – do any of those questionable virtues spring to mind?'

'You think you are being amusing, Inspector Keating, when, in point of fact, you are just being rude.'

'I'm sorry,' said Sidney. 'I know how you disapprove and I'm sure you don't like any of us very much.'

'It's not that I don't like you, Archdeacon,' Miss Morgan replied. 'I just think you are a long way from Jesus. As is the Church of England.'

'And what do you intend to do about that?' Geordie asked.

'Mr Chambers knows perfectly well. You may not think it likely, but the day will come. They are ordaining Joyce Bennett in Hong Kong at Christmas. Once you accept women into the Church everything will change.'

'Women are already in the Church.'

'But not as priests.'

'Then I must wish you good luck. I am sorry if we have let you down.'

'On the contrary, Archdeacon. You have made me more determined than ever.'

Mrs Maguire died on All Saints' Day. She had not always been popular in the community and had had her battles with people who found her too judgemental. As far as she was concerned, it was no accident that she had been born on the day that Queen Victoria died, and some of the Grantchester villagers liked to joke that, when she got on her high horse, she probably thought she was the dead monarch's reincarnation. And yet, despite the pronounced lack of a sense of humour, Sidney's former housekeeper had served God well throughout her life, expected the best of people and kept her standards up to the end.

Sidney remembered how she had helped him set up home when he had first arrived in Grantchester, and seen him right about food and routine and the demands of his parishioners. Despite her strong traditional views, she was capable of recovering from an often over-hasty first impression, changing her mind when encouraged to do so and then lovably convincing herself that this new second opinion was how she had felt from the start. There had been no malice in her, and Sidney was convinced that she had lived as well as anyone. She had put up with Dickens and Byron, grown used to Amanda, welcomed Hildegard, understood Leonard and forgiven the husband who had deserted her. It wasn't a complicated life, she hadn't had the luxury of too much introspection, but she liked to think that everyone knew where they stood when she spoke to them, and they couldn't ask for any more than that.

Sidney thought of those who might accompany her on her final journey: St Honoratus, the patron saint of bakers; St Gertrude of Nivelles, the patron saint of the fear of mice; St Eligius, the patron saint of jewellery; St Ambrose, the patron saint of argument; St Monica for the victims of adultery and St Thomas of Villanova for memory loss.

Given a healthful eternal life, Sylvia Maguire would have quite a few things to say for herself, he decided. She wouldn't care what anyone else thought. She could be herself again.

The following day, Amanda was back from Madrid, and Sidney went down to see her in London. 'I stayed in a little hotel off the Plaza de Santa Ana,' she announced. 'I lived almost entirely on garlic soup and suckling pig. The waiters at Botín, which is the oldest restaurant in the world, took pity on me. I ate every day at a table just next to the kitchens while I waited for the Prado to make up its mind. It was humiliating but necessary.'

'And you were on your own?'

'Absolutely. The trip had to be a secret. I didn't want Xavier Morata ruining it all over again. It turns out he didn't need to bother. I spent most of my time looking at paintings and trying to understand what it must have been like for Goya; to have been so much part of society, a life filled with colour and light, and then, at the end of his life, to be confined to deafness and blackness, making paintings of the living damned.'

'They refused to accredit it?'

'They believe it is, as stated in the catalogue, a painting by José de Madrazo y Agudo.'

'But what about your documentation?'

'Not specific enough, and, as Morata said, they thought it was "too crowded a composition". He might just as well have briefed them.'

'Perhaps he did?'

'They also said it didn't *feel* like a Goya – whatever that means. And so the painting is currently worth the estimate that was originally given in the first sale. Exactly £1,500.'

'What about the other bidder?'

'I think someone might have been trying to ruin me.'

'You mean they knew your tactics? But how could they tell when to stop? You went far beyond any upper limit you told anyone about. They could have ended up with the painting and been in the same situation.'

'I don't think so. You know, Sidney, I'm pretty sure that Charles was behind it all.'

'Charles? Why on earth would he do that?'

'Because I cannot love him. I told him it was hopeless.'

'You rejected him?'

'I told him I was content to be his friend, but he was expecting more.'

'It seems an extravagant and vengeful way of going about things. Why do you think it's him?'

'He was covering himself with two different options so he could get the painting without any financial outlay himself.'

'You mean that you still think it's a Goya . . .'

'Of course I do . . .'

' . . . and that this whole affair has been some kind of conspiracy?'

'Yes. It's been run by a cartel of men who wanted to take advantage of a little rich girl who got just a bit too greedy and thought that she was rather better than she was. They wanted to teach me a lesson.'

'Are you sure you're not being paranoid?'

'I don't think so, Sidney. Charles knew about the house in Chester Row. He guessed my upper limit. He was sure I wouldn't risk more than my home, but he put another bidder into the auction both to cover himself and to punish me. If the other bidder acquired the painting then presumably he had a separate deal. If I got it then he would still win either way: whether I shared the painting after the resale at a far higher price or if I was forced to give it directly to him because I couldn't pay the auction house. Charles is in it with Morata.'

'So you are saying that he'll share the final profit with Morata rather than you; that you have been betrayed?'

96

'The bribe was a bluff to throw me off the scent. They've done all this together and the Prado is in on it too. Now all they have to do is wait until I am desperate to sell.'

'Have you challenged any of them about all this?'

'I can't. Charles has disappeared. His family say he's gone abroad.'

'Leaving you to pick up the pieces?'

'There aren't very many pieces to pick up.'

'But you still have the painting.'

'I do, but if I want to sell now, without accreditation, I'll get £1,000 at best. I think I may be ruined. I had some savings and raised the money against my home, but if everything falls apart I'll be left with pennies. I can't imagine what I'm going to do or where on earth I'm going to live.'

'Will you go back to your parents'?'

'Can you imagine what that's going to be like?'

'You can always stay with us.'

'I don't think so, Sidney.'

'It need only be for a little while, until this all blows over. You're still holding the ace. You have the picture. Those men can't make any profit without it. Can you not find a way of holding out?'

'I'm already on the floor, Sidney. I never imagined how quickly I could lose not only my confidence, but every sense of who I am. I thought divorce was bad enough, but I could cope with that and with my brother dying in the war and my father becoming frail. I mean, I know people get old. Mummy's hoping that if she pretends nothing is going to go wrong and refuses to acknowledge Daddy's ill then he'll somehow get better, but I know he won't. He's mortal.

We're all mortal. But when you think you're going to lose your job you don't know who you are any more. It defines me more than being the vacuous socialite everyone used to think I was.'

'No one thought that.'

'You remember we used to joke about each other, Sidney? I used to say that because you could be amusing it didn't mean you were not serious.'

'And I used to say that just because you were rich it didn't make you stupid.'

'Well I've proved it now. I'm not so rich any more. And perhaps I am even more foolish.'

'You have made a mistake, that's all. And you can rectify it.'

'Perhaps. I could possibly make amends for the mistake but I can't undo the professional damage. People will abandon me. They will worry that any association with me will sully their reputation. I had forgotten how fickle friendship can be. You're the only one I can trust, Sidney.'

'And Hildegard.'

'Sometimes I am still not sure whether she likes me.'

'She loves you, Amanda. She doesn't have to prove it. She's only amused to think what it would have been like . . .'

'If we had married each other? Don't.'

'Those days are gone.'

'Everything's gone. I don't know how much is left of me. I don't know anything at all any more. I wish you'd stopped me getting into all this.'

'I've never been able to prevent you doing anything, Amanda.'

'But you know me best. And now I'm ruined.'

Sidney did not like to point out that Amanda could not be 'ruined' if she was still able to fall back on her parents and she had only been suspended from her job at the British Museum; he was sure that her boss liked her enough to restore her position once she had acknowledged both that Charles Beauvoir had 'led her astray' and that 'lessons had been learned'. Amanda still had her beauty, her charm and her connections. She was hardly likely to starve.

He remembered Ted the verger's point that there was a difference between being broke and being poor, and he had always rather despised people from rich families when they told him they 'had no money'. Amanda had been chastened by an experience that was fuelled, in part, by greed; just as he, too, had been humbled recently by meetings with Miss Morgan and Mrs Maguire. Still, it didn't take much to throw a life off balance. We just had to hold on tight to what made the best of us, he decided. Perhaps he would preach about that next Sunday: the illusion, or at least the confining limitations, of the self.

'Will you be able to keep the painting?' he asked.

'As you say, it's the only card I hold. I know a thousand pounds is still a lot of money, but I'm going to have to find a way of waiting until either the others come back and make me a proper offer or I can make a stronger case. Perhaps Xavier Morata will die and a new Goya expert will emerge from the shadows?'

'You're still sure you're right?'

'I'm certainly not going to let them defeat me, Sidney.'

'You're sounding better already.'

'It's a question of money and pride.'

'And vanity.'

'That too; and we both know what impostors they all are. You've taught me that, and I hope you will go on teaching me even if it takes a lifetime. I've still got so much to learn.'

'And so have I. But don't worry. I've no plans to abandon you, Amanda. We will always learn from each other. In fact, I don't think our lessons will ever stop.'

Just before catching the train back to Ely, Sidney paused to look in the window of an antiques shop near the British Museum. He had noticed a rather expensive-looking mirror (if he had raided the Sunday collection himself he would have been able to afford it easily) but, after talking to the shopkeeper, he discovered that it was cheaper than he feared because it was actually made from tin. This was perfect. He was only a month late for his wedding anniversary and Hildegard was used to the somewhat erratic timing of family celebrations. He just hoped she didn't think that he was trying to buy his way back into her good books.

She had just finished teaching and was preparing the supper when he arrived home, kissed her and presented his gift.

'This is very beautiful, *mein Lieber*. Will it tarnish?' As soon as she had spoken, Hildegard held up her hand to prevent interruption. 'Don't draw any moral conclusions from the question. Just answer it.'

'We will need to keep it in good repair. Like . . .'

'Our marriage? Yes, I know, Sidney, but I fear I am getting too old for mirrors. I do not like to look at myself too much. I do not want to turn into my mother.'

'There is little chance of that, I promise.'

'There is every chance. But I like to make an effort.'

She gave her husband a spontaneous hug and they held on to each other in front of the cooker as the potatoes bubbled away. 'I hope you are still proud of me, Sidney. I know I can be difficult.'

'We can all be difficult.'

Hildegard stepped back. 'You are not supposed to agree with me. You have to say that I am the easiest and most tolerant person in the world.'

'I don't know what I'd do without you, my darling.'

'Fortunately, you do not have to think about that.'

'Shall I put the mirror up?'

'As long as you don't bang your thumb.'

'I think I can hammer in a nail.'

Hildegard smiled. 'What is the eleventh-anniversary material?'

'Steel. I think.'

'That is good. I think there is something called "mild steel". That describes you perfectly: tough when you want to be, but responsive to pressure.'

Sidney hesitated. 'I don't suppose I could be *stainless*.'

'No, *mein Lieber*,' said Hildegard. 'That is my job.'

Insufficient Evidence

IT WAS ADVENT. ALTHOUGH Sidney was in residence at Ely Cathedral as priest on duty, presiding over the reassuringly timeless candlelit services, he still found there was an element of desperation during the festive season. His pastoral visits included a call on a woman who could no longer face the daylight and didn't get up until the middle of the afternoon; a local grocer who was terrified that his business would suffer due to the popularity of frozen food from Bejam ('If people want raspberries in December, what can I do to stop them?'); and the first wife of a local bigamist who was distressed that her husband had finally left her because he 'couldn't afford two Christmases'. One of Sidney's clerical friends, a man never knowingly filled with the joys of being alive, referred to this particular time of year, after a surfeit of carol concerts, as 'Death by Little Donkey'.

Hildegard had found last year's Christmas-card list and was making additions (and the odd subtraction) as Anna wrote her letter to Santa. Sidney knew their daughter was only pretending to continue to believe in his existence because she was afraid the number of presents might reduce if she didn't. At the same time her parents were content to play along with the idea if it meant preserving the mutual illusion of their daughter's innocence for a little while longer.

What Sidney did not need, amidst all these extremes of emotion, was a telephone call from Geordie demanding his presence in Cambridge as soon as possible.

He explained that because he was the priest on call he could not leave his post except in the case of an emergency.

'Well, what do you think this is?' said Geordie. 'If you could get the next train . . .'

'You assume I can drop everything?'

'It hasn't stopped you before.'

'I'm supposed to be spending my time in silence and meditation, reflecting on the birth that transformed history, available to anyone who comes in time of trouble.'

'Well, I'm the one that's got the trouble.'

'What is it?'

'I can't tell you over the telephone. It's about that Yorkshire trip.'

'Oh, for goodness sake, Geordie. Is it Amanda? Why didn't you tell me about it when we last spoke?'

'Because, obviously, I didn't know about it then. It's taken all this time to come to light.'

'And you're not going to give me a clue?'

'We've got a suspect who is refusing to speak.'

'And why do you think he'll talk to me?'

'Haven't we known each other long enough, Sidney, for you to realise that I already have a good enough reason and that I'm unlikely to be wasting your time?'

'At least give me something to think about on the train.'

Geordie confided that they were holding Helena Mitchell's photographer, Frank Downing, for questioning.

'On what charge?'

'Rape.'

'Of whom?'

'Helena.'

'What?'

'Exactly. Downing's pursuing his right to silence and he's not saying anything other than "no comment". However, just before he clammed up on us, he asked for you and a lawyer. We think it's his mother's idea. Apparently, you helped her once.'

'I remember there was a bit of a fracas in a pub when he was a teenager; underage drinking and a fight. Does Mrs Downing know about the charges?'

'We haven't made any yet. This is a very difficult area, Sidney. It's his word against Helena's and it was weeks ago now, when you were up at that auction.'

'And why has it taken so long for her to report it?'

'Fear.'

'Poor girl,' said Sidney. 'Are you sure my involvement with the accused will help?'

'I don't think you have much choice. You were in the vicinity.'

'We didn't all stay in the same place.'

'You were close enough, Sidney. It's hard to tell what's going on. Downing insists it was consensual.'

'I think I have to see Helena before I agree to do anything.'

'It's a grey area.'

'I'm not sure it is, Geordie.'

Sidney could not believe that their friend would make a false accusation. Risking her reputation, and possibly her career, with such a charge was not something she would do without a lot of thought (and, as a journalist, she knew the limitations of the criminal justice system). As soon as he had finished speaking to Inspector Keating he dialled Helena's number and got her husband.

'She's with her mother and sister,' said Malcolm. 'She does not want to speak to, or be in the company of, men at all.'

'Why didn't you tell me about this?'

'Because as soon as you get involved with anything, Sidney, the situation escalates . . .'

'It seems to have "escalated" perfectly well without me. I have been asked to visit the accused.'

'You'd better not tell Helena that.'

'If I do visit him, and I only say "if", then I think she'll find out anyway. But I'd like to talk to her. You too.'

'Why don't you refuse to go to the police station, Sidney? There are plenty of other clergy in Cambridge.'

'I know the man's mother. Besides, you know that we are called to respond to every challenge God sends.'

'Not *every* challenge, surely? And perhaps God didn't send this himself: aren't there times when friendship overrides duty?'

'That is why I need to speak to your wife. I want to make it clear that she can trust me.'

'Well, Sidney, you haven't made a very good start. You shouldn't have any doubt where your loyalties lie.'

Impatient to be of assistance, and in the absence of any phone call from Helena, Sidney decided to accept Geordie's request to come to Cambridge. At least he would be doing *something*.

One of the *Daily Mirror*'s top photographers, Frank Downing had covered everything from war to fashion and behaved as if he was capable of going into any situation with both arms free and a Leica round his neck. He was used to sweet-talking his way out of trouble, but this was not going well.

'I haven't said much,' he announced when Sidney arrived in the interview room. 'And I'm not sure I can speak to you.'

'You are, of course, entitled to answer "no comment" to any question, but I don't believe that it ever helps your cause.'

'The police can twist anything they like.'

'But if they only ever have the partial truth then they are bound to be partial with it.'

'I don't know why that bloody girl is causing trouble. She was keen enough at the time.'

'You are not denying the event took place?'

'It depends what you mean by "event". If you mean sex, then no, I don't deny it; not that it lasted that long.'

'Keating tells me that she asked you to stop.'

'I don't remember anything like that.'

'It's a serious accusation.'

'And easy to defend. Helena Mitchell's too embarrassed to confess to her husband, that's all. I don't know why she's told anyone anything in the first place. She knows the rules.'

'Which are?'

'What happens on location stays on location. Never apologise, never explain. Deny, deny, deny.'

'Even if you're caught?'

'We weren't caught. She's confessed. Now she's making all these accusations when she was the one who left her door unlocked.'

'Does she say that?'

'She insists she can't remember doing it. But how could I get into her room if I didn't have a key?'

'Perhaps she forgot to lock the door?'

'Do you think she's doing this to ruin my career?'

'Had you had an argument?'

'We have now. I could bloody kill her. My wife's found out.'

'How?'

'When the police came. I couldn't believe it.'

'What happened that night?'

'We were in the hotel bar. We'd been there for ages. We can both handle our drink. We're journalists, for God's sake. She kissed me goodnight and said "see you later".'

'That might have meant "in the morning".'

'She kissed me on the lips.'

'Any more than that?'

'It was enough to know what she meant.'

'And you're confident of that?'

'I know women.'

'That's not always easy.'

'Harder for a clergyman. You're not supposed to indulge in flirtation.'

'Even a clergyman can be tempted.'

The photographer leant back in his chair, the passive-aggressive attitude of a man about to go on the attack. 'I've been thinking. It must be difficult being married to a priest. There's so much you have to live up to as a vicar's wife. You have to be good all the time and set standards. When you go away from the parish it must be inviting to let it all go, behave badly. How do you lot keep it up all the time? Helena told me that her husband was the cheerful sort that never really knows what's going on. I don't know how much of the world he's seen. They live in their own little bubble. She needed a bit of excitement, and I was happy to oblige. I was probably doing her a favour when you think about it.'

Sidney did not want to think about it at all. When he got home his wife told him she was not sure that the involvement of yet another man in the case was going to improve matters.

'Don't they have any female officers, lawyers or people Helena could talk to?'

'I'm sure they do.'

'Then why don't they offer?'

'I don't know, Hildegard.'

'Perhaps they don't take them so seriously. If we had women priests that would be a bonus too.'

'Don't start on that.'

'I imagine Vanessa Morgan could do a good job.'

'But they haven't asked for her. They've asked for me.'

'Although Helena hasn't. You've volunteered and yet the victim hasn't responded at all.'

'Perhaps she is embarrassed.'

'I am sure she is. She's probably fed up talking to men about the whole thing.'

'There doesn't seem to be much of an alternative.'

'Can you imagine what Helena must be feeling?'

'I can try. But empathy is not the only way of helping someone.'

'I wonder, Sidney, what would you do if this had happened to me?'

'I can't think about that.'

'What do you mean? You don't want to confront the possibility, or you don't think it's likely?'

'I don't know what to say.'

'Do you think I am too old or not attractive enough to be raped?'

'It's not that.'

'What is it then?'

'We can't always confront our deepest fears, Hildegard, otherwise we go mad. You have to live your life optimistically. If you don't then you are always at the mercy of your own anxieties.'

'But it *could* happen to me, Sidney, or eventually to Anna.'

'She's nine years old. She is far too young.'

'She won't be soon.'

'Well, if it did happen then I'd kill the bastard.'

'Now you're beginning to understand. This will be volatile. If you are going to help then you are going to have to behave in a way that you have never known before.'

Sidney decided to risk an unannounced visit to see Malcolm, assuming that Helena might have returned home, but she was still staying with her parents in London. Apparently, her husband had said the wrong thing when he had first been told about the attack and now risked never being forgiven.

109

'What did you say, Malcolm?'

'I insinuated – I didn't say outright, mind, I promise – that *perhaps* she shouldn't have got herself into the situation in the first place . . .'

'Oh dear . . .'

'And that maybe she was a little drunk . . .'

'Does she admit to that?'

'Not really.'

'Then she wasn't. You have to trust your wife. And whatever happened in the hotel restaurant, I'm not sure she can be blamed for what went on afterwards.'

'I can't help worrying, in my heart of hearts – and I know it's wrong, Sidney, believe me, I know this is very wrong, but I just can't help it, call it insecurity or anything you like – that Helena might be making all of this up to excuse her actions.'

'You know that's a terrible thing to say.'

'I can't stop thinking it.'

'But if that is the case, then why did she need to tell you anything at all? She could have said nothing and got on with the rest of her life. Why put herself through all this? She must be innocent, Malcolm, otherwise she wouldn't have gone to the police. You have to believe her. Otherwise your marriage has no future.'

'I'm not sure it does anyway.'

'You can't give up so easily. Remember the vows you took. Helena needs your help.'

'She doesn't want it.'

'Perhaps that's because you haven't been offering it in the right way.'

'I don't know, Sidney. If you should see her . . .'

'I will. But you need to talk to her too, Malcolm. She will feel very alone.'

'She has her parents; her sister.'

'Having met them in the past, I'm not sure they are the best people to help.'

'They'll get her a good lawyer.'

'I didn't mean that. She needs you, as well as everyone else, to believe her. You have to trust her; you more than anyone else. That is your job as a husband.'

'But what if I don't? What if I can't stop worrying about it?'

'Then you must stop thinking that this is all about your reaction rather than the event itself. This is about Helena, Malcolm, not you – or your lack of confidence – or your trust in your own marriage. It requires total understanding, an utter unbreakable confidence, a solidity that cannot be broached or weakened. Anything less than the complete love and support of your wife will be a failure. Wouldn't she do the same for you? Don't doubt her, Malcolm. Love her.'

Sidney finally saw Helena at her parental home in Maida Vale. She was snuggled up under a blanket on an old sofa listening to Leonard Cohen, holding a mug of tea and wearing a loose baggy jumper and jeans.

'I was just thinking of you, Sidney.'

He remembered the first time he had met her, when she had just finished university, and was investigating a series of unusual deaths amidst the elderly in the winter of 1954. Helena had had a cold at the time and, despite being a young up-and-coming journalist, still looked like a student who wore a duffel coat not just as protection against the winter but also to hide herself against the world. Since then she had come out of her shell. Now she had been forced back into it. It didn't take long, Sidney thought, to ambush a life.

Helena said she was worried that the more she explained what had happened, the more lasting the memory would become. She had given the police three statements already.

'You don't have to go over it all again with me,' said Sidney. 'In fact you don't need to tell me anything. I am just here to be with you. You know that I will never doubt you.'

'I have asked enough of you in the past; that time when my sister had her necklace stolen on the Meadows in May Week . . .'

'That was nothing. This is something far worse. And I am here. If you want me to stay, I will. If you'd like me to leave, I'll do that too.'

'We've known each other for such a long time.'

'We can just sit here, if you like.'

'And it's easier to talk to you. I'm more used to it.'

Helena confessed that she had forgotten to lock her hotel-room door and was pretty much comatose when Frank had let himself in, climbed into her bed and raped her.

'I let my guard down, Sidney. As a journalist I'd been trained to protect myself. I made sure people always knew where I was; I didn't draw attention to myself. I didn't wear flash clothes or jewellery or anything anyone would ever want to steal. I always wear flat shoes so that I can make a run for it. But when you're with a colleague and you're back in the hotel and you've knocked off for the day, you think you're safe.

'It wasn't the most challenging assignment, and we could do it quickly; payback for all the crap we'd both had to go through, like knocking on doors and getting people to tell you about the death of their children. And so I changed for dinner and was off duty. More fool me.'

'You think you were too relaxed?'

'I probably drank a bit too much, if that's what you mean, but I wasn't drunk. I don't know if he added anything.'

'You think he might have spiked your drink?'

'I'm not sure, Sidney. All I do know is that I should never have got into the situation in the first place. Then, by the time I tried to stop it all, it was too late.'

'It's horrible.'

'It'll be my word against his. But I can't let him get away with it.'

'I understand.'

'I'm not sure that you do. Men always look after themselves.'

'Not always.'

Helena's mother popped her head round the door to ask if they wanted any more tea or if she could provide Sidney with 'something stronger'. It was clear that this was just a ruse to see how the conversation was going. Hermione Randall, so often the confident, expensively dressed, charity-lunching pillar of the community, now carried a look of helpless disappointment. This sort of thing wasn't supposed to happen in a family such as hers.

Sidney politely refused all offers of hospitality and Helena continued. 'They make you go over the story again and again. And the people asking the questions have no idea what it's like. You have to keep remembering it, reliving it even if you can't bear it, and all the time you're cementing the memory, making it last. If you make the slightest change to your statement they think it proves you're lying.'

'They probably just want to get it right.'

'Or they want to catch me out. How can I tell the story again and again in exactly the same way? They keep you for hours in a brightly lit room. It goes on into the night. You might as well have murdered someone. They give you cups of tea. A succession of different men come and go before disappearing to do something important. Sometimes you can smell their contempt. They think I asked for it. They think it's my fault. Already there have been so many times when I wanted to give up and stop and tell them they've won. There didn't seem any point in going on.

'Then one of the policemen asked if it ever felt good to be possessed so violently. Didn't women always secretly want that? He suggested that we all had intense fantasies and only claimed to have been raped because of the guilt that followed. And that was someone who was supposed to be *on my side*.'

'So what did you say?'

'I walked out.'

'But you still want the police to press charges?'

'Malcolm made me go back.'

'You've told him everything?'

'I did, Sidney. And I heard you'd spoken to Downing. I know you're trying to help. But I also have to ask – what the hell did you think you were doing seeing that bastard? You know what he's done.'

114

Sidney looked down at shoes that were in need of a polish. 'I thought I could help.'

'Well you've made it worse. Talking to the man who raped me: whose side are you on?'

'I'm not on anyone's *side*, Helena.'

'You can't sit on the fence, Sidney. You once told me that silence was consent. If you don't speak up for me then I will have to assume you are sympathetic to the man who attacked me and, if you are, this is the last time we will ever speak.'

'I'm not on his side, Helena.'

'Frank is still in his job. I've had to take time off. The paper can't afford to lose their star photographer but they can get rid of me.'

'There's only one thing I wanted to ask you, Helena.'

'Don't you dare doubt me . . .'

'I don't.'

'Then what is it?'

'Why bring the charges now? Why did you wait?'

Helena put down her mug of tea, stood up and walked to look out of the window, as if what she saw could lessen the impact of what she was going to say or make her think about something entirely different.

'Because I'm pregnant,' she said.

'As a result of the rape?'

'It's not Malcolm's. We can't have children. We only found out last year.'

'Are you sure?'

'Why would I make that up?'

'I'm not accusing you of that.'

'This, it seems, is the only way I can have a child. We had talked about adoption. There was that possibility. But now there's this. I don't know what to do. I can't bear it.'

'And have you thought about the alternative?'

'An abortion? I've already had one, Sidney, before I was married, and I don't want another. Malcolm doesn't know about that and I don't want him to know. Besides, even if I went through with it, I can't abort the experience. And if the courts ever find out that I was pregnant before I was married then there's probably no hope for a "loose woman" like me at all.'

Sidney returned home and was just about to walk Byron when he discovered that the Keatings had paid a visit while doing some Christmas shopping. Cathy and Hildegard had shared a pot of tea while Geordie made a few enquiries with regards to a different investigation and left word that he would be up for a quick pint at six in the Prince Albert.

When Sidney arrived he found his colleague in conversation with their old friend Dr Michael Robinson. They were discussing the nature of rape, the examination of women by male doctors, the problem of alcohol and consent, and the difficulty of prosecution. Dr Robinson was arguing that sometimes it was better for women to forget these things in order to avoid the further trauma of a court case and a destructive cross-examination.

'That's why so many women give up,' said Geordie. 'They can't face their attacker. It makes everything worse.'

'But then the perpetrator gets away with it,' said Sidney.

The doctor picked up his pint. 'It was possibly just a drunken fling.'

'We don't know that. Rape is an offence.'

'As is a false accusation.'

'But Michael . . .'

'I've seen it time and time again . . .'

Sidney hesitated. Was this the man who had been so compassionate as to take the palliative care of his patients to the limit of the law? Why was he being so unsympathetic? Could he once have been similarly accused?

On the third Sunday of Advent, Sidney offered to help celebrate at Malcolm's parish carol service. This was an opportunity to show his support in a practical way without making his anxiety too obvious.

'Helena's angry with me as much as with the man who attacked her. She keeps going on about why men have to punish women for their own inadequacy, and every time I try to comfort her she flares up. I wish we could stop the prosecution, but my wife wants justice. She can't think of anything else. Perhaps it stops her dwelling on the child.'

'You must let her have the time to work out what she wants to do.'

'There isn't much time left if we are going to take action.'

'I didn't know you were thinking of that?'

'It's hard not to, Sidney. I know it's a terrible thing and Helena doesn't want to pursue it. I can understand why. I went to the synod debate on abortion last year. But the child will be a constant reminder, not only of the rape but of my own inadequacy.'

'As far as we can tell.'

'And if we decide to keep the child then I will always know that I am not the real father.'

'There's always adoption.'

'It's hard to work out what Helena wants apart from justice. There's something else going on, I'm sure of it.'

'This is your adversity. This is your test of love and faith,' said Sidney. 'How will the real Malcolm behave?'

'Oh, I don't know,' his friend continued. 'I just wish everything was how it used to be. Sometimes I feel like a little boy who has been asked to sit his A levels. I look at all the questions and I haven't got a clue how to answer them. All I want to do is to leave the room, put my head under a pillow and hope that everything goes away.'

'But we can't live our lives like that, Malcolm. We have to be active in the world, no matter how much it troubles us. There's no escaping it.'

Outside, tinny Christmas music came from the town centre: from Tesco and the Co-op, Edis and Cutlacks; Crocks, Babie Care and the Ely Trophy Shop. Men in sheepskin coats carried model train sets and that year's must-have Christmas game – Mousetrap – past displays of women in low-cut Santa Claus tops and silver hot pants with glitter leggings. The New Seekers sang 'You Won't Find Another Fool Like Me', Wizzard wished 'it could be Christmas everyday' while Mott the Hoople made the almost Easter-like suggestion to 'Roll Away the Stone'.

The streets were filled with crowds, slush and winter fog. Sidney found it hard to feel a part of the enforced seasonal cheerfulness, the hope of a newborn child, a light in the darkness. Over Christmas drinks in the Prince Albert, as Byron stretched out and slept by the fire, he reported to Geordie on his conversation with Malcolm.

'Is she talking to him again?'

'He says she's frightened of intimacy.'

'You can hardly blame her.'

Keating picked up his pint and changed the subject. 'Do you think there's such a thing as knowing too much?'

'About our friends? There has to be a level of discretion, especially with marriage. I'm sure our wives wouldn't want us talking about intimate matters in a place like this.'

'I don't have to worry too much about that kind of thing these days. Cathy's lost interest.'

'I'm sorry to hear that.'

Geordie's wife had given up smoking, bought in extra vitamin pills and was taking something called Laetrile. 'Do you know what that is, Sidney? Is it for the menopause?'

'Why don't you ask?'

'She said it was nothing. But there's something she's not telling me. What do you think it can be?'

By New Year's Eve, Sidney was filled with trepidation about the year ahead. A national state of industrial unrest, a three-day week and a heating ban in public places did not help. The Chambers family had just the one hot meal a day, didn't use the washing machine, shared their bath water and walked round the house covered in rugs and blankets, with candles to light the way at night.

His parents were coming to supper (sautéed liver with orange and a rice pilaf) but any chance of an improved mood was ruined by another power cut. Sidney took his father to one side and told him about Helena.

He was worried about her volatility and her loss of confidence; how the trauma of the event had been amplified by the stress of the investigation, and the fact that the longer the case took to come to trial, the harder it would be for her to survive a prolonged interrogation in the witness box.

Alec Chambers confirmed Doctor Robinson's belief that it was going to be difficult to get the jury to believe her. In the eyes of many of his fellow professionals, Helena had put herself in a dangerous situation. The people involved were journalists – isn't that what they do? The drink, and the clothes that she was wearing, had not helped either. He only hoped that no one had access to her medical records.

'I know.'

'Even finding out what age she was when she went on the pill . . .'

'They can find that out?'

'If she's signed a consent form. It's easy enough to agree. They make you think that you are helping. Most people are trusting when it comes to medicine. And that, of course, can be a great mistake.'

'Helena needs understanding. She has to be innocent. I can't believe that she would be putting herself through all this if she wasn't.'

'I'm sure you do. But it's difficult, isn't it? One word against another. I always think infidelity is like a batsman going after a ball outside the off-stump and then getting caught out when he should have left it well alone.'

Sidney wondered whether there was any situation in human existence that his father could not explain without reference to cricket. 'It's not a case of infidelity, Dad. It's rape.'

'Very hard to prove, if she let him into her room. That's not an innocent act. Is there evidence of undue pressure? Bruising?'

'She took too long to report it.'

'It was an afterthought?'

'She's pregnant.'

'And it's too late for a termination?'

'No.'

'What's a termination?' Anna asked as the lights came back on.

'The end of a conversation,' her grandfather replied. 'I am terminating this conversation with your father in order to speak to you. How is your pony?'

'I don't have a pony. Mum and Dad never gave me one.'

'But there is one that you ride, isn't there? Don't you have a friend called Sophie who has ponies?'

'It's too cold.'

'Just like this supper,' said Hildegard. 'I might as well start again.'

'By the way,' Sidney asked his father as they searched for a warming bottle of whisky, 'I forgot to say. Do you know about Laetrile?'

'Why do you want to find out?'

'Cathy Keating's taking it. Geordie wondered why.'

'He doesn't know?'

'No, and she won't tell him. She says it's nothing to worry about.'

'Well, Sidney, I am afraid it definitely is something to worry about. It's a new and quite controversial treatment for cancer.'

'You don't prescribe it?'

'Certainly not. And I'd like to know who did.'

The next day, Helena came to see Sidney to ask him to put pressure on the police to do more. He had influence and responsibility, and he was one of the few people who had taken her seriously.

'My mother asked me how I could have "allowed this to happen"; my father thinks it's entirely my fault and my sister is relieved it's not her. I sometimes wonder if I am to blame after all; not just for the night itself but for not choosing a different career like teaching or writing or working overseas for Oxfam or the Red Cross: anything that might make a difference and change the world. But whatever I *would* have been doing, it was always going to be about getting to the truth of things. I can't just brush this all aside as if it was a mistake or part of some male fantasy.'

'You don't have to. We must continue.'

'And yet at the same time Malcolm is frightened. I have no one to talk to. You and Geordie are the only people who believe me. I don't know what to do. Perhaps I should withdraw the charge?'

'You have never given up before. Do not abandon this now.'

Helena couldn't stop going over events, particularly worrying whether she had left the door to her hotel room locked or unlocked. She kept hearing doors opening and closing, the sound of keys turning, bolts crossed and unbolted, creaks and slams.

'Is there such a thing,' she asked, 'as the fear of doors? Is there a name for it? I'm worried it's becoming a phobia. I keep checking them all the time.'

'I am sure we can find you someone to talk to; a female therapist.'

'The last one of those I saw was terrified I was going to have an abortion. She referred to it as medical rape. Keeping the child will, apparently, teach me how to forgive.'

'I think that's for you to decide.'

'I'm worried about the baby, Sidney. When will I have to tell her what has happened? How old will she be (I have to think it's a girl. I'm not ready for it to be a boy) and will it always be difficult to explain? Who else will we have to tell and how often? Perhaps it will be like giving my statement again and again. What if my child looks like the man who raped me? What if she has his smile or his laugh? I feel he will be jeering at me through her.'

'You could choose adoption.'

'I'm so terrified I don't feel I can choose anything; to have that violence growing; something evil inside me.'

'Or something to love, Helena, some fragile hope, however far away that seems.'

He wished he could talk more to Hildegard about the situation. There were so many occasions when the right words had not come out, when he could not really trust what he was saying, when he would have preferred the silence. But his wife had begun rehearsals for a performance of the *St Matthew Passion* in the cathedral. She was not only singing in one of the two choirs, but had also been offered a soprano solo, '*Aus Liebe*', which she was due to perform with her new friend Rolfe von Arnim. He was going to accompany her on the flute.

They had much in common. A small, neatly dressed man in his early sixties, Rolfe had originally come over from Hamburg in the 1930s. He taught music with his wife, Inga, and they bought a small cottage just outside Ely, where they had brought up two children very happily. Then, five years ago, Inga had been killed when out walking on a country road. The driver hadn't been drunk or anything like that. He had sneezed at the wrong moment, lost control of the car and run straight into her.

Rolfe had stayed on in Witchford to bring up his daughters. He was a popular, kindly man but demanding when it came to musical performance, insisting on extra rehearsals at Canonry House. He was helping Hildegard to control her breathing as she sang, letting the sound emerge naturally from each silence.

Sidney envied their quiet ease with each other and knew that he wasn't supposed to interrupt, but he felt that their practice had gone on for long enough. He had to ask his wife about Helena. He hoped she would be able to help him how to think. He didn't want another man in her life.

He popped his head round the door of the sitting room and offered to make a pot of tea.

'I should be going,' said Rolfe.

'No, do stay,' he said. 'Don't let me interrupt.'

(Even though he just had. Why was he doing this? he thought. Was he jealous?)

Hildegard adjusted her music on the stand. 'We won't be long, *mein Lieber*. I just have to finish this. "*Aus Liebe*".'

She nodded to Rolfe and they began to play once more. The music resounded through the house; flowing, breaking off, recapitulating, halting, continuing and then stopping again. It was a matter of examining each phrase perhaps, Sidney wondered, as if it were a piece of evidence in a crime scene.

He returned to his study and tried to work on the Lenten meditation that he was due to lead the following week, but he couldn't concentrate. He kept thinking if there was anything more he could do for Helena and, indeed, for any other of his parishioners.

It had been such a difficult time of year. The cold weather and the intermittent electricity had made his congregation fearful to leave their homes. Some of them had died in the big freeze, victims of what the undertaker called 'post-Christmas needle-drop'. Church attendance had fallen, the Valentine's Day dance at the rugby club had been cancelled, and there was chaos in town every time the traffic lights blacked out.

Sidney fell into further gloom when he took a break from his thoughts and looked to *The Times* for relaxation. There, he read that a friend who was an army chaplain, a priest with whom he had studied at Westcott House, had been killed in an IRA bomb attack at a barracks in Aldershot.

'In all times of sorrow,' he prayed as the sound of Hildegard's singing and Rolfe's flute continued.

'In all times of joy,
In the hour of death,
And at the day of judgement,
Good Lord, deliver us.'

Sometimes you just had to say the words, he reminded himself, before letting the silence fall.

'Make our hearts clean, O God,
And renew a right spirit within us.'

He prayed again for Helena. 'Support her in her grief, love her in her suffering, sustain her confidence. Assuage the doubters. Protect her child. Love her as you loved your only son.'

He heard Rolfe saying goodbye. He wondered if Hildegard had kissed him. He wouldn't ask.

When he next interviewed the accused, Keating asked if Frank Downing had ever been in a similar situation before.

'I'm no angel,' the photographer replied, 'but I'm good to the women I meet. I've never had any complaints, put it that way.'

'Always a first time . . .'

'There's no sign of any violence, though, is there? My lawyer told me that, in most cases, unless the woman's knickers are ripped, she's got no chance.'

'You'd get a lighter sentence if you confessed.'

'I don't need inducements and there's nothing to confess. Why don't you admit, Keating, that you're only doing this because Helena's such a very good friend of yours?'

'I'm doing it because it's my job. I don't know her that well.'

'I don't believe you.'

'You don't have to.'

'I just wonder, do you think you would have done the same thing if you had had the same opportunity?'

'I very much doubt it.'

'I know you fancied her once. She told me: you *and* the clergyman. She's let me know about both of you. Perhaps you're only pursuing this case because you're jealous. I've been where you can't go and you can't accept it. You probably aren't getting enough at home and you can't stand the fact that you've missed out.'

Geordie waited for a moment, uncertain how to respond to the challenge. He then punched the accused in the face, pushed him to the ground and walked out of the station.

It was impossible to go back. Downing filed a complaint and Geordie was suspended, pending an enquiry. He took a train to Ely, summoned Sidney away from a meeting about a new initiative, 'Clowning for clergy: the pursuit of holy folly', and insisted that they had a drink in the Prince Albert. But on this occasion, the open fire, warm beer and hearty exchanges of the regulars failed to provide consolation.

'What a bastard,' Geordie began, unable to concentrate on anything else. 'He provoked me deliberately, as extra insurance, knowing that it'll increase his chances of getting off. He's used to charming his way out of any situation. As far as he's concerned, this is probably just kids' stuff.'

'Any witnesses?'

'No, but he's got a black eye.'

'Don't the police have means of explaining away that kind of thing?'

'In the past. It's harder to do so these days. And Downing's well connected.'

'What will happen now?'

'I don't know, Sidney. I'll be punished in some way. At least that would give me more time in the garden. And then I could find out what's going on with Cathy.'

'There's nothing "going on", I'm sure.'

'Oh, you are, are you? You're too trusting.'

'No, I'm not.'

Geordie went on a mock attack. 'What about that German your wife's seeing?'

'I'm not worried about that. He's older than me. He's also smaller, has got a moustache and he plays the flute.'

'They're the ones you've got to watch.'

'I think she feels sorry for him.'

'Perhaps that's what she wants you to think? You can't be too careful, Sidney.'

'I'm not. And I don't think Cathy's having an affair, if that's what you're worried about.'

'How would you know?'

Sidney was surprised by his friend's change in tone. It moved abruptly away from the jovial and towards the nervily hostile. So often their friendship had survived its testing times through a strange mixture of trust and banter. Now that didn't seem to be working. 'She's just not the type,' he said.

'I thought we weren't supposed to put women into categories.'

'You know what I mean.'

'You don't know my wife.'

'All I'm saying is that I'm pretty sure it's not an affair.'

'Well, I can't be so generous with my trust.'

'You should be, Geordie.'

'Don't you tell me how to conduct my marriage.'

'I'm not.'

Sidney was dismayed. They had known each other for so long that he now thought they could say anything. But perhaps, as was the case in so many male friendships, any in-depth opinion about each other's marriage was off-limits.

'Why are you doing this?'

'It's not an affair, Geordie.'

'Then what is it?'

He couldn't say. It wasn't his business. 'Ask Cathy.'

'I bloody well have. Is there something you're not telling me?'

'Ask her.'

'Do you want a punch in the mouth?'

'Calm down, Geordie.'

'You know something, don't you, Sidney? Why does everyone tell you things? Why do you know more about my marriage than I do myself? What the *hell* has all this got to do with you?'

'Geordie, I think Cathy's got cancer.'

Sidney returned home to find that Hildegard was only just back from her rehearsals of the *St Matthew Passion* in the Lady Chapel. She muttered that they should have eaten before she left and now she was starving. ('And don't tell me that starving is a relative term.')

She was peeling the potatoes, a task she had specifically asked her husband to complete if he got back first because she knew the babysitter would never get round to them. Sidney decided to prevent further criticism by going on the attack.

'How was Rolfe?' he asked.

'Very well, thank you. There were other people at the rehearsal.'

'I should imagine there were.'

'He thinks we have a long way to go. It's difficult music. At one point, just before the end, there are nineteen bars of singing with only a quaver rest. You have to plan your breathing. It takes practice so that it sounds as if everything is natural and you haven't practised at all. That's the ironic thing. And "*Aus Liebe*" is always rehearsed at the end when everyone else has gone home.'

'I thought you said you weren't alone?'

'No, Sidney. There are two oboe da caccia players with us. But then, sometimes, we have tea afterwards or we go for a walk. It's perfectly innocent. *Sometimes*,' she repeated, 'after all that music, we don't speak at all.'

'Is Rolfe still in mourning for the loss of his wife?'

'It was five years ago. Yet I think he misses her every day.'

'And does he ask about us?'

'Not really. He knows about you. And Anna. But no, we don't talk about you, Sidney. We don't need to. Sometimes, as I've just told you, we don't say anything at all.'

'But when you do, what do you speak about?'

'Why do you need to know?'

'I'm just curious. Is it all about music and how you miss Germany?'

'Yes. And children and old age and the fear of the future. It's also about how we can become better musicians and better people too. Have you been to see Helena?'

'I was with Geordie. But we spoke about Helena: the case.'

'You know that when she has the child she will be the same age as I was when I had Anna. If it turns out as well for her then she will be blessed. Would you like a cup of tea?'

'I'd rather have a drink.'

Sidney poured himself a glass of wine from last night's bottle and Hildegard continued with the supper, deliberately making more noise than normal, pointing out Sidney's domestic failures through sound alone.

'When do you think she'll tell her child what happened?' she asked.

'I don't know,' said Sidney, laying the table in order to prove that he could at least do something. 'We still haven't told Anna everything.'

'About my first husband?'

'About any of that.'

131

'I thought eighteen . . .'

'Sometimes it is better to remain silent about these things. Perhaps she and Malcolm should bring up the child as their own.'

'Perhaps.'

'Do you think we tell each other everything?'

'Of course not,' said Hildegard. 'But I hope you feel that you know everything you need.'

'I don't always find that reassuring.'

'And why *do* we have to tell each other everything? Can't we have secrets, Sidney? Shouldn't there be an air of mystery between us? I thought you like mysteries.'

'Not in my marriage.'

'Why must you know all there is to know?'

'It's not a question of everything. It's a question of understanding what matters.'

'Perhaps there are things that will make you worry too much?'

'You think I need protecting from the truth?'

'I don't know, Sidney. Sometimes I think you need protecting from yourself.'

There was no sign of spring as the dark Lenten weather folded into March. People were still using candles for parts of the day and there was little sense of their magical ability to carry the Christmas spirit of hope towards Easter. Even the undertakers had threatened to go on strike.

Sidney left for his retreat in Walsingham. Geordie said that he fancied coming too but his friend told him that it was only for nuns and clergy; a time when he could attempt to reclaim the words 'God' and 'Christ' rather than accepting everyone else's use of them as expletives during criminal investigations.

'I do try not to blaspheme in your presence, Sidney, but it's hard.'

'We keep silence for most of the time. I'm not sure you could stand it.'

'I have plenty of silence at home,' Geordie replied. 'I think Cathy and I are frightened of telling each other too much.'

'You've had the conversation?'

'It wasn't very good. But I know now. Breast cancer. They think they can get it in time. I certainly hope so. I'm sorry I flew off the handle. I'm grateful you told me. It's difficult, though. If we speak our fears out loud we're worried they might come true.'

'You don't have to say everything.'

'I thought you were an advocate of the total truth?'

'I am. But it doesn't have to come out all at once. Sometimes it's better to do things in stages.'

'But then you never know how much more there is. I keep asking Cathy "Have you told me everything?" and she tells me that it is as much as she knows.'

'She's probably right. Do you think Helena's told us everything?'

'I hope so. They've put Dave Hills on the case now.'

'What's he like?'

'People think he's old-school, but he can still take you by surprise. If anyone can get something out of Downing, it's him.'

'If there's anything more to confess?' Sidney asked.

'We'll just have to see, won't we? Downing's probably not going to come out with very much more. It's not looking good for Helena, I have to say. She should have told us sooner.'

The police station had that winter aroma of stale gas, cigarette smoke, tea and disinfectant. It was hardly the smell of justice but, after some encouragement from his friend, Sidney still thought it worth a visit to see Dave Hills.

'Keating's told me all about you. I suppose you want to listen in?'

'If I can be of any help.'

'You'll have to watch behind the glass. I can't have you in the room. But it might be useful to have another pair of eyes. I only hope you're not shocked. My methods are a bit different.'

'You mean you don't hit people?'

'Geordie was provoked. We'll find a way of getting him off, don't you worry. We've got too much work on the go to lose a man like that.'

Dave escorted Sidney to a two-way mirror next to the interview room. It was obvious, after only a few minutes, that he was attempting the soft-cop, all-the-time-in-the-world, lull-you-into-a-false-sense-of-security routine. Downing was a victim. He had been entrapped by a woman who didn't play fair. Helena was the one who should be on trial, making a false claim like that. He was amazed Downing had been so patient. It was good of him to have put up with the investigation for so long. He hoped it wasn't damaging his career.

'It might do. But most people know that Helena Mitchell is trouble.'

'Does she put it about a bit, then?'

'You could say that.'

'I thought she was married?'

'Only to a clergyman. That doesn't count for much.'

Sidney was glad to be in a different room. Now he could understand why Geordie had punched the man.

'Is that common knowledge?' Dave Hills asked. 'Could you get other people to come forward and say it?'

'There's blokes in the newsroom who'll do it.'

'Even if it's not strictly true?'

'It's as good as. There's not much difference between a snog and what comes after.'

'She'll say there is.'

'She'll say anything.'

Dave Hills leant forward, confidentially. 'You know we're thinking of prosecuting?'

'Her rather than me, you mean?'

'False accusation. Wasting police time.'

'I'm glad about that. That woman should be punished for what she's done.'

'I just need you to go through the events.'

'Again?'

'Think of it as a fresh start. We need to get your story right so we can sort this out.'

Sidney was surprised Downing appeared to be falling into the trap. Dave Hills asked about Helena's previous behaviour, her flirtations with colleagues and her physical appearance. He concentrated on the fact that she had changed for dinner and that her dress had drawn attention to her figure. Downing said that she had touched his arm and patted him on the leg in a way that others might describe as friendly, but she surely knew what she was doing and he understood what she meant. He had been there often enough. He wasn't stupid.

'So you went upstairs?' Hills asked.

'She couldn't wait.'

'And she'd left her door unlocked.'

'I had to fiddle about a bit. But she was already lying there and waiting like a Christmas present.'

'All you had to do was tear off the paper.'

'That's right. I ripped it right off.'

'And she was grateful?'

'Yeah, I think so. She didn't say much. Women never do.'

'How much longer did you stay?'

'Not much longer. She turned away from me. I think she was whimpering. Must have been the guilt.'

'So you went back to your room?'

'That's right.'

'And did you take her nightie with you?'

'Why would I do that?'

'She said she couldn't find it afterwards.'

'I think I chucked it in the laundry basket. I couldn't imagine her needing it. It was torn and she was out for the count by then.'

'I thought you said she was whimpering?'

'She stopped before I left.'

'You calmed her down?'

'I can't remember. I suppose I did.'

'And you didn't talk to her in the morning?'

'I had to leave early.'

'You didn't want to say goodbye?'

'It was a one-night stand. I did the business and left.'

'So you didn't think anything more about it? Why should you, I suppose?'

'I never gave it a second thought until she accused me.'

'Bit of a bitch then?'

'You can say that again. I wish I'd smothered her good and proper.'

'What do you mean, "smother"?'

'You know, to calm her down when it started to get a bit frisky.'

'No, I don't know, Frank. What do you mean, "I wish I'd smothered her good and proper . . ." and by "frisky" do you mean violent?'

It was as good a confession as they were going to get. The trial was set for early April.

Helena was warned that she was going to have to be composed in the witness box. Now five months pregnant, she could still feel the suffocation, the need to vomit, the memory made physical.

'It's hard to trust anyone,' she said to Sidney. 'I'm scared to go down the street. I keep thinking people are going to attack me.'

'That's only to be expected.'

'Especially men. I can't stand the sight of them any more.'

'I'm sorry. If you'd like me to leave . . .'

'You don't count, Sidney. It's the others: the hatred of them looking you up and down; the infantile obsession with breasts and body; the lecherous condescension. *Are you all right, love? Do those legs go all the way up? I bet you don't get many of them for a pound.*'

'We're not all like that.'

'You are, Sidney. Perhaps even you. What about that jazz singer, Gloria Dee . . .'

'That was ages ago.'

'Pamela Morton . . .'

'Before I was married . . .'

'The naked woman you saw in the Fitzwilliam . . .'

'Celine Bellecourt.'

'You were certainly married then . . .'

'But nothing happened . . .'

'Then there was Barbara Wilkinson, Mary Sullivan, Amanda, I don't know, perhaps even me, for God's sake . . .'

'Helena. It's not true. I like to think that I am uxorious. Not all men are the same.'

'There're enough of them to make me think they are, Sidney. I can't even be with my husband any more. How can I ever trust anyone again?'

The *St Matthew Passion* was performed in Ely Cathedral on 26 March. Amanda brought her mother and father to the concert. Sidney was surprised to see how frail Cecil Kendall had become. This could be his last Easter.

The performance began and ended in silence and Sidney thought how much that stillness enclosed human life; before the first cry of a child and after the last breath. It was the white space around a poem, the double bar line that bordered a piece of music, the frame of a painting.

'*Aus Liebe*' had a tenderness and a beauty that he did not think he had ever experienced before. Hildegard sang without appearing to draw breath. She had learned to disguise her breathing so that her singing appeared to be continuous and without strain, a well-spring that would never run dry.

In bed that night he asked his wife if she planned to keep on seeing Rolfe now that the concert was over.

'Would you have any objections if I did?'

'Not really.'

'That means you do. Are you jealous, Sidney?'

'What do you think?'

'There's no need to be.'

'There's every need.'

'I'm not concerned about you and Amanda.'

'You are, Hildegard. You choose not to show it.'

'I'm not. You can do what you like, and if I tried to stop you it wouldn't make any difference. I've shown you that for more than ten years now.'

'And you expect me to behave in the same way? Let you do what you'd like?'

'I would rather you did. It seems fair. Unless you'd like me to stop seeing Rolfe altogether?'

'No,' Sidney replied carefully. 'I wouldn't want to force you to do anything against your will. Not that I could.'

'I'm sure you could, but I love you more if you don't. Not that love can be measured. But you'd prefer me to decide on my own accord; make a sacrifice?'

'I would. If you think it upsets me, perhaps you should stop?'

'And does it?'

'It does.'

'Then I'll stop.'

'And gracefully, willingly, with an open heart?'

'I said I'll stop, Sidney. You can't tell me how I do that. It's up to me. And I'll do it in my own way. Aren't you glad I haven't asked you to do the same?'

'Now I feel bad.'

'I should hope you do.'

'I'm sorry, darling.'

Sidney reached over and started to stroke his wife's back. She got out of bed and put on her dressing gown.

'I'm going to sleep in the spare room,' she said.

The judge began Frank Downing's trial with a cautionary instruction informing the jury that rape is a charge easily made by the accuser and yet difficult for any defendant to disprove. The law required the jurors to examine the testimony of the female named in the information with caution. This was a volatile situation with no witnesses, and the accusation had been made so long after the alleged assault that there was no admissible evidence. Their judgement depended, therefore, on the credibility of two people.

Sidney could not quite believe what he was hearing, and was aghast when the barrister for the defence asked what Helena had been wearing on the night of the incident and openly smirked as he was told that she had changed into a halter-necked cocktail dress.

'And is that the kind of thing you usually wear for dinner?'

'If I want to look nice.'

'And did you want to "look nice" for Mr Downing?'

'Not him especially.'

'Who then?'

'For myself. When you've been out all day you sometimes want to change for dinner. You don't dine in your wig, do you?'

'This isn't about me, Mrs Mitchell. Do you think you were dressed provocatively?'

'I don't know.'

'Do you like being attractive?'

'I don't think I am.'

'Come, come, Mrs Mitchell, you are too modest.'

'I like to look my best. Is that a crime?'

'We're here to establish if your clothing was a material fact in the case.'

The witness refused to rise to the barrister's attempt at a pun. 'As inanimate objects, I don't think my clothes can be responsible for anything.'

And yet, as the trial continued, Helena's personal appearance became inseparable from her credibility as a witness. Her clothes, hairstyle, posture, accent – every mannerism and each physical aspect – was either silently or vocally assessed according to its relative attractiveness. The more poised she appeared the more likely, the prosecution suggested, that she was making a false accusation; that her rapist was not so much a criminal but a victim of her sexual allure.

'What do you wear in bed, Mrs Mitchell?' the defence resumed.

The prosecution interrupted. 'I object. This is not relevant.'

'In a case of rape? I think it's much to the point.'

'Please answer,' said the judge.

'A nightie.'

'And were you wearing "a nightie" when Mr Downing came into your room?'

'I was.'

'Any underwear?'

'I don't know any women who wear underwear in bed.'

'And so it would have been a simple matter to reveal yourself to him?' the defence barrister continued. 'It was a warm night, even for October, the heating was on, you were hot, perhaps a bit thirsty, and, as a result, you could have been said to be what the French call déshabillé?'

'I was in my own room and I was just about to fall asleep.'

'Just about?'

'I woke up when I understood what was going on.'

'And what was "going on"?'

'Frank was kissing my breasts. I told him to stop. He said it was too late for that. I said: "Please stop." "Don't you like it?" he said. I was frightened. I thought if I answered back he would hurt me.'

'So you didn't say you didn't like it?'

'I told him to stop.'

'How hard did you try to tell him?'

'I didn't want him to be angry. I was afraid he would hurt me.'

'So you asked him nicely. Perhaps you didn't mean it?'

'I did mean it.'

'So why didn't you tell him in a way that he understood?'

'I did.'

'And what did he say?'

'Something about us both wanting it; that it was inevitable. I should just relax and enjoy the ride.'

'Enjoy the ride?'

'That's what he said. I tried to move out from under him and asked him again . . .'

'To stop?'

'Yes.'

'More than once?'

'Yes.'

'How many more times than once?'

'I can't remember. A lot.'

'You can remember saying no, but you can't remember how many times?'

'I know I said it.'

'But you can't remember much else?'

'I don't WANT to remember it.'

'Why didn't you scream?'

'I don't know. I can't recall.'

'If you bring these charges, Mrs Mitchell, I am afraid you are going to have to recall every detail. Were you a virgin when you married your husband?'

'That is none of your business.'

'Everything is my business, Mrs Mitchell.' (He kept repeating her name as if this, too, was a fault.) 'A woman that dresses deliberately and provocatively . . .'

'OBJECTION,' the prosecution shouted.

'. . . away from home, in a hotel with a very close friend, as she has done before if the evidence provided by her colleagues is anything to go by . . .'

'OBJECTION.'

'. . . shouldn't be surprised if, after drinking far too much, that close friend draws his own conclusions. How can you explain saying to my client "see you later"?'

'I meant "in the morning".'

'But you didn't say that, did you? You said "see you later", meaning that night.'

'It's an expression.'

'Then I suggest you should be more careful using it.'

'I didn't know it was going to lead to this.'

'What did you think it was going to lead to?'

'I didn't think anything at all. It was meant in all innocence.'

'I am not sure the jury is going to believe that.'

'It's the truth. That's all I'm saying.'

'I'm sorry, Mrs Mitchell, I think you're going to have to be saying a lot more.'

'I was tired. Nothing more. I didn't mean sex.'

'I think you were tired, drunk and flirtatious. That is a very different matter. You led Mr Downing on.

'OBJECTION.'

'I expected my colleague to behave well. That was my only mistake.'

'You kissed him on the lips.'

'I was being affectionate.'

'And you weren't surprised when he expected more?'

'I don't know. I thought I could trust him.'

144

'Have you been in similar situations before?'

'OBJECTION.'

'I don't think so . . .'

'A situation when you are in the company of a man, dressed provocatively, kiss them, tell them to "see you later" and NOTHING HAPPENED?'

'That's not what I meant.'

'But you accept, Mrs Mitchell, that such a remark could be open to misinterpretation, or rather to only one interpretation?'

'I don't know what to think any more. I just want it to stop. Just like I wanted that night to end. I started crying.'

'Out of shame?'

'Then he put a pillow over my face. I thought he was going to suffocate me.'

'I don't see how a man can put a pillow over your face and rape you at the same time.'

'It wasn't at the same time. It was after . . .'

'I thought you said it was before.'

'You're confusing me . . .'

There was nothing Helena could do to mitigate the defence barrister's inquisition.

Geordie was called as a character witness and asked if he had ever been intimate with Helena.

'I have not.'

'But did she ever lead you on?'

'Of course not.'

'You are sure about that, Inspector Keating?'

'Yes.'

'Were you ever keen on her yourself?'

'I have always liked her, but that doesn't mean . . .'

'What does it mean?'

'Nothing more than what I have said. I am a married man.'

'That hasn't stopped men in the past.'

'It stopped me.'

'Even when Mrs Mitchell encouraged your attentions?'

'I'm not sure she did. There is a difference between flirtation and action.'

'And do you know what that difference is?'

'Everything blurs after a few drinks.'

'But if you had been asked to put her to bed, what would you have done?'

'That is a hypothetical question.'

'Would you mind answering it?'

'I would have done as the lady asked.'

'Nothing more?'

'No.'

'You would have been able to resist the temptation of a half-naked woman . . .'

'OBJECTION.'

'. . . almost certainly drunk, available and in the privacy of a hotel room?'

'I hope I would have behaved as a gentleman, laid her on her side, and left.'

'And did you behave "as a gentleman" when interviewing the accused?'

'I was angry with him.'

'You admit that you hit him.'

'There was an altercation.'

146

'You were defending your girlfriend's honour.'

'She's not my girlfriend. She is a married woman.'

'Sorry; your *former* girlfriend.'

'Mrs Mitchell was never my girlfriend. We have always behaved well in each other's company and I have never taken her to be the kind of woman you are implying that she is.'

'I'm not implying anything, Inspector Keating. I am asking questions in order to prevent a miscarriage of justice.'

'Mrs Mitchell's the one who is most likely to suffer . . .'

'That will be for this court to decide.'

When the time came for the jury to consider its verdict it was clear that, despite the ripped nightie, and the alleged attempt to stifle Helena's sobs with a pillow, their judgement would be that there was 'insufficient evidence' for a prosecution. It was not enough for her to have said 'no'; Frank Downing had to understand that she was saying 'no'. Helena had not made her feelings sufficiently clear. In conclusion, the judge said that there had been 'mixed messages' and that, although the situation had been 'unfortunate', there was nothing he could do apart from draw attention to the 'lessons learned'. There was no point in ruining a man's entire career for the sake of a single night of passion.

Downing was 'impassive' as he left court in his best suit and navy tie, only telling the press that he wanted 'to leave this nightmare behind me' and that he bore Helena 'no ill will' for her 'false accusation'.

Helena said that the fierceness of the interrogation at the trial and the not guilty verdict had been like a second assault. She resigned from her job, particularly after her newspaper's coverage of the trial and their lukewarm response to having her back. Some of her colleagues even spoke to her as if rape was some kind of initiation ritual that she had failed. She was branded as a troublemaker, a woman who had broken ranks. Downing was 'just being Frank'. Was it really that serious? Couldn't she just have toughed it out and got on with her job? It wasn't that bad.

That night Sidney tried to understand the limitations of the criminal justice system and how inadequate he had been in helping Helena. He couldn't think of a single thing he had done that had improved the situation.

He smashed a glass of water.

Hildegard asked him what was wrong.

'You know the Puritans used to punish women who had been raped for fornication,' he said. 'They thought it was their fault. Not much has changed.'

On Midsummer Day, just after seven o'clock in the morning, Mercy Mitchell, conceived the previous October, was born in the Middlesex Hospital in central London. She weighed six pounds, ten ounces.

'One wouldn't want to call this a happy ending,' said Malcolm, 'but at least it's a new beginning.'

'Seven hours of labour,' said Helena. 'I suppose it could have been worse.'

'Are you all right?' Sidney asked. 'I'm sorry to be banal. I have to know.'

'Of course I thought about what happened. It all came back. Not that it's ever gone away. But Mercy gives me something different to care about; something other than myself. I've shut out everything else.'

'Have your parents come?'

'Not yet. And we haven't told them the truth. But we'll bring Mercy up as our own. People can think what they like.'

'She *is* our own,' said Malcolm.

'But that doesn't mean I'll always be silent about what happened,' said Helena. 'I'll speak when the time is right. And so, I hope, will Mercy.'

'I like the name.'

'Her middle name is Victoria. We think they go well together, don't we, Malcolm?'

'She will be our victory.'

'And will you go back to work?'

'I will,' said Helena, 'although not for that paper. I want to tell stories differently. When Mercy is a young woman I hope she'll go out to work in a very different world to the one I grew up in. Frank Downing may have started with his right to silence. I want us to have the right to noise.'

'Then I hope that I will live to see the day.'

'And I hope,' said Malcolm, 'that one day you will celebrate Mercy's wedding.'

'Oh, you don't think she'll do something as conventional as that?' Sidney replied.

'Would you like to hold her?' Helena asked.

'I can't think of anything I'd rather do.'

Despite a reprimand, Geordie was reinstated in his job almost as quickly as he had left it. There were, he said, still some advantages to old-fashioned policing and now, having seen Helena himself, the only thing he regretted was that he had not hit Frank Downing harder.

'Still unrepentant then?' Sidney asked.

'I'd trust that girl with my life. She's a fighter.'

'Woman, Geordie. We're supposed to say "woman".'

'She'll always be a "girl" to me.'

'Then she'll keep on saying that, despite your sympathy and support, as a man you have still got a lot to learn.'

'I don't mind about that. I just want to get that bastard. His card's marked, I can tell you.'

'Helena will keep up the fight, as must we all.' Sidney gestured towards the bar. 'I presume I'm getting the pints in?'

'If you don't mind. I have lost three months' pay.'

'And Cathy?'

'On the mend, I hope. She's ditched that drug you asked your father about and the surgeon thinks he's got it all out. And her GP's paying more attention now he realises that if he doesn't come up to scratch Cathy will go off and see some expensive quack.'

'Is that where she got the Laetrile?'

'Her sister married an American who knew someone in London who organised it all for her. Cathy's too embarrassed or anxious to tell me everything, but I wouldn't mind sorting the bugger out.'

'One thing at a time, Geordie. You're hardly back at work.'

'Couldn't have come soon enough. I'd go mad sitting at home all the time.'

Although it had been a dull day for late June, it was still warm enough to stay out in the pub garden and enjoy what little of the light was left.

'You know, I didn't demand to be reinstated,' Geordie continued. 'They just did it. But then I've never asked for anything in my life; not this, not that, not Cathy, not her cancer, not our friendship, nothing. I suppose I should learn to pray. That's asking.'

'And receiving.'

'But I'm frightened that if God gives you one thing, he'll take away something else. He gives me Cathy. He takes her away.'

'It doesn't work like that, Geordie. She'll pull through.'

'I hope so. It's a hell of a treatment.'

'And sometimes when things are taken away, other things are given back.'

'What are you talking about?'

'Helena's child. I don't want another argument, but at least *something* good has come out of all this.'

'I don't agree at all, Sidney. I think nothing happening at all would have been a hell of a lot better than what actually took place. You say no incident, no child. But I say no child, no incident. You always see the silver lining, not the bloody great cloud.'

'That's what makes us a team, though, Geordie. You see the cloud, I see the lining.'

'And none of us get the sunshine.'

Sidney picked up his pint. 'You know that, whatever happens, with Cathy or anything else, I will always be your friend.'

'You'd bloody better be. You know I'd be lost without you.'

The two men resumed their drinking. For a short while they sat in a companionable silence that neither had any desire to interrupt. Geordie unpacked a box of backgammon.

There was a flicker in the sky, a trick of the light, perhaps, and the sun made a final appearance that day, low on the horizon, sending a brief beam across their garden table, the silver lining in the cloud.

Sidney looked up and smiled at the warmth on their faces.

'Don't,' said Geordie. 'Don't even think about speaking.'

Ex Libris

EVERY TIME SIDNEY RETURNED to Corpus Christi, Cambridge, the college where he had been both student and chaplain, he felt inadequate, intimidated by history, architecture, scholarship and tradition. He worried that he could never live up to the university's intellectual expectations, that he had only ever had temporary membership of such an august institution, and that his presence never counted for very much at all.

This was odd, because he did not have the same feelings when he entered a cathedral, even though the sense of human transience amidst so much ancient stone might have provoked a similar response. Perhaps ecclesiastical buildings were welcoming because they were open to all of the faithful, whereas a university could close its doors to anyone it chose. Simply through its admissions process it was more likely to reject than accept you, and even if you did manage to make it through the front door, you were still greeted as a temporary member, bounded either by length of degree or security of tenure.

The fact was that, no matter how often he was welcomed, Sidney never felt that he belonged, and there was something added to his uneasiness each time he made his way past the Porters' Lodge and looked out over the finely mown grass of

New Court. He tried to pin it down. Was it the issue that the university was a self-governing organisation that considered itself outside the laws of the land? Was it the elite confidence that only the cleverest and the fittest were worthy of admission and that those less fortunate, privileged or intelligent could simply be locked out? Or was it, he wondered, the inhabitants themselves? Could it perhaps be the combination of intellectual superiority and social unease that so many of the university Fellows displayed, particularly in the presence of a clergyman whom, they made plain, could never be given academic respect: for how could anyone with rational intelligence believe in God?

Sidney wondered if he could do anything to improve his chances of intellectual acceptance. Perhaps he was being a touch paranoid; yet he couldn't help but dwell on the matter. Was the apparent disapproval of the dons due to the fact that Sidney had a sense of humour and that his delight in the absurd demonstrated an alarming partiality to the trivial? Did his meddling in detection and the cares of the world leave him on the nursery slopes of the icy heights of academe? Or was the disdain of his colleagues the result of jealousy; a situation in which the Fellows who had deliberately incarcerated themselves within the privileges of the past envied Sidney's freedom of movement in the world outside, his easy friendships and genial curiosity?

After a moment of what he now had to dismiss as ungrateful nervousness, Sidney pulled himself together and made his way around Front Court to the Parker Library, one of the most valuable collections of medieval manuscripts in the world.

Matthew Parker had been a pupil at Corpus Christi in the early sixteenth century. He was chaplain to Anne Boleyn, King Henry VIII's second wife, and Archbishop of Canterbury to her daughter, Elizabeth I. A book-collecting scholar, he edited the Bishop's Bible of 1568, and established the Thirty-nine Articles as the official definition of the beliefs and obligations of the Church in England: a Church separate from Rome which, Parker argued, Pope Gregory the Great had always intended when he first sent Christian missionaries to Britain.

On his death Parker had left over five hundred manuscripts and several thousand printed books to his old college; a series of priceless documents that showed the unbroken continuity of the English Church from earliest times, including the *Chronica Maiora* of Matthew Paris, Bede's *Life of St Cuthbert*, Alfred's *Laws*, *The Anglo-Saxon Chronicle* and the finest copy of Chaucer in England.

The most prized possession in the collection was the gospel book that St Augustine brought from Pope Gregory in Rome to the county of Kent in 597 AD in order to found English Christianity. This was the first book ever known to have been in England, the forerunner to all the Christian art that followed and the oldest object that had been in continuous use since the sixth century. Many thought it to be the most precious artefact in English culture.

It was also the religious text upon which Archbishops of Canterbury took their solemn oaths of office and now, following Michael Ramsey's retirement, it was due to be pressed into service at the enthronement of his successor, Donald Coggan.

155

Before this could be done, the library had to undergo its annual audit, for it was a condition of Matthew Parker's original bequest, made in an age when literary kleptomania was rife, to confirm the collection was still complete.

The auditors were allowed to inflict a penalty of four pennies for every leaf of a manuscript found wanting and two shillings for every absent sheet. For every printed book or manuscript missing, and not restored within six months of admonition, they could levy whatever sum they thought proper. More crucially, if six manuscripts in folio, eight in quarto and twelve of lesser size had been removed due to negligence, and were not restored within six months, then the whole collection, together with the college silver given by Parker, would be forfeit to Gonville and Caius within a month, and should that college be found similarly wanting, then they were to pass to Trinity Hall.

Although not a single item had been lost since Parker's time, it was therefore in the interests of both Gonville and Caius and Trinity Hall to find manuscripts missing and become beneficiaries. The Masters of both these colleges were almost amused by their potential to ruin another at the annual feast, attended by Fellows, friends, benefactors and representatives from all three colleges, which was given in celebration of the bequest.

The evening that required the pleasure of Sidney's company took place in early September and began with a display of the most valuable manuscripts in the library followed by drinks in Old Court and dinner in the Great Hall.

Sidney's host was the librarian, Dr Ralph Mumford, an expert in Anglo-Saxon and the development of the

156

English language from the Corpus glossary of 800 AD to the Norman Conquest. A tall, enthusiastic man dressed in clothes that he looked as if he was trying to escape, Ralph acted with surprising clumsiness for an archivist entrusted with the care of fragile objects. Some of his colleagues treated him as a bit of a joke, but he was more of a scholar than he let on; patiently allowing people who worked in the glitzy world of painting and sculpture to patronise him; only bristling when they pronounced his Christian name incorrectly. 'It's Rafe, as in *strafe*,' he would say, 'not Ralph as in *Alf*.'

After looking at a series of images from medieval bestiaries depicting horses, donkeys, eagles and dragons, Sidney was told how many of the inks used in the illustrations contained poisons (canary-yellow orpiment, for example, included arsenic; vermilion: mercury) and Ralph ventured that perhaps, had he lived in medieval times, he would have been called to solve crimes even then?

After replying that this was no joking matter, he was shown a 1572 edition of *The Bishops' Bible* that Parker had edited and an English Romanesque manuscript that illustrated one of the earliest examples of musical notes on a stave: a hymn for the Feast of St Augustine.

'Something to tell Hildegard when you get home.'

'I'm sure she'd like to have come, but she knows the college doesn't encourage women.'

'Nonsense. Bring her next year.'

'She'd like that,' said Sidney, thinking that this was at least one thing he could offer her that Rolfe von Arnim couldn't.

The Gospel Book of St Augustine was given a prominent position in a display case at the far end of the library. It was not a large manuscript, some ten and a half by eight and a half inches, bound in plain oak boards, slightly bevelled on their inner edges, with a spine of creamy alum-tawed goatskin. The condition of the manuscript was remarkable, the Latin text written in the same uncial script used by St Jerome, separated out into clauses that were each designed to be read aloud in one breath: '*per cola et commata*'. Sidney remembered that Winston Churchill had set out his speeches in a similar way, with rhetorical performance in mind.

The manuscript lay open at the illustrated page at the start of Luke's gospel, showing the Evangelist beneath his attribute as an ox. The colours were soft yet persistent, like those found on old Roman frescoes – indigo, vermilion, hematite and orange red lead – and the painted architectural design that framed the scene looked both back to Pompeii and forward to the Bayeux Tapestry.

'After the dinner,' Ralph Mumford promised, 'when everyone's gone, I'll bring you back here and we can take it out of its case. Then you can handle it yourself. To think that you will have history in your hands, Sidney: our sacred Christian heritage. You know that in the Middle Ages they thought it had miraculous powers? There's a 1414 reference to a peasant in Thanet who lied when swearing an oath on it and who was then struck blind as a result.'

'I'll be careful how I handle it, Ralph.'

'I should hope so. It is almost a talismanic object, Sidney, more valuable than the relic of any saint.'

'Not that many of those *are* relics. Shall I wear gloves?'

'No. We prefer clean, dry hands, but you need to be careful. We'd rather not have to mend a tear. But let me start gathering up the troops for the drinks. I'll leave Julian to lock up.'

'The chaplain? Is he entitled?'

'He can do it in his capacity as Fellow. He's perfectly competent; unless you'd like to take charge of security yourself?'

'I think I'd rather have a drink.'

'Good man.'

They made their way to the most ancient part of the college and the oldest surviving enclosed court in Cambridge; a series of fourteenth-century buildings that still contained the sills and jambs used to hold oil-soaked linen before the arrival of glass. A long table with a fluttering white cloth was staffed by four waiters preparing jugs of Pimm's, and glasses of red and white wine, together with orange juice and elderflower cordial. It was the last knockings of summer, with the students not yet back, and the small gathering of some sixty or seventy friends and benefactors had an air of secluded privilege.

The only drama of the evening came when Sir Leslie Manning, the recently appointed cathedral agent of Canterbury, the man responsible for the safekeeping of *The Gospel Book of St Augustine* during the enthronement of the next archbishop, arrived late. The unfortunate chaplain had not seen him when he was locking up and had therefore managed to trap him in the library. Manning had then had to telephone the Porters' Lodge to be released. As a result, he was not in the best of moods when he arrived in Old Court and only calmed down towards the end of his second glass of Pimm's.

It was a noisy dinner, despite the relatively small number of guests, as the Dining Hall was something of an echo chamber. Sidney was seated between Kenrich Prescott, the Master of Gonville and Caius, and Sir Leslie Manning, and he had to lean forward to hear their guest of honour repeat the story of his brief incarceration.

'I thought it was some kind of practical joke at first. I didn't know what to do. I'm too old to start jumping out of windows.'

'They are locked and alarmed,' Ralph Mumford observed, 'so I am afraid you would have had no joy there.'

'Actually I'm not sure they were,' said Manning. 'The chaplain made quite a fuss when the head porter informed him that the alarms were off. He swore he had switched them on.'

'But they're on now?'

'Oh yes. There was a great to-do about it.'

Ralph Mumford stood up. 'Will you please excuse me for a minute? I'll just check with the porters.'

'He gets very anxious about these things,' said Sidney as the librarian left. 'In another life I think he must have been St Jerome.'

'I thought you people didn't believe in reincarnation?' the Master of Caius asked.

'It was a figure of speech.'

'According to St Augustine, "What Jerome was ignorant of no mortal has ever known,"' said Sir Leslie. 'He is the patron saint of librarians. It's his saint's day at the end of the month.'

'The gospel book is his translation,' Sidney continued, 'so I think Ralph feels he is as responsible as any archbishop in preserving our inheritance.'

'Apparently Jerome had a terrible temper,' the cathedral agent went on. 'Is that something they might have in common?'

'Ralph can be curt in matters of scholarship, though that is sometimes the Cambridge way, the abrupt dismissal of folly, but I don't think he shouts unless he is very angry.'

'Or when someone forgets to set an alarm?'

As soon as the librarian returned, and reported that all was in order, the party stood to say grace and settled in to a hot vichyssoise, followed by smoked salmon, cucumber sorbet, a venison stew and a blackberry and apple sponge that was washed down with four different decanters of port, madeira, and red and white dessert wine.

Given the nature of the dinner, and the forthcoming enthronement of Donald Coggan, the conversation resumed with a debate on Parker's legacy and the Anglican tradition. How much, the Master of Trinity Hall asked, could the Church of England respond to the modern world while retaining its historic values?

The cathedral agent argued that the Church should not be distracted by modernity or reject its ancient language and ceremony. He detested the New English Bible and was worried that the next archbishop might make further reforms which would dilute the Anglican tradition.

'You can't discard history so easily. Take *The Gospel Book of St Augustine*,' he argued. 'When an archbishop touches the manuscript he is in communion with a series of oaths that stretch back to the saint. He is no longer an individual but part of the larger Christian body of both the living and the dead, supported by tradition and buoyed up by hundreds of years of devotion and faith.'

Kenrich Prescott was unimpressed, arguing that tradition was no guarantee of truth. He initiated a discussion on the concept of holy folly, and raised the idea that no scientist worth his salt could *seriously* believe in God. 'There is no empirical evidence.'

'Science is not the only truth,' Sidney observed. 'There can be poetic truth, metaphorical truth . . .'

'But aren't you supposed to believe that it's all *literally* true?'

'Not necessarily . . .'

'Anglican hair-splitting.'

'Perhaps faith can be as complicated and as detailed as a scientific experiment.'

'Science deals in outcomes.'

'As do we.'

'But you do not have the empirical evidence. How can you believe in something you cannot judge?'

'We can test our faith,' said Sidney, 'through prayer and through our lives. And we have the historical record of Jesus.'

'That, too, is open to question, I would have thought. The gospels were written long after his life.'

'Not that long.'

'Who is to say they are not made up; that the whole thing is not a fraud? Even your precious gospel book could be a fake, couldn't it, Ralph?'

'I don't think so, Master. Although we have commissioned a facsimile.'

'A duplicate?'

'For academic study. It preserves the pages of the original.'

'Then your scholars won't be studying the real thing.'

'But they can be much more hands-on, and you can get away with so much these days. Some of the items tonight were facsimiles.'

The cathedral agent put down his glass of wine. 'Do you mean to say that the book on display tonight could have been the duplicate?'

'It could have been,' Ralph Mumford smiled, 'but it wasn't. I can assure you.'

'That's a relief. We wouldn't want the next archbishop swearing his oaths of office on a fake.'

'No, we most certainly would not.'

'I wouldn't have thought that it would make too much difference,' Kenrich Prescott continued. 'Provide enough smoke and mirrors at the ceremony and people will believe anything.'

'It is the most ancient of rituals,' the cathedral agent concluded, 'a fitting tribute to the sacred nature of the priesthood. If you choose to dismiss it then that is your prerogative. But I prefer a sense of the transcendent; to dwell in mystery. The earth alone is not enough.'

Sir Leslie then asked the Master of Corpus if he could go over a few details about the forthcoming enthronement service in private before his driver took him back to Canterbury.

'It would be my pleasure. I've just received this rather fine book. I thought you might like to have a look at it. Fascinating stuff. It sheds new light on the Chalcedonian definition of faith . . .'

The two men retired to the Lodge and the Master of Gonville and Caius took their departure as his own cue to leave, saying that he had a few things to tidy up before the morning. There was, however, still plenty of time amongst those who remained for further conversation on the current state of medieval scholarship, paper conservation and the creation of facsimiles. And so it wasn't until well after ten-thirty that Sidney was able to return to the library for his own private view of the great and sacred document.

Ralph Mumford undid the double-locked outer doors, climbed the stairs, and then used a second set of keys for the upper room. He switched off the burglar alarm and turned on the lights.

The gold of the illuminated manuscripts sparked into life as if awoken from slumber. Sidney was struck by the quiet beauty of the room, awed by its reverential stillness, the hallowed history of literacy and faith laid out before him.

It was not until the two men reached the far end of the library that the extent of the catastrophe was revealed.

The lock on the final display case had been forced. The vitrine was empty. *The Gospel Book of St Augustine* had been stolen.

Ralph Mumford checked all the other cases and the cupboard in which it was kept when not on display. He asked Sidney to test all the windows to see that none had been disturbed and that the manuscript had not been thrown down to an accomplice below.

'I feel sick. It's like a death,' he said.

'Let's try and take stock.'

'I don't know what to do. How could this have happened?' Ralph began searching through the shelves, as if the thief might have hidden the gospel book amidst them and was planning on collecting it at a later date.

'Do you think it's the cathedral agent?' Sidney asked.

'You mean he stole the book while he was locked in? But how did he take it out? We saw him at the dinner.'

'He could have hidden it.'

'I relocked the library. I checked everything.'

'Even the gospel book?'

'Yes. It was there.'

'Are you sure?'

'Well, now, of course, I'm not sure of anything,' the librarian replied. 'I can't even trust myself. I made a sweeping glance at the room. I know that. I didn't go up to the cabinet and inspect it carefully, but nothing seemed amiss. The room had been well locked and the alarms were on. Julian is not as hopeless as everyone seems to think he is. Perhaps the book *had* already been stolen. But I am sure I would have noticed. I *felt* it this time, as I came into the room, in a way that I didn't sense that anything was wrong a few hours earlier.'

'Perhaps it's because you're with me, or that it's late at night?'

'But if it was stolen earlier that does beg the question: why on earth would the cathedral agent want to steal such a precious object that he can borrow any time he likes?'

'Perhaps he wants it for himself.'

'No proper antiquarian takes pleasure in a stolen book. They never feel it's theirs.'

'Perhaps he's an improper antiquarian.'

'The cathedral agent? I don't believe it.'

'Or he wanted to get it back for Canterbury?'

'But then he would have to tell them and everyone would know that he had taken it without due process and they would have to return it. He would be a laughing stock.'

'He left early,' Sidney remembered.

'To see the Master, and not with the book.'

'You don't suppose there could have been someone else hiding in the library?'

'You mean that two people were trapped, and one of them kept on hiding? But where?'

'There are no hidden doorways, secret drawers, loose floorboards, concealed alcoves or fake bookshelves?'

'None.'

'And I don't suppose,' Sidney continued, 'anyone could climb the library steps and lie low on top of the stacks?'

'They'd have to be quite an athlete. But in any case, when would they have been able to get out with the book? The only time would have been after I had locked up. As you saw when we came in, the library was as secure as when I left it.'

'You don't think it's still here, do you?'

'If it is, I don't know how we're going to find it. I just can't understand it, Sidney. There are two mysteries. The first is how the theft was managed. The second is why anyone would want to do it. As you know, *The Gospel Book of St Augustine* is our most precious possession. Its loss endangers our ownership of the entire library and the Church of England will be unable to enthrone its next archbishop. But it is also far too famous to sell. If the thief takes it to an auction house or a rare-book dealer then any expert will be able to tell what it is straight away. There is no market in which it can be sold.'

'I presume it's insured?'

'For £150,000.'

'That doesn't sound very much.'

'You must be the first person to think so, Sidney. Up until now, the highest price paid for a medieval manuscript has been £90,000. A sum of £150,000 is a perfectly respectable amount for an object that is neither painting nor sculpture. In the past some of our Fellows had even suggested that we sell it. They'd rather have the money for something else. Wine, probably. But you can't put a price on a possession until it's gone.'

'Would the thief know the insurance value?'

'He would if he worked either for the library, the college or the insurance company.'

'I suppose,' said Sidney, 'it could also be one of our friends in either Gonville and Caius or Trinity Hall, hoping to deprive us of the collection.'

'You don't mean the Masters?'

'Not directly. But they might have arranged the theft. Corpus forfeits the collection and then, miraculously, the stolen volume is found and restored.'

'That's devious but possible,' Ralph Mumford replied. 'Although we still don't know how anyone could have done this, either practically or morally.'

He kept searching through the stacks and on the shelves as if *The Gospel Book of St Augustine* had simply been misplaced.

As he did so, he looked through piles of manuscripts that were waiting to be catalogued and found what seemed to be a rogue book without its dust jacket: *An Illustrated History of the Coptic Church.*

'I've never seen that before. Goodness knows what it's doing here. One book disappears and another one arrives.'

'Perhaps one of the guests left it?'

The librarian was no longer listening. 'I suppose I'd better check on the facsimile. It's such a pity we didn't put that on display instead. I thought of doing it, but then I would have been too ashamed to pass it off as the original in front of my scholarly friends.'

'They would have been able to tell?' Sidney asked.

'At fifty paces.' Ralph opened a series of cabinets without appearing to concentrate. 'I wonder where it's got to?'

'You can't find it?'

'Extraordinary. Someone seems to have stolen both the original *and* the facsimile. Why would anyone want to do that?'

'Perhaps they couldn't tell the difference and wanted to be sure?'

'That would involve a thief who had little knowledge of medieval vellum. It seems unlikely.'

'Unless it was stolen to order. The bibliographical equivalent of a hitman.' Sidney thought for a moment. 'Perhaps the thief had other motives. It seems far-fetched, but perhaps it could be someone wanting to stop or delay the enthronement of the next Archbishop of Canterbury?'

'A protest by someone who disapproves of Dr Coggan's modernisation of the language of the Church of England

and his hopes to ordain women? Then the suspects would have to include our own chaplain.'

'Julian already had the keys. Perhaps he's stolen the book and hidden it?'

'But why would he do that?' Ralph Mumford almost wailed. 'He can't have such a serious objection to the next archbishop. It's ridiculous. You might as well accuse me! There is a history of librarians stealing from their own collections.'

'I think you are just about the only person we can discount,' said Sidney.

'There's the Master as well,' the librarian replied. 'He also has a key and could remove the book at any time.'

'Surely, Ralph, we have to consider why the book was taken on this night rather than any other and if the theft was planned or opportunistic?'

'Taken in the chaos, as people were leaving for the drinks, you mean? But if anyone did that, where would they hide it and how would they not be seen?'

'Sir Leslie managed to lock himself in the library without anyone noticing.'

'That was unfortunate.'

'We'll have to go and see him,' said Sidney.

'We can't. If he's not the culprit then he'll know the book has been stolen and all hell will break loose.'

'We could consult the police.'

'I don't think we want them involved just yet.'

'But I can't see us solving this case on our own, Ralph.'

'It's going to be bad enough telling the Master. I don't want anyone else to know what's happened. *The Gospel Book of St Augustine* is not on permanent display. We need to establish the timeframe during which it was stolen, who had what keys, and when and if the porters have seen anything suspicious. Good heavens, Sidney, it's going to be a long night. It's just as well you are staying.'

'I should warn Hildegard that I might be late back tomorrow.'

'No! You can't tell anyone.'

'Then how are we going to question people?'

'We'll start with the porters and then go on to Julian. Goodness knows, I was cross enough with him about the locking-up earlier in the evening. Now he's going to feel the full force of my fury.'

Sidney established that there were only three sets of keys: one belonging to the librarian (subsequently used and returned by the chaplain); one held at the Porters' Lodge; and one kept by the Master.

He thought through the possibilities. Even though Ralph Mumford could easily have stolen the book when he went back to check on the alarm, why would he have needed to force the lock on the display case when he had a perfectly good key himself? And why would he want to take the manuscript in the first place, unless it was a complex attempt to frame someone else for burglary?

As for the Master, how could he have left the dinner without being seen and, like Ralph, what motive could he have for stealing a precious object that was already in his possession and which he could peruse whenever he chose?

Did he carry the keys to the library with him at all times or were they left in his study so that anyone could walk into the Master's Lodge, pick them up, steal the gospel book and then return them as if nothing had happened?

Could the head porter have stolen the book during the dinner? But again, why would he have needed to break the lock on the display case and what could be his motive?

Could anyone have taken the keys from the Porters' Lodge? Were they marked in any way to make them identifiable?

Sidney wondered if the chaplain might be culpable. Did Julian Wells lock the cathedral agent in the library on purpose? Perhaps it wasn't an oversight after all, but a deliberate attempt to implicate Sir Leslie Manning in the theft and take attention away from himself? Did the chaplain then steal the gospel book in the brouhaha after the cathedral agent had been released? When *exactly* did he return the keys to the librarian? And what could *his* motivation be? Given the opportunity, Sidney felt that his colleague could soon be the prime suspect.

He then asked himself if Sir Leslie had deliberately trapped himself in the library. Could he have thrown the book out of the window to an accomplice in St Botolph's churchyard while the alarms were off?

Could further people not previously considered have been hiding in the room or have gained access afterwards?

And why did the thief take both the original and the facsimile?

All these questions needed to be answered, but the central problem was common to all. What would anyone want with a manuscript that was impossible to resell and could never be shown by a collector, even in secret, for fear of betrayal? What was *the point* of stealing such an object?

Could there be a reason that lay beyond its financial value?

The chaplain's college eyrie was a cross between a don's room and a vestry, filled with books and gowns, a prie-dieu before an image of Christ and the Virgin Mary, and an eclectic mix of images on the walls. There was a reproduction of a Matthew Paris manuscript showing a trip to Jerusalem and a thirteenth-century portrait of an elephant in the Tower of London; icons both ancient and modern; a framed photograph of a Greek patriarch and a letter pinned to a corkboard outlining a future trip to Mount Athos.

Julian Wells was a High Anglican who took a dim view of any modernisation in the Church of England, disapproving of the ordination of women, colloquial liturgical language and the ascent of informality. He believed in ritual, mystery and the pomp of birettas, bells and smells. Although he wouldn't be drawn into any direct criticism of the next archbishop, he admitted that he was anxious about any descent into the rigorous simplicity of a new puritanism.

Once the chaplain had been appraised of the situation (and had recovered), Ralph Mumford asked whether he had locked up properly when Sir Leslie had been trapped; that there could be no possibility of the man engaging in some kind of trickery to let himself in and out of the building.

'None at all. I can't think how this has happened.'

'How did the cathedral agent behave?'

'He was perfectly charming. He was only agitated when the porters rescued him.'

'And where was he at the time?'

'By the windows.'

'And they were locked?'

'Absolutely.'

'Although the alarm was off.'

'Only for a short time. I got confused about the system just before we all left; but it was a matter of moments.'

'Long enough for the cathedral agent to open a window and drop the book down to an accomplice?'

'Possibly. But if he did it then, I'm sure that someone would have seen him. There were still eight or nine people left in the room. I don't see how he could have done it. And besides, didn't Ralph check when he locked up for a second time? The gospel book was still in its rightful place.'

Sidney suggested, once more, that they might have to bring in Geordie.

'I'd rather you didn't,' said the librarian. 'We still haven't told the Master. Things tend to escalate when the police arrive.'

'A crime has been committed.'

'You don't suppose it could be a misunderstanding, or that it's someone with a grievance that can be addressed without recourse to prosecution?'

'We'll have to interview everyone who was at the dinner.'

'That would mean making the crime public.'

'I can't see any alternative.'

'We could ask the guests to keep the news to themselves.'

'I don't think we can rely on seventy people to keep the theft a secret. One of them is the editor of a national newspaper.'

'Which one?'

'The *Daily Telegraph*.'

'I see what you mean.'

Before he did anything else, Sidney visited the chapel. He wanted to pray, and also to check if, in some mad way, the thief might have had an ironical sense of humour in hiding the gospel book there.

It was a fine building, dating from 1822, in the English Perpendicular style, although the floor was Elizabethan and some of the stalls seventeenth century. A single candle burned in the sanctuary lamp; the altar was dressed in Trinity green.

Sidney searched the cupboards by the entrance and in the vestry and organ loft. Then he made his way into the nave, looking amidst the pews and under the blue cushions in the Fellows' stalls. He proceeded to the chancel, and even had a look beneath the altar. He was just about to kneel down to pray when he felt the presence of another.

He turned to see that the chaplain had been watching him. 'I didn't do it, Sidney. I don't know how any of you could think that I might have been capable of such a thing.'

Sidney took the train home on the Saturday and apologised to Hildegard for his late arrival. She was busy, she said, and barely spoke, only asking if she should give up worrying about him and walk the dog since it was clear that no one else was going to do it.

Now he'd returned, Sidney decided not to force an argument but to change into his civvies. After a revitalising bath, he dried himself and got dressed, only to notice that the favourite pair of cashmere socks he had intended to wear that day had shrunk in the wash. He was annoyed but knew that he could not express any irritation because Amanda had given them to him for his birthday. If he complained he would, at best, be informed that he could have handwashed them himself if they meant that much to him, and at worst, it would lead to an unnecessary row.

Hildegard had already set their daughter to work on piano practice for her Grade Three exam: scales, arpeggios, a Scarlatti minuet, a Witches' Dance and a Spanish ballad which seemed to be about the death of a donkey.

When Sidney finally came downstairs he noticed that there was a vase of sweet peas on the kitchen table. He had not seen them when he had left the day before. He remarked that it was late in the year for them and that he didn't think they had any left in the garden.

'We don't. Rolfe brought them.'

'I suppose his wife used to grow them.'

'No. He does. He's the one with the green fingers. But now he's going to put them to use on the piano. He wants to brush up his playing. I offered to help.'

'I'm sure you did.'

'What is that supposed to mean, Sidney?'

'It doesn't matter, Hildegard.'

'You only call me by my full name when you are cross with me. What are you insinuating?'

'I said it was nothing.'

'If it was nothing, don't speak. I have done nothing wrong, Sidney. If I called you to account for all your whereabouts and misdeeds, we'd be here for ever.'

'My conscience is clear.'

'And so is mine.'

Hildegard started to check that everything was in her handbag, taking out objects one at a time and then putting them back. Sidney had never quite understood the process and was just about to make light of the situation when he thought better of it.

'I must go,' said Hildegard.

'Where?'

'To teach.'

'I thought people had to come here for their lessons?'

'Rolfe has a piano. It makes a change. You're not the only one who can leave the house in a mystery.'

'I thought you had decided to stop seeing him?'

'I changed my mind.'

'You never told me that.'

'I didn't know I had to. Really, Sidney, it doesn't matter. By the way, you need to telephone Amanda.'

'What is it?'

'It's her father.'

'Has his condition deteriorated?'

'He's dying.'

'Does she want me to go and see him?'

'I said I didn't know when you would be back. You can't go now, as it's your turn to look after Anna. What about Thursday?'

'I said I'd go back to Corpus.'

'Then you'll have to decide what matters most, won't you?'

Hildegard left with a brief, and what Sidney took to be an automatic but unmeant kiss on the lips. Anna hardly helped the domestic mood by continuing with her dogmatic vegetarianism. It wasn't that Sidney minded the idea, but his daughter had hitherto disliked every single vegetable known to humanity apart from buttered carrots.

'How can you be a vegetarian if you don't like vegetables?' he had asked, only to be told by both wife and daughter to shut up.

There was also the question of his daughter's preparation for the eleven-plus. Because Hildegard taught Anna the piano (and her friend Rolfe von Arnim now appeared to be teaching her the flute) it was left to Sidney to take over certain aspects of the homework, not least, mathematics and verbal reasoning. And so, that evening, while they were waiting for his first attempt at a nut roast to bake, Sidney devised a missing-word game on a library theme which enabled him to keep thinking about the case while secretly recruiting his child into his investigation – the jumbled words were *Library*, *Villain*, *Forgery*, *Fake*, and even *Gospel*, which he was proud to see that Anna got immediately.

Despite this success, Sidney still felt curiously lonely, both at home and in the world. Perhaps it was the destiny of a priest to be an outsider (as Jesus was, he reminded himself) and if he did 'belong' somewhere, then he would be guilty of membership of a club that excluded others. It was therefore his task to be 'at large', to be as inclusive as possible, even if it meant that both his identity and his loyalties were always going to be stretched.

Waiting for Geordie's arrival in the Prince Albert, with Byron by his side, he listened to the everyday conversation of those around him: a man was saying that he preferred small women – 'half-pint jobs' he called them – because they normally had more of a sense of humour. It made up for their deficiency in height. Another was boasting that it would be a long time before his children received any money because his family had a history of longevity: 'much to their disgust'.

Geordie was quiet on arrival, but he had been subdued for a few months now, both after Helena's rape case and his temporary suspension. Sidney also suspected that he was still worried about his wife's cancer scare, even though Cathy had recently been given an all-clear and was suggesting a recuperative holiday in North Wales. Good news was not, however, something that Geordie ever quite trusted; like life itself, it could never be relied upon to last. He said he was 'counting the days until his retirement' which, at the age of fifty-four, was far too young. Had he really had enough or was he just jaded?

Sidney decided to find out how possible it might be to revive his friend's interests by telling him about the theft of the gospel book. He did so on the condition that any information provided was treated in confidence.

'Yet another locked-room mystery,' Geordie replied.

'It seems that way.'

'Then you just have to establish when the library was locked and when it wasn't. These crimes are nearly always about timing and distraction; either the book was not stolen when everyone thinks it was; or the utterly convincing alibi is a fake. Like magicians, the criminal has to mislead the audience. It's your job, Sidney, to study the whole thing from backstage rather than out front. Are you ever going to inform the police officially or are you just going to carry on as usual, chatting away to me as if nothing is wrong until I have to come in at the last moment and save the day?'

'As I've already said, we're not planning on reporting anything just yet.'

'Even though a crime has been committed.'

'We are trying to pretend that it's been "mislaid".'

'I'm sure people will believe that.'

'Perhaps there has been a misunderstanding? No one can sell the gospel book. It's hard to see what anyone could want out of it.'

'Has anyone asked for a ransom?'

'I don't think so.'

'That'll probably be next.'

'You've known such a case before?'

'I've experienced just about everything, Sidney. When I've seen the lot it'll be time to retire.'

'I wish you wouldn't go on about that.'

'And then it'll be a few short steps to the grave. Once your parents have gone, the sky feels a whole lot lower. You're lucky you still have yours.'

'Amanda's about to lose her father.'

'I presume you'll be taking the service.'

'It's the least I can do.'

'These days, every time I see a hole in the ground I think I might as well get in it. Save everyone the bother.'

'Don't be ridiculous. You're a much-loved man.'

'It doesn't feel that way, Sidney.'

'I think we have to stop being so grumpy. Cheerfulness is an underrated virtue.'

'Well you can "cheer me up" by getting another round in. Are you busy? I'm not planning on letting you go just yet. You can tell me what makes this book of yours so valuable.'

'That may involve religion.'

'It's not too late,' said Geordie, 'and there's always hope. Isn't that your mantra?'

Despite a thorough search of the library, Ralph Mumford confessed that they were going to have to tell the Master and delay their plans to take *The Gospel Book of St Augustine* to Canterbury for the enthronement. He also asked Sidney's advice on what they might offer as a replacement volume for the ceremony should the worst come to the worst.

'We have Augustine's own *Confessions*, of course, and his commentary on the Gospel of John. We also have Gregory the Great's *Homilies* and MS 361, his *De Cura Pastoralis*, but I don't suppose the new archbishop could take an oath on that. What about MS 33, *The Glossed Gospels of Mark and John*? These are twelfth century, possibly from St Albans. They are larger and more richly illustrated.'

'But they are only two gospels, rather than four, and they are five hundred years too late.'

'We do have a whole Bible, MS 48, twelfth century, also from St Albans. It has double, triple and quadruple columns of sixty-three lines. *The Book of Lamentations* is headed by a fine table of the Hebrew alphabet. Eton College has something very similar. And the initials to the gospels, I think on page 205, contain illustrations of the evangelists' emblems. Isn't it marvellous?'

Sidney turned the fragile pages. The intricate Latin text had been written by a small hand, dark ink on vellum, with occasional illuminations. He found a half-length figure of Christ holding a book with a silver sword across his mouth.

'Do you really think they'll accept it?' he asked.

'That depends if the cathedral agent has seen the original book before. Is there any chance he would think that most medieval manuscripts look alike? He has never been to an enthronement and we're only likely to run into trouble if one of the clergy is an expert. Are you going yourself, Sidney?'

'I think so.'

'And would it worry you if we provided a substitute?'

'Not if it is a Bible. If the archbishop takes an oath on this, then it surely counts?'

'But does it? If you swear on a fake are your vows valid?'

'It's not technically a "fake". It's just not what people think it is. It's still a Bible.'

'There are others that I could think about: new additions.'

'I thought the Parker bequest was one complete set. What do you mean by "additions"? Have there been "subtractions"?'

'I'm afraid so.'

'You have made some substitutions?'

'Parker's son did it all the time.'

'That doesn't excuse it, Ralph. And I think it means that books are missing after all. How many?'

'Four. But no one knows that yet.'

'So you think. How did you get away with the recent audit?'

'There was a bit of sleight of hand, Sidney.'

'You mean a cover-up.'

'I wouldn't put it as strongly as that.'

'Your rivals might. They only have one more to go and then, if they find out, the collection is forfeit.'

'Exactly. Which could implicate someone from Caius. They stand to benefit the most.'

'Then we had better go and see the Master. Do you think he knows already?'

'About the theft? He certainly does if he's done it; and if he has, then he's only one book away from inheriting the whole lot. That would be a disaster for Corpus. What did you think of him, Sidney? That's partly why I put you next to him.'

'He seems too irascible to be a criminal.'

'Do you think he could be responsible?'

'He could have delegated the task, and he did leave the dinner early.'

'Do you think that's what he meant by "tidying up"?'

'Would you like me to go and see him, Ralph? I don't think I am ever going to be one of his greatest friends, but I'll see what I can get out of him if you like.'

The next day Sidney made his way down King's Parade and into Trinity Street where he turned through the Gate of Humility, passed the Porters' Lodge and crossed Caius

Court before finding himself, just beyond the chapel, in the Master's Lodge.

Kenrich Prescott's rooms were decorated as a nineteenth-century cabinet of curiosities, filled with Victorian taxidermy, Ancient Greek heads, several anatomical figures and a model of the double helix, as if it had been staged by the admissions tutor as a prompt for questions to prospective undergraduates.

It was made clear, very early on, that this would not be a long meeting. 'I wasn't expecting to see you so soon, Archdeacon,' the Master began. 'Has someone died?'

'Not exactly.'

'I'm afraid you're too late to convert me.'

'It's not that. I need your discretion.'

'I am used to providing it.'

'You cannot tell anyone that you know what I am about to say to you.'

'Intriguing. Very well.'

'*The Gospel Book of St Augustine* has been stolen.'

'I know.'

'How?'

'Ralph Mumford telephoned.'

'Already? He didn't tell me he was going to do that.'

'I don't think he could wait. Perhaps he doesn't quite trust you . . .'

'But . . .'

'He thinks I'm behind the whole thing.'

'I'm sure he doesn't.'

'Bloody nerve. We already have the best library in Cambridge. I don't see why I would want to steal anything else.'

'I suppose so,' Sidney replied, unable to hold back his desire to be rude. 'It's only that I thought the Wren was the finest, then the Parker, the Pepys and St John's.'

'The Parker may be a fine medieval collection, Archdeacon, but that's as far as it goes. We have 90,000 volumes: law, theology, medicine, illuminated Books of Hours and Psalters, over one hundred fifteenth-century *incunabula* or cradle books, the *Nuremburg Chronicle*, the plays of Terence, Gratian's *Decretum* . . .'

As the Master spoke, Sidney wondered whether some small part of his energy could be pointed in the direction of personal hygiene. It was extraordinary how many Fellows were unfamiliar with toothpaste, deodorant or the advantages of dry-cleaning.

Kenrich Prescott expressed his astonishment that Sidney was bothering with his questions when it was perfectly obvious who the guilty party was. 'You don't think the cathedral agent was so absent-minded as to get stuck in the library by accident? The whole thing was staged. Either he took the book or manufactured a crisis as a diversionary tactic. The chaplain was misled and let him get away with it. He's not exactly one of nature's Einsteins. I wouldn't trust him to lock himself in his own lavatory. Where did you get him from?'

'Julian is a good and holy man.'

'I think he's a fool.'

'Then we will have to agree to differ.'

'If you ask me, you should see that cathedral agent as soon as possible. The evidence of his guilt is all too clear.'

'But if he knows we've lost the gospel book, there'll be the most almighty fuss.'

'Nothing you haven't dealt with before, if your reputation is anything to go by, Mr Archdeacon. Besides, what other choice do you have?'

Before he could pursue his investigations any further, Sidney knew he had to go to London to visit Amanda's dying father. The once-proud rooms in Chelsea were a depressing contrast to the Master of Caius's exhibitionism. Muted in grief, the only sounds came from a fire in the hall and an ancient grandfather clock. A couple of typed letters remained unopened on the hall table. Sir Cecil, it seemed, had no more need to communicate with the world.

His voice was high and faint and he only had a few words left in him. He told Sidney he had developed insomnia because he had got to that age and frailty when he feared that any sleep might be his last.

'It's good of you to come,' he said. 'I know we have had our differences.'

'Not at all.'

'Keeping busy?'

'There's been a theft in a Cambridge library.'

'I meant *in the Church*.'

'Oh yes, that too.'

'I'm glad you've come. There's just one thing I wanted to say to you, Sidney. You know that, after Robert, I have always thought of you as another son.' (Amanda's elder brother had been killed in Italy, just before the war had ended.)

Sidney was not sure that was the case at all, but he wasn't going to argue with a man on his deathbed.

'I want you to promise that you'll look after Amanda.'

Sidney thought he had spent most of his life trying, and failing, to do that. 'Of course. I'll do the best I can, Sir Cecil.'

'She's always been a wayward girl. That business with the Goya hardly helped.'

'I didn't think she wanted to tell you about that.'

'Ah yes, she thinks she has secrets. She told her mother. That's as good as telling me. Dreadful business.'

'I haven't seen her recently to talk about it.'

'I hope you haven't abandoned her?'

'I would never do that.'

'I'm glad to hear it. Her godfather sorted the situation out. Sir Giles Norrell – do you know him, by any chance?'

'I'm afraid not.'

'Good man. He believes in her. He offered the price she paid and ten per cent of any future profit. The plan is to hold on to the painting for a while and then sell it in America. They have their own experts and it'll get one over on the Spaniards.'

'I thought Charles Beauvoir was more to blame?'

'That little shit? His father was no better. Amanda should have known.'

'She likes to think the best of people.'

'I suppose that helps all of us in the end.'

'She's very lovable.'

'No one knows that more than we do, Sidney. I sometimes think I've been too hard on her, but I didn't want her wasting herself. It turns out she's done that anyway.'

'She's still young.'

'You know I always wanted her to marry you?'

'I thought you disapproved.'

'Amanda *imagined* I did. But she never asked me directly. Perhaps she didn't have enough faith in me. Or perhaps she didn't trust herself. It's a pity when love lacks confidence. So many people let the possibility slide away from them. Then it was all too late. I suppose it doesn't really matter. You would have made a good couple.'

'But it wasn't to be.'

'You have a fine wife now.'

'I'm a lucky man.'

'You chose well.'

'I have been blessed.'

'You took your chance when it came, just as I did. Marriage makes a man, don't you think?'

'People generally only say that when it's been a success. Amanda tried with Henry.'

'He had too much of a past. But I'm tired now. Will you pass me that water?'

Sidney did so.

'I suppose you are going to tell me that no one is beyond redemption?'

'The belief is there to help us all.'

'I hope it's more than a *belief*, Sidney. The trumpet shall sound. And we shall be saved.'

'And death shall have no more dominion over us.'

'Will you pray for me?'

'I will, Sir Cecil.'

'Just Cecil, if you don't mind. And, as I ask, please do look after Amanda. You can't deny a dying man his wish, can you?'

'I have already promised you that.'

Sidney's stay in London was cut short by a summons from the Master of Corpus. Sir David Montgomery had received a ransom demand for a book no one had told him had been stolen: a request made by someone who clearly knew the insurance value of the missing manuscript as well as the size of the college's endowment. The demand was for £50,000 to prevent the theft of another book (*The Bury Bible* or *The Anglo-Saxon Chronicle*) and another £50,000 for the return of *The Gospel Book of St Augustine*.

Attached was the opening illustration of St Luke's Gospel. It had been cut into tiny fragments. The note read: 'This is from the facsimile. The next time it will come from the original manuscript.'

Ralph Mumford had also been called in to explain the situation. 'So that's why the thief took the reproduction as well,' he said. 'It must be someone who can't bear to desecrate the original.'

'Or someone who doesn't have it at all and is bluffing,' said the Master.

'But who else knows about this?' Sidney asked.

'Only us, the chaplain, the Master of Caius and the thief.'

The Master paced the room. 'We cannot give in to such a demand.'

'Then how will we get the gospel book back?'

'Do you think the cathedral agent knows too?' the Master asked.

'I think he would be quick to telephone us if he did,' the librarian replied.

'How long do you think we can keep the news from him?'

'I still think Sir Leslie could have stolen it,' said Sidney. 'The book was removed after he had been trapped in the library.'

'He went straight back to the dinner, and then he was with me for the rest of the evening,' the Master concluded.

'What did he want?' Sidney asked.

'We had a very interesting conversation on the future of the Anglican communion and its relationship with Rome. Sir Leslie wants to invite the Pope to Canterbury. You know he's never been? The gospel book has the potential to be one of the great attractions of his visit. He could see, touch and study something sent by his predecessor, Gregory.'

'And now he can't unless we pay the ransom.'

'In the likely event that it's not the cathedral agent,' the Master replied, 'are there any clues as to who might be behind all this?'

'I have a friend who might have an idea,' said Sidney. 'Quentin Torrens is an antiquarian bookseller. People often try to sell to him, although I fear this might be out of his league. But I can make a few discreet enquiries. Otherwise we will have to bring in the police.'

'You mean your man Keating? I don't think we're ready for that.'

'He gets results.'

'I've heard he can be a little rough.'

'He's determined,' said Sidney, 'and enthusiastic, but I'll try my antiquarian first.'

Quentin Torrens was, it had to be admitted, something of a long shot. He was a genial, scholarly but other-worldly pipe smoker who had once, famously and in Sidney's presence, set fire to the beard that he had grown to compensate for his baldness. An Italian liqueur, Sambuca, had been involved. Quentin had been at Corpus and had stayed on to do a PhD on the revisions to Dr Johnson's dictionary and had a penchant for quoting the great doctor's more obscure words to describe the dons at their old college. (Thus the Professor of Chemistry was a 'fopdoodle', the Professor of Modern History was a 'bedpresser' and the Professor of Law was a 'bellygod'.)

After the initial 'hail-fellow-well-met', Quentin took the opportunity to explain a little bit about the nature and philosophy of book thievery in order to try and understand who might have committed the crime. It certainly couldn't have been a serious book-lover, he argued, because, as Ralph Mumford had already pointed out, none of them would take pleasure in possessing a stolen object. It was like owning a time-share, Quentin maintained: you couldn't ever feel that the property was yours.

'And that's no good to a collector. Although it's possible someone may have "borrowed" it for a while just to see what it's like. There's a history of that. People stopped lending books to Dr Johnson because they knew they'd never get them back. He'd either mutilate them in order to rip out quotations for his dictionary, or lose them, or forget that he had them. Matthew Parker's own son, John, was notoriously vague and unreliable, even rewriting the bequest to suit books that he wanted back or wasn't sure his father had meant to include in the first place. But I suppose the children of archbishops are bound to be unreliable. They've enjoyed such privilege, it's hard to recover.'

'But if someone has borrowed it,' Sidney replied, 'how long is "a while"? For some people that could be twenty years. The book could deteriorate badly during that time.'

'There must be a degree of covetousness, I think. It's more than a question of money. It's the fact that there's only one copy, and that it's fragile. These are words that speak of eternity written on a surface that has survived the centuries but can still prove transient. It would be hard not to be moved by it.'

'And so you're confident the thief will be careful with what he's got?'

'As much as I can be. But there have been vandals in the past. I wouldn't take him for granted.'

'You think we should pay?'

'I am afraid so.'

By the time Sidney returned to Corpus a second ransom demand had been made: £100,000 was to be left in the Reading Room of the British Library for the safe return of the gospel book. To prove that the thief had the original, the demand came with page seventy-eight of the original folio: a half-length figure of a winged being with lion's claws and ears, and human face, holding a book.

'Is this the real thing?' Sidney asked.

Ralph Mumford found it difficult to answer. 'It is.'

The ransom note suggested that if the money were not paid then the next image would either be cut, torn or burned.

'Then this cannot be a serious book-lover after all,' said Sidney.

'But it is the work of someone who is determined to extract money,' the Master reminded them. 'What are we going to do?'

'Pay them,' said Ralph. 'Please.'

'Do you think the British Library request means that the gospel book is now in London?'

'Possibly.'

'We must get it back before the cathedral agent finds out.' The Master turned to the librarian. 'When are you seeing him?'

'Thursday.'

'You'll have to put him off.'

'I've done that twice already.'

'Then you'll have to think of something. We can't give in to this. I suppose it's time to notify the police.'

'I'll talk to Geordie,' said Sidney, but before he could do anything, Amanda telephoned. Her father had died.

He made the journey to London and offered to take the funeral. Before he entered the room to console his friend, he remembered the words of his pastoral director, Simon Opie, telling him that it was always best to arrive slightly late, to give a family time to get ready.

'No matter how much warning you have, the end still comes as a shock,' Amanda said. 'I wasn't prepared for the guilt or the relief.'

'Relief that it's over at last?'

'And guilt that I never loved him enough.'

'He didn't make it easy.'

'He never recovered from my brother's death. And I suppose I resented that. So now I don't know what to say.'

'You're not expected to say anything. The silence and the attention is enough.'

'Will you teach me how to pray?' Amanda asked. 'I mean *properly.*'

'If it will help. There aren't always answers.'

'Just the silence?'

'Yes, Amanda. Just the silence. Although that too can be an answer.'

The following day, Sidney joined Ralph Mumford on a train down to Canterbury. The librarian was carrying a secure attaché case containing an alternative book from the seventh century: *The Northumbrian Gospels.*

On entering the Chapter office on the first floor of a Georgian building within the cathedral precincts, they were asked to wait. After three minutes a short man with sandy hair, dressed in a grey pinstriped double-breasted suit, came out into the hall, shook their hands and introduced himself as Sir Leslie Manning, the agent of Canterbury Cathedral.

This was not the man who had attended the audit dinner. It was also not the man who had been trapped in the Parker Library. And it was not the man who had talked so movingly about the continuity of tradition and the sacred nature of ancient manuscripts.

Sidney and Ralph introduced themselves, accepted Sir Leslie's offer of tea and biscuits and couldn't think what to say.

'We were so sorry not to see you at the audit dinner,' Ralph Mumford began.

'I didn't know I was invited.'

'You were.'

'It must be the new secretary.'

'Yes,' said Sidney, 'it has to be, unless we made a mistake. Perhaps the invitation was sent elsewhere. You are the cathedral agent, are you not?'

'That's what it says on the door to my office.'

'There's not a similar title that could be confused with your own?'

'Certainly not. Who did you think I was?'

'Sorry,' said Sidney. 'I'm not sure I'm quite myself today.'

'Have you brought the book?' Sir Leslie asked.

'We have.' Ralph Mumford took out *The Northumbrian Gospels*. 'I'm afraid it's not what you were expecting. But these gospels were also held at St Augustine's, Canterbury and have a very fine frontispiece. We thought this might look better on television.'

'But why haven't you brought *The Gospel Book of St Augustine?*'

Sidney cut short the pain. 'Because it's been stolen.'

'By whom?'

'Almost certainly someone who was pretending to be you.'

'Then what the devil's going on?'

Sidney reported how convincing the impersonation had been; how the fake cathedral agent had spoken of the unbroken tradition of archbishops since 597 AD, all being sworn in on this holy text.

'But that's not true,' said the real Sir Leslie; or rather, the man who now said he was real.

'What?'

'We've only been doing this part of the ceremony since 1945. It's all a bit of a fraud, if you ask me. Dr Coggan is only the third archbishop to be enthroned in this way. The dean and the Master of Corpus were having dinner at the Athenaeum after the war and thought it might be a rather spiritual thing to do. It's amazing how modern some traditions are. I think it was part of a bid to get the gospel book back.'

'Even though it was never yours in the first place,' Ralph jumped in. 'It belonged to St Augustine's Abbey, not the cathedral.'

'I don't think this is the time to bring up points of principle,' the cathedral agent replied. 'I'm alarmed that someone has been impersonating me and that you believed him. How he did so, why no one caught on, and how he managed to steal the book, God alone knows. Have you any clues?'

'Tell me about your secretary . . .' Sidney asked.

'What about her?'

'Does she open your post?'

'That is part of her job.'

'As well as running your diary and answering your telephone calls?'

'Isn't that what a secretary is for?'

'I think we need to meet her . . .'

'That may be difficult. She's just handed in her notice.'

'That doesn't surprise me at all,' said Sidney.

It was clear that Sir Leslie's secretary had passed on the invitation to the audit dinner and helped brief the man who had been impersonating the cathedral agent. But who was he and how had he stolen the manuscript? He had definitely left the dinner early, and could well have picked up the book from a prearranged hiding place and hidden it under his cloak while passing the Porters' Lodge. But it would have taken some nerve, and it would almost certainly have required an accomplice.

Sidney returned to see his old friend Quentin Torrens. The antiquarian bookseller was in the middle of lighting a pipe that had been hand-carved in Ethiopia by a gnostic sect. 'What was this fake cathedral agent like?' he asked.

'The man was very well tailored, I must say. His dinner suit had silk lapels and he wore rather too much cologne – more than any man would normally do, come to think of it. It was strange, but he knew his stuff. For example, when looking at the Bury Bible from the twelfth century – the first book in the collection that names its artist, Master Hugh – he remembered that the parchment used came from Scotland rather than East Anglia. But, at the same time, he didn't seem to know much about the broader English culture. He pronounced Caius College as "Kai-ous", rather than "Keys", which was unusual for a member of the establishment.'

'Could he have been Italian?' Quentin suggested.

'Why do you ask?'

'There is a renowned book thief called Luca Simeone,' Torrens continued. The police have nearly caught him on a number of occasions, but he's always managed to give them the slip. His mother is English aristocracy, so he knows how to fit in. His father is one of those dubious Italian counts from around Verona. Simeone is more of a Renaissance specialist, but I wouldn't put it past him . . .'

'Why would he want to take the gospel book?'

'For pleasure, for money or, perhaps, to return it to what he considers to be its rightful place.'

'Which is?'

'The Vatican Library in Rome; amongst Pope Gregory the Great's possessions. You know what these people think: that the book was given to the English as an act of faith and trust. We broke that trust when Henry VIII severed our ties with Rome. As well as raising cash, the theft could be, in part, a punishment for the foundation of the Church of England, the Dissolution of the Monasteries, the persecution of Catholics and the fact that we no longer recognise the Pope.'

'Seems a bit extreme. Although I would think that the demand for cash is paramount,' said Sidney.

'But the ecclesiastical politics provide moral justification.'

'I didn't know thieves were so scrupulous.'

'If they are anything like Luca Simeone, then they are. It will all have been planned very carefully. The secretary at Canterbury was clearly in on it; and he must have had someone at the college too. What about the chaplain? Do you think he could have taken a bribe?'

'Julian Wells? I very much doubt it,' said Sidney.

'It's amazing how the man fooled you all. In plain view.'

'Even the scientists were taken in.'

'Perhaps it only goes to show how gullible intellectuals can be,' said Quentin. 'They may not believe in God, but they trust a man who says he comes from Canterbury without there being any empirical evidence.'

'Where do you think the manuscript could be?' Sidney asked.

'If Luca Simeone *is* behind the ransom demand, he's probably still in England, unless he's decided to take the book to the Vatican. But if he did that, then he wouldn't get the money.'

'I don't know if he'll get it anyway,' said Sidney.

'You mean the college won't pay up?'

'They don't intend to.'

'Then I wonder how long they'll hold their nerve. The stakes are high enough already, Sidney. I just hope they realise who they might be dealing with.'

'Well, if they don't, then we'll just have to tell them, won't we, Quentin?'

Back at Corpus, the Master was slow to take in the latest development, embarrassed that so many intelligent men had been duped, especially now that he found himself in the presence of Inspector Keating. 'Do you mean to say that we have been visited by an impostor?'

'Exactly that.'

'But I lent him my *Illustrated History of the Coptic Church*! The man was so convincing I can hardly believe it.'

'And was he ever alone in the Lodge?' Sidney asked.

'Only for a minute or two.'

'Enough time to take the key?'

'It must have been when I went to fetch the book from the living room.'

'Was your guest in the study?'

'*Our* guest,' the Master insisted. 'He was.'

'And is that where you keep the keys to the library?'

'It is. But they were never missing.' He walked over to the sideboard and picked them off the rack. 'I still have them.'

'Are you sure those are the right keys?' Geordie asked.

'I think so. I haven't checked them in the lock. Are you implying the thief might have swapped them over when I was out of the room?'

'It's been done before,' said Geordie. 'He probably had some help from inside too; perhaps your cleaner or one of the kitchen staff. We'll make some enquiries. You do hire temporary staff, Master?'

'All the time. They come highly recommended.'

'Yes,' said Geordie. 'I bet they do.'

Sir Cecil Kendall's funeral took place in Holy Trinity, Sloane Street, a church where some thirteen years previously Sidney had stopped Amanda marrying a bigamist. Then the priest had asked the family to be careful with the confetti in order to spare the feelings of those who were due to attend a memorial service the next day. Now, the situation was reversed.

There were some two hundred people in attendance; one of the few advantages of Sir Cecil dying at the comparatively young age of seventy-four meant that most of his friends and colleagues were still alive. The last autumn flowers

(November roses, winter chrysanthemums) were bulked out with ivy and other assorted greenery in expansive decorations throughout the church, but the atmosphere was uneasy, caught between mourning and thanksgiving.

Because it was such an establishment 'do', Sidney took great pains over his appearance, making sure that his funeral Oxfords had a proper 'army polish', remembering his pastoral director's other great dictum: 'Always clean your shoes before a funeral because the family will certainly have polished theirs.'

He preached on the theme of love, duty and a life well lived. Sir Cecil Kendall had been determined to pack as much into his time on earth as possible. He was a straight-backed man with what might be called 'old-fashioned values', believing in manners, decency and respect. He was slow to judgement and quick to praise. Despite his achievements he remained modest, hoping that, like great cricketers, when you returned to the pavilion after your innings people should not be able to tell from your demeanour whether you had scored a duck or a hundred.

Sidney ended with Cardinal Newman's great prayer for God's blessing: 'May He support us all the day long, till the shades lengthen and the evening comes, and the busy world is hushed, and the fever of life is over, and our work is done. Then in His mercy may He give us a safe lodging, and a holy rest and peace at the last.'

He then told the congregation that Sir Cecil had asked him, on his last visit, what he thought 'a safe lodging was'. When Sidney had paused for thought, the dying man had said simply: 'I think it's probably a rather good B&B.'

Amanda had asked if Hildegard could sing. Her father had enjoyed the *St Matthew Passion* and he had specifically requested a reprise of '*Aus Liebe*' when planning the order of service before his death. As a result, Rolfe arrived with two oboe da caccia players and accompanied the choir for the '*Pie Jesu*' from Fauré's *Requiem*.

Sidney tried not to mind.

They held the wake in Chester Row. Amanda soon tired at the relentless meeting and greeting, the loud concerns ('Poor you'), the quiet solicitations ('If there's anything I can do . . .') and even the suggestive invitations ('We really should have dinner together. Just the two of us. It would help take your mind off things. I know this little place . . .').

She kept her bright face on for as long as possible but collapsed onto the sofa with a stiff whisky as soon as the last of the guests had gone.

'In the past when people lost their parents I tried to be as sympathetic as I could, but I knew nothing. All my sympathy was superficial.'

'We cannot know what we don't know.'

'We can make a better effort, Sidney. Your sister told me that Daddy was proud of me, but I didn't really believe her because he never told me himself. I always thought I was a disappointment. I wanted to impress him: with money, achievement, property, even my career. And I didn't manage any of those things. What did you talk about when you saw him near the end?'

'We spoke mainly about you. He told me about your godfather bailing you out. You should have said, Amanda. I was worried about you.'

'I was too embarrassed. It would only prove your theory that I'm spoilt.'

'I don't think that.'

'You don't really approve of money, though, do you, Sidney?'

'I don't know. Perhaps I'm just jealous.'

'There's no need to be. The rich do have their problems.'

'It's just that poverty isn't one of them, and, for the poor, that's all that matters. But let's not spoil the day. Wealth is a relative term. Compared to most of the world's population I'm rich too. Any revolutionary coming into this room wouldn't be able to tell us apart. We'd both be rounded up and shot.'

'Is this your normal funeral chitchat, Sidney?'

'I think it's because I'm with you. I can be myself.'

'You preached a good sermon. I'm so glad we asked you. It was Daddy's idea. I think he knew you'd smooth over his faults. You were very kind.'

'The occasion does rather demand it.'

'I know. But my father was wrong about so much: how Britain should never have come off the gold standard; how we would have won the war without the Americans. Goodness, he was even anti-Semitic when he could be sure of the company. But none of his mistakes ever seemed to trouble him, perhaps because my mother never contradicted him. She just wanted everything to be "lovely".'

'Or nothing was ever as bad as the death of your brother?'

'Yes, "the thing we never spoke about". Daddy wouldn't countenance it. So they've been living in some kind of afterlife since 1944 when everything in this house came to a halt. Nothing mattered: not my job, my marriage, my life. I just had to be the dutiful daughter.'

'And you've done that. Now you can stop.'

'And find myself again. Not that there's anything left to find any more. I think I'm lost, Sidney. My life is as mislaid as your gospel book. Have you had any joy in finding it?'

'Let's not talk about that now.'

'I don't know. I rather miss your investigations.'

'Not when you are the subject of them.'

'I think book thievery is beyond me. Will you show me the scene of the crime?'

'You can come to Corpus any time you like.'

'We can have lunch, like the old days. Take in the Fitzwilliam . . .'

'We were so young. Now look at us.'

'You've done well, Sidney. You're so lucky. I never did have good judgement. With Hildegard you knew straight away, didn't you?'

'No. It took me nearly seven years to make up my mind. And I still don't really understand her.'

'She likes an air of mystery.'

'I wish she wouldn't. Sometimes I don't know what's going on at all. I can't read her, Amanda. I never know what she really thinks.'

'You're not worried about her friend Rolfe, are you?'

'I try not to be.'

'Because that would be double standards.'

'I don't know. I have a clear conscience.'

'So you *are* worried?'

'Not so much about him or whatever they do or say; but the fact that she seems to need him. He can offer something I cannot.'

'And has she told you what it is?'

'"Time", she says, although I think it's more than that. The fact that he's German must help. And music is very much a part of it and I can't do anything about that. I can't play any kind of instrument and it's too late to start now.'

'I presume you don't like talking to her about it?'

'No, I don't.'

'Isn't it strange,' said Amanda, 'that you should be so curious about the lives of other people and yet so reluctant to get to grips with your own?'

By the time Sidney was next in Corpus a third ransom demand had been made.

Cut from the manuscript was an illustration of the Last Supper and a warning: 'It's autumn. The leaves disappear. This is your last chance before I destroy the gospel book page by page.'

'My God,' said the librarian. 'This is desecration.'

'We still can't pay,' said the Master.

'We have to.' Ralph Mumford spoke with a desperation that suggested he might kill anyone who disagreed with him. 'Otherwise we will lose the entire manuscript.'

Enclosed with the demand was the key to a locker in the London Library. Inside, when they left the money, they would find a shelf mark telling them where the gospel book was waiting.

204

'It must be a library member,' said Sidney. 'I wonder how many people belong both to the University and the London Libraries and have a ticket to the Reading Room in the British Library?'

'It would take too long to correlate.'

'The London Library is the smallest. There can only be three or four thousand members. We could, perhaps, get your friend Quentin Torrens to go through the list?'

'But if it is Luca Simeone he is unlikely to be using his real name,' said the Master.

'And we can't even be sure it's him,' Ralph continued. 'Why would a bibliophile want money rather than the book? Any true lover of the manuscript would want to keep it. I don't think it's him.'

'But who else can it be?' Sidney asked.

'We don't have any time to worry about who is responsible,' said Ralph. 'The important thing is to get the book back. Then we can worry about the finances and who might have done it.'

'It's all very well for you to say that,' said the Master. 'The insurance company is creating one hell of a stink. They are accusing us of carelessness and threatening not to pay up.'

'That is all the more reason to get the book back safely. Then we can get the police to recover the money.'

'And how easy do you imagine that's going to be?' Sidney asked. 'Don't you think we should ask Geordie to keep watch on the lockers at the London Library and make our move when the thief does?'

'But if he makes a mistake, everything is ruined,' said Ralph.

'The book, our endowment and our reputation,' the Master agreed. 'All in one crime. It doesn't bear thinking about.'

After a long consultation about how much to involve the police, it was agreed not to tell them anything and simply pay the ransom. However, there still remained the question of how much they could trust the thief to hand the book back safely after the money had been collected.

The cash was to be left as the London Library closed and no one was to remain in the building. The thief presumably planned to stay on after hours and then make his escape.

Sidney offered to spend three or four hours with Ralph on the lookout, but when they opened the locker to leave the money they found a further note. 'No witnesses. I can see you watching.'

'Where *is* he?' Ralph asked.

'I don't know. Perhaps we should do what he says?'

They heard a noise, footsteps receding on the stairs, a crack, and the smell of burning. A fire was starting outside the Reading Room.

'My God, what the hell is he doing?' Ralph shouted. 'We have to put it out.'

He ran with Sidney to get extinguishers and then, when they realised the fire was out of control, they telephoned for assistance. An incendiary device had been left behind the enquiry desk, conveniently placed to enable the flames to take advantage of the draught up the stairs, the dry paper of books waiting to be collected, the soft leather chairs and the oak library tables that might just as well have been ready-chopped for the blaze.

It was twenty minutes before the fire brigade arrived. By that time, the flames had reached the Reading Room. It took six men to get the main hose going and, for a while, it looked as though the London Library was undergoing its second Blitz.

'My God,' said Ralph, 'how could anyone who loves books do this?'

Any chance of keeping tabs on the suspect was lost in the pursuit of a greater good: putting out the fire.

Once the conflagration had been quelled, Ralph and Sidney returned to the lockers, where they found another note: 'That's better.'

The money was gone but *The Gospel Book of St Augustine* had been returned. As the firemen sorted through the rubble and a distraught librarian tried to feel grateful that the situation had not been worse, they went up the back stairs to the fifth floor, across a vertiginous walkway, following an eccentric cataloguing system (Eccles. Hist. Tithes, Unitarianism, Vulgate, Wales, Wiclif, Zephania, Zoroaster) to find the stolen book shelved in Religion, Quarto, next to *The Missal of St Augustine's Canterbury, with excerpts from the antiphonary and lectionary of the same monastery, from a manuscript in the library of Corpus Christi College, Cambridge.*

A few days later, Quentin Torrens telephoned to say that he had an intriguing possibility. An Italian book dealer had asked if he might be interested in acquiring a series of Renaissance volumes that he had picked up 'on his travels'.

On checking the list of prospective volumes, he was pretty sure that they had been stolen from the Bodleian Library in Oxford and that there was a high chance the seller was none other than Luca Simeone in one of his guises. Perhaps Sidney would like to come along with his friend Geordie, make a few enquiries and even an arrest?

It was a late morning of mist and tired rain. The windows of Antiquaria Torrensiana had steamed so that only a few precious items on display were visible beside drying umbrellas and tables of second-hand books that still had to be sorted and priced: editions of Anselm, Aristotle and Aquinas, a medieval Book of Hours, Geoffrey of Monmouth's *History of the Kings of Britain* and a Kelmscott Chaucer. Torrens was so keen to avoid any suspicion of a sting that he had taken his idea of 'normality' to eccentric levels, with yesterday's tea and cake together with last night's whisky glass lying on top of precarious piles of books, maps, letters and bills. He appeared to have little interest in tidying. There were no customers in his shop other than the man who had pretended to be Sir Leslie Manning.

'We've met before,' said Sidney on being introduced, 'at the audit dinner in Corpus.'

'You must be mistaken.'

'I don't think so. It was on the fifth of September, when *The Gospel Book of St Augustine* was on display.'

'I don't know what you mean.'

'In Cambridge.'

'I can assure you that I was not there.'

'Not in your current guise.'

'What on earth do you mean by that?'

'You impersonated the cathedral agent of Canterbury.'

'And why would I do a thing like that?'

'You tell me.'

'I do not know who you are,' the man continued. 'We have never met. We haven't even been introduced correctly. I am here to do some business with Mr Torrens. Please do excuse us. I am sure you have other concerns that take up your time.'

'This is my only *concern*, Mr Simeone. You made sure that you were locked into the Parker Library at Corpus not because you wanted to steal the gospel book but because you had to check the burglar alarm and security system,' Sidney explained. 'You watched the chaplain lock up and set the alarm, and then questioned the porters closely when they came to rescue you. Later, when you were having your night-cap with the Master, you asked if you could borrow a book. I am guessing that it was an *Illustrated History of the Coptic Church*. While the Master went to fetch it you took his library key from the rack and replaced it with a similar key so that he would not notice the loss. The front door of the Lodge could hardly be closer to the Library. It would take moments to slip in, steal the gospel book and use the dustcover of the book on the Coptic Church to disguise it. You then left the college with what appeared to be a recent publication under your cloak.'

'That is very interesting, Archdeacon. I don't know how you can ever prove it.'

'And that's where I come in,' said Geordie, stepping forward to introduce himself.

The enthronement of Donald Coggan took place in Canterbury Cathedral on 24 January 1975. The new archbishop passed a small, silent, anti-Roman Catholic protest outside the cathedral and knocked three times with his pastoral staff on the great West Door to gain admittance. He was dressed in a gold and red cope decorated with the arms of the towns, cities and colleges with which he had been associated throughout his life and processed up the Nave to make his solemn vows on the gospel book, and then be twice enthroned, blessed by the Archbishop of Kenya and welcomed by representatives of the Anglican communion and other faiths from across the globe. He preached on the text of John 16:33: 'In the world you shall have tribulation. But be of good cheer. I have overcome the world.' He spoke of how the Church militant expects wounds, for it follows a wounded Lord, but that we should be filled with the confidence to overcome our fears. 'We are on the victory side of Calvary,' he concluded. 'We are children of the Resurrection.'

The pale winter light gave the stained glass an even luminosity, the low sun hitting the tops of the well-worn steps that led up to the High Altar. The sheer volume of the hymn-singing, 'Immortal, Invisible,' caused the pages of the gospel book to flutter lightly, as if the breath of God were upon them. The final organ voluntary resounded through the stone, its deep bass affirming that a church had survived on this spot through the centuries and would continue to occupy holy ground until the end of time, greater than any individual life or congregation that filled it, offering up one final Hallelujah to the promise of redemption from death and the joy of life everlasting.

Sidney stood between his wife and Ralph Mumford, and looked at all the other clergy in their pomp, their ceremonial roles stretching back across history, enjoying their moment amidst the glory and the splendour, and wondered what his life would be like when the next Archbishop of Canterbury was appointed, and how much more tribulation he would have to overcome before then.

The Long Hot Summer

IN THE SUMMER OF 1976 it never seemed to rain at all. There was a nationwide hosepipe ban, water rationing in Wales and fires in the New Forest. A specially appointed Minister for Drought demanded that Britain halve its water consumption. Car washes were outlawed, fountains were shut off and most people were unable to find an open swimming pool. Sidney noticed in *The Times* that the Kensington Institute was taking advantage of the conditions to advertise a course in 'water divining'. He wondered who would sign up.

He was on a train to London to see Gloria Dee's 'Farewell to Europe' tour at the club owned by his brother-in-law, Johnny Johnson. He had first heard the great singer over twenty-five years ago when she had been a still-youthful firecracker. Now she had turned into a diva, 'the Cleopatra of Jazz'.

Hildegard was with him, and they opened all the windows in their carriage to create as much of a breeze as possible. Outside lay the wilting flowers, parched earth and brown lawns of England's once-proud gardens. There were a few exceptions, where owners had either been canny with their bathwater or had taken to illicit watering at night, but there was enough green grass and blooming roses to make Sidney remark that if only it was as straightforward to spot a murder suspect then his life, and Geordie's, would be a lot easier.

'Do you ever stop?' Hildegard asked.

'I've stopped now.'

'You promise?'

'Always on duty. You know that.'

'As a priest. Not as a detective.'

'I am always on duty as a husband.'

'Good.' Hildegard smiled. 'I am intrigued to see the woman you once admired so much. I hope she does not distract you.'

Sidney was glad that he could take his wife to hear the legendary performer before she retired. He only hoped that Gloria was not ill. Weren't jazz singers supposed to go on until they dropped?

There was no air conditioning in the club, but Johnny had installed a series of fans and kept the doors open between acts. It was still, however, a hot and crowded occasion, with men in summer shirts and women in light cotton dresses, sleeveless tops and billowing skirts. There were few young faces. Gloria's fans had aged with her. And so, as Sidney sat beside his wife and sister Jennifer, he wondered if jazz music was becoming rather like the Church of England, an acquired taste, soon to be out of date, replaced by an easier, popular, secular culture?

Gloria was wearing a yellow silk trouser suit with a matching rose in her dark hair that had been swept up to give her height an extra three inches. Sidney remembered how intoxicated he had felt when he had first met her, the exhilaration of her presence, the sensual smell of sweat, gardenia and tuberose, and, as she sang, he surrendered once more to a voice that had mellowed like a 25-year-old malt whisky. It was all honey-smoke, peat and flame.

The first set was a straight run through some of the old standards – 'Satin Doll', 'The Girl from Ipanema', 'How High the Moon', 'Caravan', 'Mean to Me' – and although she took them at what was, perhaps, a slower tempo than her recordings, Gloria replaced speed with a languorous seduc-tiveness that seemed to suit the Alabama heat of the evening.

Hildegard was impressed by the singing and amused by her husband's adoration, and remembered that this was what it had been like the first time they had gone to a jazz concert together, the Eric Dolphy Quintet in Berlin in 1961. It was when she had first known for sure that she would marry him, and as she recalled that night, her husband seemed fifteen years younger, the man she had found at last and knew that she would always love. She reached for his hand and held it as Gloria sang, smiling as her husband occasionally clicked his fingers and even, at one point, shouted out: 'Yeah!'

In the break between sets, as everyone cooled down and ordered more drinks, Jennifer took them to meet the great performer backstage. Every time Sidney saw his sister he was perplexed at how similar and fond they were of each other and yet how little time they spent together. How could it be that families could drift apart so easily over the years?

As soon as Gloria spotted Sidney she put her hand to her mouth in mock-horror at the sight of him. 'Careful, boys, there's been a murder.'

'Nothing like that, I'm pleased to report.'

'You surprise me, Preacher Man.'

'You remember me?'

'You're kinda hard to forget. I only hope you haven't brought trouble. I seem to remember how it follows you around.'

Twenty years ago, Gloria had been singing when there was a murder in the toilets. She informed Sidney that she had seen plenty of suffering and it was always about love or money. 'Those things go together the whole damn time.'

Now he told her that he hoped London wasn't proving too hot. The weather had been extremely oppressive lately.

'Too hot?' Gloria almost spat. 'Do you think a woman who comes from where I'm from can ever be too hot? Is there such a thing as being too darn hot?'

'I'm sorry. I should have expressed myself differently.'

Hildegard changed the subject by saying what a pleasure it was to be there. As a musician she appreciated both Gloria's voice and her piano playing.

'Perhaps you should accompany me, honey?'

'I'm only a teacher. It's nothing glamorous. I trained as a classical pianist.'

'And so did I. Studied classical. I can play that stuff too.'

'I can tell.'

'You're too kind, sweetheart. Although I'm not sure if I can keep it up for much longer. I'm too old for touring. Going to be seventy come December.'

'You don't look it,' said Jennifer.

'I used to lie about my age in the past,' Gloria continued. 'I had to say I was so much *older* than I really was so I could play in the clubs that served liquor. Then I started to lie that

I was *younger* than I was so no one would think I was past caring. That's what my life has been, honey, a pack of lies.'

She turned back to Hildegard. 'So you're the woman that tamed the preacher?'

'And you're the woman that got away?'

'He didn't run fast enough to catch me, baby.'

'It didn't feel like that at the time,' said Sidney.

'Oh, you know, preacher, I was only kidding you. That flirting never meant a damned thing.'

Gloria returned to do her final set – 'April in Paris', 'How Long Has This Been Going On?', 'Let's Do It', and 'Ain't Nobody's Business' – while Hildegard smiled at her husband and gave him a little nudge.

'"Never meant a damned thing" . . . Poor you.'

'She also said she was an habitual liar.'

'Are you disappointed?'

'Of course not. I love you and only you.'

'It's so good to hear you say that.'

'You think I don't say it often enough?'

'I think we should remind each other as much as we can. It's my fault as much as yours.'

They looked steadfastly at each other, surprised by the moment, and kissed each other on the lips.

Despite the exhilaration of the music Sidney felt nostalgic, thinking that this celebratory liveliness was locked in the past, already swept away by relentless disco and the emerging anger of punk. Gloria's singing seemed like the end of an era or the conclusion of a holiday in a beautiful landscape to which he would never return.

She finished with three encores, the last being 'It Don't Mean a Thing If It Ain't Got That Swing', and it was almost two in the morning when the family finally got back to Kentish Town. Sidney was still holding the gardenia his heroine had thrown to him at the culmination of the show.

'Let me put that in some water,' said Hildegard. 'Unless you'd like to take it to bed with you?'

'Thank you,' her husband replied, handing it over. 'You know *you're* all that I need.'

'You say the nicest things when you're feeling guilty, Sidney.'

They were awoken next morning by a commotion at breakfast. Jennifer was quizzing her youngest son Dan about his elder brother's whereabouts. It seemed that Louis Johnson had not come home the previous evening.

'He's not allowed to stay out overnight without asking us first,' said Jennifer, 'even in the school holidays. What the hell's he playing at? Do you know where he went?'

Dan was finishing his bowl of Weetabix. 'He didn't say.'

'When did you last see him?' Sidney asked.

'It was after *Are You Being Served?* He said he wouldn't be long but I shouldn't wait up.'

'Was Louis supposed to be your babysitter?'

'I'm not a baby.'

'Sorry. But he *was* responsible for looking after you.'

Jennifer interrupted. 'It's bloody *irr*esponsible, if you ask me.'

217

'Are you taking me to tennis coaching?' Dan asked.

'You can get the bus,' his mother replied.

'I'll be late.'

'Don't you care about your brother?'

'He's probably with Amy.'

'I thought they'd split up.'

Once Dan had left for tennis and Amy's mother had been telephoned and expressed surprise, and not a little anger, that the Johnson family would think their son would be allowed to stay over with her daughter on any night at all, let alone the last one, it was clear that something was wrong.

'Where the hell has that little shit got to then?' said Johnny.

'Don't call him that,' said Jennifer.

'Well, he is. Selfish bastard. Only thinks of himself.'

'I wonder where he gets it from.'

The Johnsons spent the rest of the morning ringing round everyone they knew.

No one had seen their son.

He was fifteen years old.

Missing.

'Please,' said Hildegard, 'let Sidney stay and help you.'

'I'm sure it's nothing,' her husband replied.

'Will you stay, though?' Jennifer asked. 'I'm worried.'

Sidney looked to his wife for an answer. Hildegard had to get home for her teaching and to pick up Anna from her friend Sophie's house. She offered to let the dean know about the situation and cancel Sidney's appointments for the next twenty-four hours. Members of the cathedral staff were all too familiar with such absences, but they could hardly object when this was a family matter and, in any case, most of them were away in August.

Sidney searched his nephew's room for clues. There was a corkboard with Louis's ticket to a free festival at Watchfield; a Polaroid photo showing some friends gathered around a punch bowl in the kitchen at a party; and a *Shoot* magazine centrefold of the Arsenal team for the season 1975–6.

As well as his O-level textbooks (biology, maths and physics) and files for English, history, French and geography, Louis's bookshelf contained *Zen and the Art of Motorcycle Maintenance*, Kerouac's *On the Road* and Sartre's *Nausea*. By his bed and on the floor were scattered old copies of *NME*, punk fanzines, leaflets and alternative magazines – *Black Flag*, *Freedom*, *Outa Control* – together with a 30p handbook for student militants: *The Little Red Struggler*.

In the rest of the room, despite the overwhelming evidence of teenage taste, there were still reminders of Louis's younger self: a junior athletics trophy, a framed family photograph from a Normandy holiday and a teddy bear that had been given a punk make-over with an eye-patch, slashed T-shirt and a pair of safety pins.

Sidney noticed the Hendrix recording of 'Hey Joe' on top of an Amstrad amplifier. He remembered that it was a song about a man on the run after killing his wife.

Jennifer was in the little back washroom, trying to work out what her son had been wearing by going through his clothes.

'I knew there was something wrong,' she told her brother as they re-gathered in the kitchen and thought about what to do next. 'I told myself not to let him out of my sight. But what can I do? Louis's so wilful, Johnny's out the whole bloody time. The holidays are just a nightmare.'

Her husband tried to defend himself by going on the attack. 'You nag him too much.'

'Oh, so you're saying it's my fault?'

'It's nobody's fault,' Sidney interrupted, 'and we don't know for certain that anything's wrong. Has there been any evidence of truancy?'

'None as far as we know,' Johnny replied. 'We thought he was all right. He's got good friends.'

'Any new ones? Older ones?'

'Don't, Sidney . . .' said Jennifer.

'Let him ask what he needs to ask,' said Johnny. 'He's had enough practice. Do you mean people not at the school? Someone who might have led him astray?'

'That is a possibility.'

'I don't think so.'

'We can't discount anything.'

'He joined CND, if that means something.'

'It will to Louis. What about drink, smoking?'

'And drugs,' said Johnny. 'I suppose you're going to ask about them too?'

'The police will want to know everything. We had better get our story right.'

'The police?'

It was not as if the Johnson family were unknown to the authorities. Johnny's father had been an infamous burglar; his sister, Claudette, had been murdered; and there had even been a shoplifting scare with Louis when he'd got in with the wrong people in his first year at secondary school.

'We can't lose any more time. I think you'd both better come with me. They'll want to know everything about Louis, the good as well as the bad.'

'I don't care what they find out,' said Jennifer, 'just as long as my son's all right. What on earth can he have been thinking of?'

'I'm afraid it's unlikely to be about us.'

'Do you think we haven't loved him enough?' Johnny asked.

They went out into the streets of Kentish Town with a photograph of Louis that Jennifer had taken the previous summer. The boy was shielding his eyes from the sun and he was wearing a T-shirt and jeans. He looked so thin, Sidney thought. He was just a scrap.

He had had enough experience with Geordie to know that the first twenty-four hours were crucial. It was Louis's sixteenth birthday next week, the age at which he could leave home without his parents' consent. Had he decided to strike out early, and, if so, could Johnny and Jen order him home after he had come of age? At the moment it did not matter if they could or couldn't.

The police station in Holmes Road was a Victorian building that looked as if it had originally been intended to be something else (swimming baths? a library?) and its current occupants seemed equally uncertain, greeting each new arrival with unimpressed suspicion, as if they preferred to be left alone. They had plenty to be getting on with.

Sidney thought it must have been the heat. The sergeant on duty was a large sweaty man who would have failed an audition for *Z Cars* but had kept his job because it probably would have been too much trouble to sack him. He was holding a manila folder and a between-meals snack of a white corned-beef roll with the healthy addition of a slice of lettuce and a dollop of salad cream that had spilled onto his trousers.

Terry Allen asked for details of every friend and relative; places that Louis was known to frequent (had they checked all of them?), and if he had a particular medical or mental-health problem. Had he been silent or withdrawn, had his behaviour changed recently, how much money was likely to be on him and did he have his own bank account? Had there been any family arguments? Was there trouble at school? Would Louis have wanted to run away for any reason? What about his exam results? Had he had them yet? (He had not.) Was he expecting to do badly? How secretive was he and how well did the family understand him?

'I think I know my own son,' said Jennifer.

'I'm not saying you don't. It's just the young sometimes like to have their secrets.'

'I don't read his diary, if that's what you're asking. But I think I can always tell when my boy's unhappy.'

'And he's not been that, Mrs Johnson, as far as you are aware?'

'He can be moody. But isn't that part of being a teen-ager?'

'Any trouble with his love-life?'

'There's his girlfriend. It's been a bit on-off.'

'Have you spoken to her?'

'Just her mother. Amy says she doesn't know where Louis is. He told his brother he was going round to hers but he didn't turn up.'

'And that's the last anyone saw of him?'

'Yes. Around eight o'clock last night.'

'You live in Falkland Road. And this Amy . . .'

'Grieve. She lives just up past Tufnell Park: Cathcart Hill.'

'So we think he went missing in the area between those two roads; unless he went somewhere completely different. Does your son often lie to his brother?'

'I don't think Dan could tell.'

'We'll need to talk to him too. How old is he?'

'Twelve.'

'And they get on?'

'As much as any brothers do. We try not to interfere when they're talking. It's best to let them get on with it rather than ask too many direct questions ourselves.'

'They find me embarrassing,' said Johnny. 'Dads always are. I try to be friendly, but it never seems to work unless he wants money.'

'You give him pocket money?'

'Fifty pence a week. But he helps himself occasionally,' said Johnny. 'You know. Goes through my pockets for loose change. He thinks I don't notice but I do. Honestly, we give him the most liberal upbringing. He has anything he needs within reason. Now he goes and does this.'

'Any trouble in the past?'

'I don't know. Not much. There was a bit of . . .'

Jennifer tried to interrupt her husband but it was too late.

'Shoplifting?' the policeman asked.

'How do you know?'

'It's common.'

Jennifer became agitated. 'Why are you telling him that, Johnny?'

Terry Allen's response was more kindly than it might have been. 'We were always going to find out about that. We do have records. It doesn't matter so much now, unless he's got bigger plans.'

'He's not like that.'

Johnny did not share his wife's confidence. 'I don't know what he's like any more. I used to think I could get through to him about anything. We were friends.'

'It's hard for parents to be mates with their children,' said Terry. 'They're two different jobs. What do you think, Vicar?'

'It's probably too early to tell what's happened,' Sidney replied. 'I just hope he's gone somewhere of his own choosing.'

'I hope so too,' said Johnny.

Sidney answered the unspoken question. 'I don't think Louis is the type to take his own life, if that's what you are thinking.'

'I was just wondering when we were going to get round to that,' said Terry.

'You don't . . .' said Jennifer.

'No, I don't,' said Sidney. 'That's why I raised it, so that we could all be clear that we are discarding the possibility.'

'We'll do a search of the area,' said Terry, avoiding a detailed answer. It was clear that neither parent had thought of suicide at all. Sidney tried to take this as an encouraging sign but couldn't be sure. It only took a moment to do something rash: to walk in front of a car, jump from a bridge or throw yourself under a train. He felt a sudden, deep fear.

The policeman continued. 'We'll need to start with a description and a photo. Have you got one? We'll have to have as many as possible.'

'I brought one out with me to show to all the people we've met in the street,' said Jennifer. 'It's the first I could find. We took it last summer.'

Terry Allen studied the picture; a pale young boy with one hand up in his tousled but gelled black hair, sleepy eyes – taken at a party – and a nose that he probably thought was too thin and too long. Louis had a little bit of acne on his chin and right cheek, an uncertain smile that looked like it wouldn't last, and he was wearing the north London adolescent uniform of a leather jacket, white T-shirt, jeans and Doc Martens.

'Seems like a nice lad,' the policeman said, without wanting to give anything away. How many similar photos had he seen? Sidney wondered. And how many young men had either killed themselves or been abducted recently? Was there an ongoing investigation? How much were the police prepared to share information and was there anything about this new case that would commit them to urgency?

'Is he a trusting sort?' Terry asked.

'He'd help anyone,' said Jennifer.

'Ah,' the policeman replied. 'That's not so good.'

A few hours later, Sidney's father telephoned from Budleigh Salterton. He wanted to talk to Sidney about the cricket. He had seen three days of the recent Test Match at the Oval but now wanted to come up to watch Viv Richards bat and have another look at the West Indian fast bowlers in the Prudential Trophy game at Lord's. Despite his retirement, Alec Chambers was determined, as he put it, 'not to slope away into the long grass'.

'I can't imagine you ever doing that, Dad.'

'You never know, son. You have to keep interested in life before life loses interest in you.'

The only real indication of Alec Chambers's age was a slight loss of hearing and an increased impatience with the opinions of other people. He had to get his point of view in first (lest there be any misunderstanding) and made any follow-up question sound like an accusation.

'Hildegard said you were at Jennifer's,' he continued. 'But I didn't think you'd still be there. Is something wrong?'

Should Sidney tell his father what was going on? If they didn't find Louis that day then there would be an appeal in the papers and the news would reach Devon soon enough. He decided to come clean.

'I'll get the next train.'

'You can't do that, Dad. It won't help.'

'Why not? Don't tell me what I can and cannot do, Sidney. I'm not going to abandon my daughter's child. Jennifer will need me. Louis is my first grandson. What kind of a man do you think I am?'

'I don't want you to worry.'

'I'll be more anxious down here, away from everything that's going on. Have you any idea where he's got to?'

'Not really.'

'He once told me he'd always wanted to go to New York. You don't think he's managed that, do you?'

'I don't think he's got the money. But how did you know that?'

'You see, Sidney, perhaps I can be of assistance after all? I know my grandson better than everyone thinks.'

'All right. If you can spare the time . . .'

'What else am I going to do? The only thing is, Sidney, I'll have to pretend I'm coming up for some cricket. I don't want to alarm your mother.'

'You mean you won't tell her?'

'I can't.'

'I don't think that's fair, Dad.'

'Iris is a little fragile these days.'

'I know that. But she's all right mentally, isn't she?'

'I don't want to alarm her.'

'But how can you keep it from her? It'll be in the papers if it goes on like this. Wouldn't it be better if you explained?'

'We're very isolated.'

'Someone will tell her and you won't be with her. That isn't right. We can't keep it from her.'

'You were trying to keep it from me.'

'That's different. And anyway, you found out soon enough.'

'I don't see how it is, Sidney. And I think I know what's best for your mother.'

'But you can't just leave her down in Devon. She knows London. If you're coming up to town then she should come too.'

'It's a bit more complicated than that.'

'What do you mean? Is there something you haven't been telling us?'

'Iris has had a few setbacks recently: little bits of dizziness.'

'Then you can't leave her on her own. Why didn't you say?'

'We didn't want to alarm you.'

'That's what I was trying to do for you with Louis, Dad. Stay with Mum. Look after her.'

'But I have to do something.'

'You are doing something. You're looking after Mum.'

Sidney was irritated all over again by the partial knowledge within families; how truths were revealed to a son or a daughter, a brother or a sister who were then instructed not to pass things on. This meant that no one could ever tell how much other family members ever knew and whether they were able to say anything out loud or not. It was a hopeless situation and one, he thought, that was particularly British. He couldn't imagine Hildegard putting up with such nonsense. No wonder children had secrets. They got the idea from their parents.

He was just beginning to consider how and why Louis might have chosen to rebel when Helena Mitchell arrived at the front door of the Johnson house with sweat in her hair and a notebook and tape recorder at the ready.

'I'm sorry, Sidney.'

'You've heard?'

'I work in a newsroom.'

'I thought you were freelance now? And what about Mercy? I didn't realise you planned to be back at work so soon.'

'I have to earn a living, Sidney, and, like you, I do have my contacts. They put two and two together.'

'Louis has a different surname.'

'It's not hard and I wasn't expecting to find you here – although I should have guessed. I've met Johnny in the past at his club. Is he in?'

'I don't think this is a good time, Helena.'

'No, it certainly isn't. That's why you need me.'

'What do you mean?'

'We have to blow this story up, Sidney.'

'I think the family will want to keep a low profile.'

'That's the last thing you need. You've got to realise how dangerous this situation is. Hundreds of young children go missing and they're never found. No one even knows about them. It's so common they are hardly reported. If you want to see your nephew again then we have to act big and fast. We have to shout it out all over the country. This boy matters. This boy is missing. You've got to make this as urgent and as public as you can. It's the only way. Believe me. And it's the least I can do for you.'

'How do you think you can help?'

'We have to make the story personal. The police will do their bit. There'll be a press conference. But I need one member of the family to make a direct and heartfelt appeal. Who is the boy most likely to listen to? His mother?'

'I'm not sure. I think that's who he might be running away from.'

'His father?'

'No.'

'His brother?'

'I don't think so.'

'His girlfriend?'

'Possible but not ideal.'

'Then it has to be you, Sidney.'

'Really? Me?'

'Yes, you. You'd better start writing. It has to be the most moving thing you've ever written. It has to appeal both to the public and to your nephew. I'm not leaving until you've done it.'

Jennifer and Johnny agreed that Sidney had the finest way with words and that he had the best chance of getting the tone right. It had to be loving and yet forceful, emphasising how much distress and anxiety Louis had caused without making him feel guilty. It had to be free of blame, offer a promise of a welcome return without any punitive consequences and even, Sidney thought, contain a joke or two to make his nephew smile. Through force of rhetoric, Sidney had to make Louis miss his family in a way that he had never realised.

He could not dwell at this time on the possibility that the child was already dead. He had to convince himself, and others, that Louis was still alive, that there was still hope. To doubt that, in a superstitious world, would only increase the possibility of disaster.

It took more than an hour to write a simple paragraph.

'Will this do?' he asked.

Helena read it through. 'It's good enough for now. There'll need to be more. We have to keep this story in the news for as long as it takes to find him.'

'And how will we do that?'

'You leave that to me.'

Sidney walked north to Cathcart Hill to try and extract information from Louis's girlfriend. There was no respite from the London heat and traffic, the fumes and the gridlock, the desire every time anyone left home to return as soon as possible for a shower, a cold beer and a sofa in the shade. Sidney was forced to a halt when a swarm of ladybirds emerged from nowhere in front of his face. He didn't know what to do. A group of workmen stopped to watch and laugh at him.

'Go on, Vic, take 'em on! Show 'em what you're made of !'

Sidney fended off the blur of red and black and tried to pretend it had been a deliberate attempt to attract good luck. He smiled at the workmen and gave them what he hoped would be taken as a cheery wave. They were resurfacing the road but the heat and steam off the fresh tarmac already had an exhausted air.

Amy was a worryingly thin girl with dyed red hair. The family had only agreed to let Sidney meet her because he was a vicar. The Johnsons were considered a bad lot, even though the Grieves seemed perfectly capable of inflicting damage on their children without any outside influence.

Amy sat cross-legged on the sofa with a cigarette and a can of lager. She showed no signs of wanting to go anywhere. She avoided eye contact and spoke as if human interaction was nothing but an irritating interruption to a preferred solitude.

'I hope you can help,' Sidney began. 'I'm very fond of my nephew, and I think, in a way, you are too.'

'He spoke about you.'

'Oh dear.'

'He thought you were quite cool for a vicar.'

'That may not be saying very much.'

'It isn't. It doesn't matter. You do your best, I suppose.'

'I try.'

'I don't know what to call you.'

'"Mr Chambers" is fine. "Sidney" if you prefer.'

'It wasn't a serious thing with Louis, you know? I just felt sorry for him.'

'And you broke it off?'

Amy smiled, almost sorrowfully. 'There was nothing to break. I couldn't ever be what Louis wanted me to be. Although I never found out what that was. He was so serious it was scary. He'd ask me a load of questions, tell me I wasn't like anyone else, try to kiss me and then leave as soon as he could. It wasn't like it was a relationship or anything.'

'He thought it was.'

'I don't know how he can have felt that.'

'Perhaps, Amy, you were the only person that was kind to him?'

'He had friends, Mr Chambers. He wasn't a total waste of space.'

'What kind of friends?'

'People interested in CND, politics, rallies. I think they lived in a squat. They made a magazine and stuff. Louis went on some kind of march with them. I think it was the Anti-Nazi League. Then he went on a coach. He wouldn't say where it was going. It was a Magical Mystery Tour of some kind. He said he'd never been with so many people he agreed with in his life.'

'I saw a ticket to a free festival in his room. Watchfield. Did you go with him?'

'He asked me. But my parents took me to France. It was boring. I should have gone with Louis, but you don't know these things, do you?'

'Was he anxious about anything in particular? His exam results, for example, or losing you?'

'He was always worried about something; but I don't think it was anything about his family. It was more about the state of the world, the fact that we're all going to die in a nuclear war and so what's the point slaving away to be bank managers or accountants or whatever we're supposed to become when we're older. You'll have to ask him, if you can find him. I don't think he'll take much notice of his mother or father. They're not going to help.'

'They're trying their best. They were young once too. We all rebelled against our parents at some stage.'

'It doesn't look like that now.'

'What do you mean?'

'You lot go on about the sixties and how cool it all was but what have you got to show for it? A semi in Tufnell Park? A new car? A fridge-freezer? A double garage? Is that it?'

'As a Christian I have to think differently . . .'

233

'No wonder Louis was depressed.'

'Not depressed in such a way as to want to do himself harm?'

'No, it wasn't that. He wanted to make something of his life. He wanted to go away and surprise people. "I'll show them," he said. "I'll even show you. Then you'll know." I told him I didn't want to know. I just wanted to do my music.'

'And what's that?'

'I'm in a band. We're called the Angels of Destiny.'

'Did Louis want to be in it?'

'How do you know?'

'Did you say he couldn't?' Sidney asked.

'He offered to write some lyrics. Then it turned out that they were all about the end of the world. It was embarrassing. Who's going to listen to that? Still, I wouldn't want anything horrible to happen to him and I'll do anything you want to help you find him. I'm not a bad person, despite what my parents say.'

'And what do they say?'

'You'll have to ask. But I wouldn't believe them. They don't know anything. Have you got children, Mr Chambers?'

The police search was confined to a large but narrow area: north up to Tufnell Park and on to Cathcart Hill and into Highgate; west to Haverstock Hill and Belsize Park; east to Holloway and south down to King's Cross. They said that, although Sidney should not share this information with the rest of his family, they would also keep a lookout at the most popular suicide spots: the Hornsey Lane Bridge, Kentish Town Lock and the Regent's Canal; building sites, homeless shelters and pub car parks; scrubland and parkland.

It was almost evening by the time Sidney left Amy and there was still too much heat in the day. He kept seeing 'Missing' posters for his own nephew. He had always been intrigued by these sudden desperate pleas in the past. Now he tried to avoid them.

The headmaster of the boy's north London school was away on his annual holiday in the Lake District, but his secretary had put Sidney in touch with the English teacher, Robert Ellis, a relatively recent graduate who was also Louis's form-master. He lived just up the road.

A thin, bald man with aquiline features that reminded Sidney of the white marble bust of a Roman emperor, Ellis was dressed in a pale-blue cotton summer suit that he wore without a tie, reclining in a deckchair in a book-lined room with open windows, venetian blinds and two fans on the go. He turned off Radio Three and promised to help in any way he could in the search for a child whom he described as 'continually perplexed'.

He said that Louis had a natural gift for English, and that he had an unusual approach to J. D. Salinger's novel *The Catcher in the Rye*.

'It always goes down well with that year, but Louis was particularly perceptive about it. They were not just the feelings of adolescent alienation. He was the only pupil to ask me if Holden Caulfield might be gay.'

'I'd never thought of that.'

'Novels with outsiders are popular; just as, if you ever think of writing a children's book, it's best to start with an orphan. Most children feel that they are alone.'

'I'll remember that.'

'Look at the New Testament. Jesus had brothers and sisters but they're hardly ever mentioned. The hero has to be alone in order to find himself. I think that's what Louis understood.'

Sidney was tempted to reply that the New Testament was 'more than a story' but thought he'd better stick to the matter in hand. 'You're not surprised he's gone missing?'

'I'm more concerned he hasn't told anyone. He's a thoughtful young man.'

'You can't imagine where he might have gone?'

'Have you asked his girlfriend?'

'No luck there, I'm afraid, unless she's lying.'

'I don't think that either of them have much guile. But you might like to take a look at one of Louis's essays. I'd asked them to write their own version of *The Catcher in the Rye*. It's a good way of making them all think about style and tone of voice. We put Louis's contribution up on Prize Day. Rather a bold decision, given what it says and how it starts. I think I've got it somewhere.'

Once found, Sidney started to read:

Everyone's trying to be someone they're not. That's the trouble. We're all phonies. Even me. We're all pretending to belong when we don't. It's like we're all supposed to be different pieces from the same jigsaw and when we're put together we form one beautiful giant picture, the whole of humanity, and only God can see it and only he can put the jigsaw back together again because he made it in the first place.

But I think we all come from different jigsaws. We're pieces from different sets, and we'll never fit together. The edges are wrong. Sometimes two pieces might go together like people in love but they don't belong anywhere else and they're not anything anyone else would be impressed by . . .

'Could I take this home with me?' Sidney asked.

When he returned to Falkland Road he heard there had been developments. A hoax call to Helena's newspaper claimed that Louis had been the victim of an IRA kidnap; a clairvoyant who smelled of bath salts and came all the way down from Seaforth had offered what she called 'mystic anticipation', and the police had received sightings of young men on the cross-Channel ferry at Beachy Head, in Manchester's Lesser Free Trade Hall and again at Old Trafford.

Sidney was infuriated. 'Why would Louis go to Manchester? He supports Arsenal.'

The most useful news was that cash was missing from the club. It was around £11, and Louis had been seen there on the day of his disappearance.

His father didn't know what to make of it. 'Normally I'd want to strap the little bastard, but the police say that this is an encouraging sign. If he had a plan that needed money then there's less chance he's killed himself or been abducted. Things are looking up, Sidney, even if we don't have anything positive. We just have to work out where the hell Louis is.'

Jennifer served up the supper. 'This salad is rubbish. God knows why I thought pineapple would freshen it up. I can't concentrate on anything. I don't even want to eat it.'

'I'll have yours,' said Dan. 'I'm still here. Your other son. Just in case you'd forgotten.'

'Yes, all right.'

'Glad to know I'm appreciated.'

'Don't start . . .' said Johnny.

Jennifer shared out the food. 'It's so hot. I'm surprised anyone's got any appetite. By the way, Sidney, Hildegard phoned. They want you back at the cathedral in the morning. There's an important meeting, apparently. She explained the situation, but the dean asked if you could pop in.'

'I don't want to abandon you.'

'You can leave after breakfast. The police are doing what they can. Perhaps you could talk to Geordie? We know how you two spark ideas off each other.'

'We should only be concerned about Louis.'

'How's his wife?' Johnny asked, trying to take the focus away from his missing son. 'I know she had a cancer scare.'

'She's better, so far. We hope.'

'Lucky, then . . .'

'You could say that,' said Sidney. 'We all prayed for her.'

'Then pray for Louis.'

'I know he isn't a great believer in prayer,' said Sidney. 'But I am. And it's my job. You don't have to ask.'

The following morning, Sidney used the train journey back to Ely to read through his nephew's anarchist magazines and the essay on *The Catcher in the Rye*:

So who are we all anyway? Sometimes people think
they belong in the same jigsaw or whatever metaphor
you want to use. The boys are the sporting heroes, the
jocks and the lads; then there are the nerds, the pseuds

and the weeds. The girls are the tarts and the swots and the in-between who hope that no one notices them too much until they wake up and find they've turned into their mothers.

But at school it doesn't matter who we are. We're all treated the same. We all go into the school chapel and pray to a God who never speaks. 'We are not worthy to gather up the crumbs under thy table?' Who wrote that? And, if it's true, why do we bother? If he doesn't answer, what's the point of prayer? You just have to work everything out for yourself and not listen to what anyone else has to say, as the only thing other people are going to do is to try and make you think like them. Faith doesn't give you answers. It only stops you asking questions.

So you have to be free of everything that's gone before and make your own way. No Gods. No Masters. There's more than one kind of freedom.

Sidney went straight to the meeting at the deanery, came back for a shower, and then updated his wife and daughter over a vegetarian lunch of lettuce soup and risotto. He decided not to comment on the vegetarianism any more (was he expected to convert?) but couldn't resist remarking on a dessert that he had never been served before. It was called Lemon Snow.

'This is good,' he said. 'Very refreshing. Where did you get the recipe?'

'Oh, a friend. No one special.'

Rolfe, Sidney thought. Perhaps it was one of his dead wife's.

'It's important that it's properly chilled,' Hildegard continued. 'I think the name alone is supposed to help us think it's colder.'

'I'm still hot,' said Anna.

'You could have a little siesta?' Sidney suggested

'I don't want to go to bed. I can't sleep. And I want you to tell me about Louis, Dad. What's happened to him?'

'Nothing's happened. We just don't know where he is.'

'Then how do you know nothing's happened?'

'We don't.'

'Then why did you say nothing had happened when something has?'

'So you wouldn't worry.'

Hildegard cleared away the plates. 'You're not handling this very well, Sidney.'

'Why is it always me that has to deal with these things?'

'I won't answer that.'

'Has he run away?' Anna asked.

'Possibly.'

'Oh.'

'Why do you think he might do that, Anna?'

'Because he's unhappy?'

'Did he tell you he was?' Sidney asked, hopefully.

'He doesn't say anything to me. Perhaps he wanted his parents to notice him more.'

'I think his mother nags him all the time.'

'Nagging's not the same as listening.'

Hildegard interrupted. 'Do you think we listen to you enough, my darling?'

'Dad doesn't. He's too busy listening to other people.'

'That's not true.'

'It is.'

'Well if it is Anna, then I'll try and do better.'

240

'You always say that.'

Sidney tried to hold on to his patience. 'I'm listening now. What have you been up to?'

'Nothing.'

'You must have done something.'

'I've been bored.'

'Then what would you like to do tomorrow?'

'I don't know. I'm going swimming with Sophie. Then we're going riding. I have to go to Sophie's because I don't have a pony of my own, even though you promised after we found that dead man.'

'We didn't actually promise. And we've been through all this, Anna. They're very expensive.'

'No, they're not.'

'Quite costly to run.'

'I could keep mine at Sophie's.'

'That would be complicated.'

'If I ran away you might give me one.'

Sidney smiled. 'That's blackmail, darling.'

'Well, at least that's something you know how to deal with,' said Hildegard.

'Dad?' Anna asked. 'Do you prefer Louis to me? Do you ever wish you had a son?'

In bed that night, Sidney decided not to take issue with either wife or daughter but looked over Louis's home-work:

How do you know who's writing this essay? It
might be me, Louis Johnson, or I could have got
someone else to write it for me, like Holden wrote

about his brother's baseball mitt for Stradlater
and put in spelling errors to throw his teacher off
the scent; except that Holden didn't write any of
it. J. D. Salinger did and we don't even know if it
was him because that might not be his real name,
he might be using a pseudonym or someone else
might be writing it for him. That's the moral of
the story: you never know what's true. You never
know if people really are who they say they are.
You can't trust anyone, not even your friends, your
family or your girlfriend, because they're always
putting on a show, pretending to be someone
they're not. So perhaps one day you have to go
some place where nobody knows you and find out
who you really are. But even then you'll find you
have to keep pretending to be someone you're not
because you have to be someone for Chrissakes –
that's just the way of things. But, like I said, you
never know what's true.

Sidney acknowledged that Geordie was probably the only
person who would tell him the truth about the possible out-
come of Louis's disappearance: the likelihood of abduction
and murder; the possibility that his nephew was still in
London, somewhere else or abroad; the average length of
time for which underage boys went missing and the chances
of a hopeful return. He would also reveal what the police
would and would not tell the family.

The next day, they sat in the shade of an umbrella in the
garden of the Prince Albert, enjoying a pub lunch, as Byron
drank down bowl after bowl of water. Although Geordie was
relatively optimistic, saying that the theft of the money was a

positive sign, there was nothing he could offer to ease Sidney's tension or to help the suspicion that no one was doing enough.

'I feel so helpless and I'm still frightened of suicide,' said Sidney. 'I told the police I wasn't, but I suppose that at least I put enough pressure on them to instigate an immediate search.'

'They would have done that anyway.'

'You know what I mean. I was worried they would think it was a family tiff.'

'Don't think the police aren't doing all they can. We always worry about young men going missing. With girls it's more obvious what to expect, I'm afraid. With men it could be anything. But don't give up. More boys run away than kill themselves. Was your nephew on drugs?'

'I don't think so.'

'And he wasn't depressed?'

'His parents say not.'

'But you think he might have been?'

'People hide it so well. I've been reading one of his English essays. He's not impressed with our generation.'

'Few young people are.'

'Where would you go, Geordie, if you were his age and wanted just to run away?'

'It would have to be somewhere I could be anonymous; a place where young people go; safer than London; somewhere with a proper alternative community where I wouldn't be nagged and with a lot of young people who were there already: the coast, probably.'

'Somewhere like Brighton?'

243

'That's right.'

'I thought so.'

Geordie had the familiar look of someone trying and failing to be patient; it was that of an indulgent and loving parent whose child had let him down once again. 'You mean to say, Sidney, that you've already thought of all this and just want to check if you're right?'

'One of Louis's anarchist magazines was printed there: the *Brighton Voice.*'

'Seems a long way to go for a hunch.'

'He'd underlined stuff.'

'Then why didn't he take it with him?'

'Perhaps he remembered it, or he had a more recent edition. This was from May.'

'I'm amazed anarchists are organised enough to print a magazine in the first place. Does the writing contain anything we should worry about; things like violent resistance?'

'Not really; it's the usual class-war stuff. "Stuff" being the operative word. "Stuff the Police", "Stuff the Politicians", "Stuff Fascism".'

'I thought we'd already done that.'

'Our generation still has a lot to learn.'

'There are times, Sidney, when I look at this country and wonder if we won the war or not.'

Geordie finished his pint. The people grouped around them in the garden did not seem particularly aware that their freedom had been hard-won, content to sunbathe, eat burgers with chips, and down as much lager as possible in order to stave off the heat.

'I saw something Louis had written in one of his exercise books. GODDAM MONEY. Do you think it's some kind of slogan?'

'It might be; unless it's the name of a band.'

'I'm just going to assume he's in Brighton.'

Sidney took out a handkerchief and wiped his forehead, momentarily irritated by the drip-dry shirt Hildegard had bought, which only seemed to make him sweat all the more.

He would have to change before evensong. There he would pray for his nephew, imagining him out in the streets with friends, or underneath Brighton Pier, throwing stones into the sea, or performing with a band, or lounging on a sofa in a squat: anything to keep the thought of him alive rather than dead.

'Do you want me to come with you?' Geordie asked.

'I don't think Louis is too keen on the police. Not that he's wild about the Church, either.'

'But do you want me to give the boys down there a ring?'

'That would be helpful; just in case I get into any trouble.'

'Do you think Louis is a bit like you?' Geordie asked.

'Why do you say that? I do feel a kind of kinship with him; an understanding that he may want to do something unexpected.'

'Well, he's certainly done that.'

'I know the Church of England is an institution, Geordie, but it was quite an act of rebellion to become a priest. I was supposed to be a doctor like my father.'

'At least that's one thing the world's managed to avoid.'

'You're too kind.'

'I'm sure you'd have been very good. But if you were as absent as you are from the Church, then God help your patients. At least as a priest you can do less damage.'

Sidney drove down to London and on to Brighton in a recently acquired fourth-hand Rover from the early 1960s. It had over 50,000 miles on the clock and was, the salesman had promised, 'the most sensible choice' for his budget even though he had been quite tempted by a bright-red Lancia Flaminia coupé that had 'needed a bit of work'. That would have been far more his kind of thing, but Hildegard had said that if he bought it she would be embarrassed to be seen with him. Who did he think he was?

So now he drove a dull car in which he took little pleasure. It was the kind of vehicle that a sales executive who had missed out on promotion might drive, Sidney thought, unable to trade up to a newer model and on his way out. It was just that no one had yet had the heart to tell him.

He wasn't sure how long he was going to be in Brighton for, or even where he might stay if he had to, but flexibility of time and movement were crucial. He could always find a B&B, even if it didn't confine itself to Sir Cecil Kendall's definition of a heavenly safe lodging.

There were far more people in Brighton than he had anticipated, both day-trippers and holidaymakers, and once he had parked his car he found the town to be louder, hotter and brighter than he had expected. He walked down Surrey Street and was assailed by gaggles of people toiling to the seafront, their voices drowned out by seagulls, their nostrils full of the familiar coastal smell of salt, petrol, fried fish and candyfloss. He turned into Buckingham Road (someone had scrawled EAT THE RICH on a house at the end) and then up into Victoria Road and Temple Gardens. The church of St Michael and All Angels was just visible. Sidney couldn't picture his nephew at worship, but at least the priest might be able to help find him.

The *Brighton Voice* was based in Victoria Road near the Open Café, an anarchist wholefood restaurant with small Formica-topped tables, mostly for two, offering tea, Coke and lemonade with a vegetarian menu of lentil soup and home-made bread, spinach omelettes, stuffed mushrooms, ratatouille and brown rice, nut loaf, apple tarts and chocolate-brownie specials.

Advertisements in the window proposed '£50 Adventure Holidays to Morocco' with a man called Eddie Brazil, a forthcoming Hawkwind concert and a touring production of David Hare's *Fanshen* at Brighton Combination.

Inside people were smoking, flirting, and reading *NME*, *Catch-22* and *The Anarchist Basis of Pacifism*. The woman behind the counter had dyed blonde hair and a faraway look in her turquoise-shadowed eyes that Sidney mistook for disinterest but then realised was unhappiness. She was holding a swatter to keep the flies off yesterday's fairy cakes.

'Odd to see a vicar in here,' she said.

Sidney had thought it best to come in uniform. It lent an air of authority and people wouldn't have to readjust when they found out later. 'I hope it's not unusual.' (He didn't bother to tell her that he was actually an archdeacon.)

'"To be loved by anyone . . ." You're probably more of a Tom Jones fan than the music we have in here.'

247

'Jazz is more my thing.'

'I thought we'd moved on from that.'

'Is there any chance of a glass of lemonade?'

Although all the doors and windows of the café were open to let in as much of the sea breeze as possible, the air was still languid with heat.

'I had you down as a shandy man.'

The woman poured out the lemonade from a large bottle. It looked a bit flat. A wasp now joined a second fly above the counter in a miniature aerial ballet. 'These creatures drive me crazy. Do you think Jesus was the first anarchist?'

'He might well have been.'

'Where do you think it went wrong then, Vicar?'

'I'm not sure it's "gone wrong".'

'Probably when the early Church got too much money. That'll be fifteen pence.'

Sidney felt in his jacket for change. It would be good, he thought, to take it off, but he worried there were sweat stains on his shirt. 'Here you are.'

'When it was *accepted*. When it had *authority*. When it *sold out*. You lot should have stayed as monks. Then you wouldn't have got into so much trouble. Did you ever consider that?'

'I did, as a matter of fact. Do you think I could have some ice?'

'We've just about run out. That's all anyone wants. But then,' the woman continued, adding an unasked-for slice of lemon as if that compensated for the lack of ice, 'perhaps, you thought of all those vicarages you could live in. A nice house, two kids, a wife called Veronica who is good at baking and has a bright smile, and a dog. There's your lemonade.'

'It's not quite like that.'

'Bet I'm close, though.'

'You're not far off, I must admit.'

The woman lit a cigarette. 'Do you want a Numbie?'

'I'm sorry?'

'Player's No. 6. It's what we call them. My dad's a vicar. That's how I get to ask you all these questions. Being brought up in a vicarage is a passport to atheism, if you ask me. Our dads rebelled against their parents by joining the Church; now we rebel against you lot. What brings you down to sunny Brighton?'

'I'm looking for my nephew, Louis Johnson.'

'Never heard of him.'

'I wasn't expecting that you had.'

'And why might he be here?'

'He's one of your readers.'

'The *Brighton Voice*? Not one of mine – one of Jason's. Well, there aren't too many of them.'

Sidney could not imagine too many anarchists called Jason either.

'What do you want with him?' The woman was positively chatty now. 'Are you really his uncle? Perhaps you're a pervert that likes pretending to be a vicar?'

'I can assure you I'm not. He does know who I am.'

'Have you come to take him back to Mummy and Daddy then?'

'He's not yet sixteen. He's still at school. I do have a responsibility.'

'Then he's old enough to make up his own mind about what he does.'

'Not legally.'

'And you value the law?'

'Without it, society falls apart.'

'We believe that "without it" society has the chance to reinvent itself. Have you got a photo?'

Sidney took out his wallet. 'Here.'

The woman inspected the image of Louis laughing with a friend, bringing it close to her face. 'I need my glasses.'

'It's from last year.'

'He looks a bit young. You know that's an anarchist badge he's wearing?'

'I wasn't sure.'

'They sell them down the road.'

'I don't think Louis's ever been to Brighton.'

'They post them out. Even anarchists use the post office.'

'Have you seen him before?'

'I'm afraid not.'

Sidney made his way towards the seafront, past the Peace House, a shop selling incense and Indian cottons, joss-sticks and miniature wooden elephants in bright colours. A girl in a sleeveless white dress sat on a stool outside, in front of a glass-bead curtain, shuffling a pack of tarot cards, asking people if they wanted their fortune told. A sign in the window of a furniture shop read:

LAST DAYS!

This shop will be closing soon due to the impending collapse of Western Capitalism

In an arcade set back from the main road, two or three boys were working slot machines; any one of them could have been Louis. Sidney showed them a photograph and asked if they had seen him. They hadn't.

Closer to the seafront, people were sitting out at wooden tables eating chips with cheese and burgers served on green school china. Two of the men were shirtless, their chests sunburnt like badly grilled ham. Sidney wondered why he couldn't see any fishermen, or indeed any signs of fishing at all. Perhaps the town had been entirely taken over by holidaymakers?

A vagrant was raging at an old army veteran who was feeding breadcrumbs to pigeons and seagulls. He shouted out that they were vermin; rats in the sky. Sidney showed him a photograph, tried to be friendly, engage in conversation, because perhaps Louis was homeless too, but the man just swore at him, saying that the young still had so much possibility while he had none. His life was over. Unless Sidney could buy him a drink . . .

A drunk woman with her skirt halfway up her thighs was being helped into a taxi and a young man in a denim suit was saying: 'Look at the state of her. You wouldn't think she was my mum.'

The town was a confusion of heat, noise and alcohol. Sidney began to sweat with the strain of not knowing where he was going or how to proceed. He knew that he should, perhaps, ask the police for help, but this trip to Brighton was still nothing other than a hunch, and would they really care about a boy who might not be in their town at all?

251

He wondered how much Louis, if he was still alive, might have turned to drink or drugs instead of political action, but he was confident that his nephew's youthful energy was still concentrated on an alternative version of saving the world: from nuclear disaster, environmental catastrophe, capitalist exploitation, economic collapse and social injustice.

He looked for listings of activist meetings, collective calls to protest, and came across a group of men and women selling the *Socialist Worker*. He asked where a young political idealist might hang out in Brighton and, even as he said the words 'hang out', he felt embarrassed by sounding like an out-of-touch would-be trendy vicar.

But this wasn't about him; Sidney didn't care about his reputation or what people thought: he just wanted to find his nephew.

'Is he gay?' they asked.

'I don't know. I don't think so.'

He passed a burned-out bus, a boarded-up newsagent's and a dead fox on the street corner. He asked everyone he thought might be likely to give him an answer – *have you seen this boy?* – groups of skinheads with dogs; poor girls with greasy hair and knackered faces begging for money; Pakistani boys trying not to get mugged; old men shuffling between the pub, the pawnbroker and the bookie's, stopping either for breath or to smoke their next roll-up; bikers and bored heavy-metal fans looking for something to do or somewhere to kick off; drug dealers with Alsatians; and then, as he moved across towards Hove, he passed affluent middle-aged couples walking their fastest, on their way home to their villas in Tongdean Avenue, making no eye contact, fearing that if they slowed down they might catch the disease known as poverty.

No one had seen Louis at all.

Sidney looked at the town as if no one in it was innocent. Every single person could have had something to do with his nephew's disappearance. Any stranger could be a criminal or a suspect or someone who knew something and yet, it seemed, no one was going to tell him anything: not the man going into the bookie's or the women waiting for their washing in the launderette or the people at the bus stop; not the busker outside Sainsbury's, the estate agents renting out rooms, the people in the bingo hall, in the record shop, at the grocer's, or in the takeaway kebab joint; not the drivers queuing at the Shell petrol station, early lunchers in the Golden Egg; not the families in the estates, around the terraces and amidst the squats in Granville Road and Temple Gardens; not the rock bands with their feedback and dodgy amplifiers in abandoned buildings waiting for demolition; not the drinkers in the Gold Ship Inn, the Sussex Arms, the Southern Cross and the Fiddler's Elbow.

Surely they had to know something – for how, amidst the noise of the town, provided he'd got the right one; how, when there were so many people, could no one have noticed this boy?

He thought of driving over to Beachy Head, and tried to imagine Louis looking out towards the coast of France, a sunny day, a blue sky, a calm sea, the run and the jump, but he did not think it possible. He *could* not think it possible, because if he could, then he might possibly dream it into reality.

Then a student in a *No Nukes* T-shirt told him about an alternative café in Kemptown, off St George's Road. It was a cheap restaurant filled with young people sitting round wooden tables eating paella and spaghetti bolognaise and listening to King Crimson.

And there, at last, he saw his nephew lying on a beaten-up armchair at the back by the toilets.

He could be dead, but then if he was, surely the restaurant would have done something about it? He had to be asleep or stoned. No one paid Louis any attention.

Sidney stood for a moment in a slight daze. Had all their trouble and anxiety been for this? Did Louis have any idea of the terrors he had put everyone through? How dare he sleep so soundly?

He asked the barmaid for two pints of tap water and woke his nephew up.

Louis did not seem surprised. 'I thought they might send you.'

'Your mother's worried sick. We all are.'

'Mum's nervous all the time. That's why I had to leave.'

'It's in the papers. We made an appeal.'

'I don't read them.'

'Where are you staying?'

'There's a squat. Have you come to take me home?'

'I can't force you.'

The boy laughed to himself, and spoke slowly and with amazement, as if he had only just learned how to talk and was still surprised by the sounds coming out of his mouth. Sidney recognised that his nephew must be on *something* but couldn't think what it might be.

'I like it here,' Louis continued, gesturing without purpose. 'There's no one to order you around. That's what the word "anarchy" means. No rulers. You can do what you want. As long as you don't harm anyone, nobody minds how you behave.'

'It's hard to build a society that way.'

'Not if it's a *different* kind of society, Uncle Sidney. We *trust* and *rely* on our friends, neighbours and workmates more than on *teachers* or *bosses* or *politicians*. Everyone here tries to do everything for *themselves* and for each *other*. It's a different way of *thinking* about money and the economy; you just *trade* the things you need. People don't have to *pretend* to be what they're not. They can *be themselves*. Life has to be about more than working so hard for exams that one day I'll be good enough to get a job I hate.'

'It might not be like that. I don't hate my job.'

'You're *lucky*. You have *faith*.'

'But I don't have money.'

'You probably have enough, Uncle Sidney.'

'Yes, I do. And what about your father? He likes his job.'

'More than his family, I'll say that. He's never home.'

'He works hard. Drink this.'

Louis took long hungry gulps of water. 'You know he's got another girlfriend? He thinks I don't know, but I do. And anyway you don't really like your job either, Uncle Sidney, otherwise you wouldn't spend all your time being a detective. You and my dad are the same. Everyone thinks you work at your jobs, but what you work hardest at is avoiding them.'

'There may be some truth in that. How long were you planning on staying here?'

'I don't know. Until my money runs out.'

'Have you got much left?'

'A few quid. I suppose you know I stole from my dad?'

'He has noticed.'

'Is he angry?'

'He just wants you home. Your parents love you.'

'Then they should show it.'

'Parents aren't always good at that kind of thing. They don't know how much to protect you or how much to let go . . .'

'Or how to pay any attention in the first place.'

'I thought you were running away to avoid their attention?'

'*Very good*, Uncle Sidney. You reason well.'

'You could have been the victim of a terrible crime, Louis. That's why everyone has been worried about you.'

'And now you probably think I've committed some kind of crime myself.'

'I'm not sure what the law is on young people going absent. Perhaps it all depends on why you went . . .'

'Whether I was "corrupted" or not; the supposed "fact" that I'm too young to know what's best for me, you mean?'

'There are types of crime and shades of criminality,' Sidney continued, hoping that his nephew would understand and take him seriously. 'People might suggest that you have been "criminal" in leaving your family without saying anything and causing so much anxiety. At the same time, someone else might think that an oppressive parental regime, which is, perhaps, a confusion of nagging and neglect, is

256

equally "criminal". And then there are your anarchist friends, planning what might be called "crimes against the state", acts of violence and protest against a governmental system they don't even recognise; so are they breaking any law if they consider the laws of society to be, in themselves, criminally unjust?'

'That's *right*, Uncle Sidney.'

'So what is a "crime"? Can it only be defined in terms of a breach in the law? Or can it be extended to include the idea of hurting other people, letting them down, being thoughtless, careless and unloving?'

'I suppose it could be.'

'Let's go for a walk, Louis. I think we need some air.'

'I'm *very tired*.'

'Then this will wake you up.'

They went to the pier, bought fish and chips and passed a woman who was prophesying that this was the exact spot where Jesus was going to return to earth, walking out of the water to reclaim his kingdom. In Brighton. She was offering free chip butties. Those who stayed with her now and prayed and believed with her could become his first modern disciples.

'That is always an alternative,' said Sidney.

Louis picked out the fattest chip. 'I don't think I'd fit in.'

'The first followers of Jesus probably felt the same. But many of them believed they had nothing to lose.'

'They took a risk, you mean.'

'They did. And so you're not so far away from them, Louis.'

257

'Thank you for understanding. I suppose I'll have to come home now. At least I didn't kill myself.'

'Did you think you might?'

'I thought how easy it would be. But I'm not the type to do that.'

'I don't think you are either. But people can change. So you need to be aware and seek help if those feelings ever develop. You have to remember that your family loves you – although . . .' and here Sidney gave his nephew a little nudge, 'having said that, I can't guarantee a completely loving welcome when you get home. But I will protect you from any fallout.'

'Mum can be radioactive.'

'I know. I've had over forty more years of her than you.'

They drove up the A23 with all the windows open, past Hickstead and Handcross, Crawley, Horley and the turns to Gatwick Airport. After stopping to get lemonade and cheese and tomato rolls, they watched an over of cricket in the village of Outwood. Then it was back to the car. The continual pulse of the traffic marked a victory for the urban over the rural; tarmac across the fields, exhaust fumes in clean air, the sound of engines over birdsong. A woman in the back seat of the vehicle in front threw a dirty nappy onto the hard shoulder.

'Louts,' said Louis. 'Thoughtless bastards.'

'The driver might have refused to stop. Perhaps they're in a hurry.'

'There's no point in impatience. You only get delayed further on. The whole country's come to a standstill.'

'At least we're moving. I suppose if you stopped them they'd only claim that it was a free country.'

258

'There has to be a difference between freedom and selfish-ness.'

'I'll have to ask you to start writing my sermons. Oh, bloody hell, what is it now?'

There was a blare of a horn and Sidney was forced to switch to the inside lane even when he was already overtak-ing at speed. Louis asked if they could listen to Radio One, but after a straight run of Abba, Dr Hook and the Bay City Rollers he couldn't stand it any more.

'What a load of old crap.'

Sidney smiled but kept his eyes on the road. 'Jazz does have its advantages.'

'But if we tune in to Radio Two we'll get Perry Como and Cliff Richard.'

'Well, we wouldn't want that.'

Sidney hoped that he hadn't forced Louis to come home.

'It's all right. You gave me the illusion of choice. I know I'm still underage. My parents are responsible for me.'

'Not for much longer.'

'I suppose I'd better stick it out.'

'You can always go back when you're older.'

'Do you think so?'

'You just have to tell us next time.'

'Sorry about that.'

Sidney stared out at the hot road ahead and thought he should keep lightening the tone. 'Your school could probably do with some anarchy. It might shake them up a bit.'

'Do you think they'd notice?' Louis asked.

There was further traffic and a burst water main ahead, so the journey through London took longer than expected. As a result they had to stop at a garage for more petrol, where Sidney found a phone box to give his sister a revised ETA.

'I've been so worried I think I'll kill him,' she said.

'I wouldn't advise that,' said Sidney. 'I've taken the trouble to bring him home safely. It's important nobody blames Louis for what he's done. Our overwhelming emotion must be one of gratitude and relief. Promise me you won't go mad, Jennifer?'

'I'll do my best.'

'I don't think that's a promise.'

'I've said what I've said.'

And, for about a minute and a half, she managed just that. She held her son close as soon as he walked through the door of the family home, telling him how frightened she had been and how anxious and that he was more precious than he ever knew, and Louis waited limply until it was over, embarrassed by all the fuss, unable to apologise, so that, at last, enraged by her son's lack of reaction, Jennifer took a step back and slapped him across the face: 'Don't you bloody ever dare do that to me again.'

'Do you think that's going to help?' her husband asked.

As soon as Helena discovered that Louis was home she wanted an exclusive interview for her paper. 'Don't let him sell his story to anyone else, Sidney.'

'His parents don't want him to give it to anyone.'

'I will help them with a bit of cash.'

'That won't be necessary.'

'You'd be surprised. Most people take the money.'

'What would be your angle?'

'Anarchy as the new alternative in a dying Britain. The death of the old guard. I want to hear what your boy's got to say. The people he met. "My Story".'

'I don't think your readers are likely to sympathise with an anarchist. Anyway, I'm not sure he ran away for that particular cause. Although he did definitely run away. His mother thought it was a plea for attention. He's certainly getting that now.'

Helena already had her story sketched out. 'People believe all sorts of things. Think of the Germans in the 1930s . . .'

'Please don't talk to Hildegard about this kind of thing . . .'

'And now children of Nazis have joined the Baader-Meinhof. Each generation rebels against its predecessor. You can't protect yourself from rejection. Then, if you're not careful, violence ensues. It's so hot, people are talking about riots . . .'

'I don't think the Baader-Meinhof is the same as Louis linking up with a few vegetarian anarchists in Brighton.'

'I know you don't have to give me this, Sidney, especially after all you've done for me already.'

'All we've done for each other,' he corrected.

'I'm just doing my job. And if Louis doesn't speak to me then I might have to talk to you.'

'Oh, don't do that, Helena. What if I refuse to speak?'

'I think I know you well enough to make it up if you don't.'

'You wouldn't, Helena . . .'

'I'm teasing.'

'I'm not sure you are.'

'I like to keep you guessing.'

'That's not fair. But I should thank you for your help. You know I look upon you as a daughter.'

'A daughter? I don't think that's right.'

'It's probably better than any alternative, don't you think?'

Johnny decided to close his club at the end of the year. 'I know it's a failure to keep pace with the times but if this is the country we have to live in, I'm not sure I can put up with it any longer.'

'What will you do?' Sidney asked.

'We're going abroad. Holland, probably. There's a good jazz scene in Amsterdam; everyone's at the Melkweg: Cab Kaye, Wilbur Little, Michael Moore . . .'

'I've never heard of any of them.'

'Then you should visit and find out. I think it will be good for us all. Certainly Louis.'

'You're going to move your entire family because of him? I'm not sure he's into jazz.' Later that week his nephew was going to hear The Clash with Siouxsie and the Banshees at the 100 Club Punk Special.

'But it gives us alternatives,' said Johnny. 'You have to agree London's a bit shit. You've walked around Kentish Town. Would you want to bring Anna up here?'

'Probably not. But Ely is very sheltered.'

'I want to be a better dad before it's too late; a better husband, too.'

'I think we both want that. Being aware of our failings is just the beginning.'

'And then we have to do something about them, Sidney. I know people keep telling you to stop all that detective work, change your life, concentrate on your main job . . .'

'People have been saying that for twenty years.'

'But I'm glad you didn't. Otherwise I might never have found my son again.'

'I am sure he would have come home.'

'Not without you.'

'There's no way of knowing that, Johnny. But fortunately we don't have to put these things to the test.'

It was yet another hot evening. Louis came downstairs to talk to his uncle. He was quite looking forward to Amsterdam, he said. It would be a change for all of them.

'Sometimes you have to go away to come home,' said Sidney.

'That's true enough. I'm a bit sorry about it all, though.'

'No one's blaming you for what you did.'

'I bet they are when I'm not around.'

'That doesn't matter,' said Sidney. 'The secret is not to be too hard on yourself.'

'I'll try not to be.'

'There is such a thing as too much thinking.'

'Do you think so?'

'I "think" there can be too much "thinking"?' Sidney smiled. 'Why, yes, I "think" I "think" I do.' He gave his nephew a hug. 'They say there's going to be a storm tonight: a break in the weather.'

'England can be itself again,' said Louis. 'Everyone goes mad in the sunshine.'

The rains came and the newly appointed Minister for Drought became the Minister for Floods. The last of the summer butterflies hovered over ripening blackberries on the brambles. The telephone wires saw the first pre-migration gatherings of swallows and house martins. The Harvest Festival was near.

People could still sit out of an evening and Sidney and Geordie switched back from their summer lager and enjoyed a couple of pints of bitter in the garden of the Prince Albert, thankful that this case, at least, had ended with such little harm done.

Sidney took time to enjoy his pint. He wanted to savour the moment. (What was that play his mother had once wanted to see? *Stop the World – I Want to Get Off*.)

'I'm grateful to you, Geordie.'

'I didn't do very much.'

'You helped me to have confidence . . .'

'. . . that your nephew hadn't killed himself? We have to give people hope – even if that's supposed to be your job. As long as you missed me . . .'

'Whenever I work with anyone else, whether it's Terry Allen in London or Dave Hills up here, it's never the same. I've been very lucky to have known you.'

'I'm not so sure about that. If you'd met Dave or Tel first you might never have got involved in crime. Think how peaceful your life would have been.'

'I am aware of my good fortune.'

'It's not just that, though, is it? Do you know, Sidney, that ever since the war I've felt we've been on borrowed time? There were moments then when we could, and perhaps should, have been killed. We were lucky. And so we have a responsibility to make the most of being spared.'

'I hope we have.'

'Only sometimes, when I look at the younger generation, it gets to me. To think that we went through all that bloodshed so that layabouts like your nephew could run away to Brighton. Did our best mates really give their lives so that their children and grandchildren could sit around eating brown rice and smoking dope all day?'

'That's the thing about liberty, Geordie. You can't dictate how others choose to use it. Otherwise, it isn't freedom.'

'You just have to know what to do with it, I suppose. But it doesn't seem fair.'

'They're trying to find a better world too.'

'I can't see it.'

'Just because they don't have to fight, it doesn't mean they don't care. We're too hard on the young.'

'I don't think we're hard enough.'

'We have to allow them to rebel and then let them come back. They'll be old soon enough.'

'And we'll be dead. I suppose it's my round?'

'It's always your round when you have to ask, Geordie.'

Flocks of swallows and martins whirled in the sky. Soon the redwings, fieldfares and song thrushes would follow them. Sidney could never remember at this time of year if they were leaving or coming home or where they really belonged. What was their place in the world and how aware of it were they? In the great scheme of things, he wondered how much it mattered.

All he knew was that sometimes a man had to be grateful for normality, that a story could end less dramatically, and not half as badly as it might have done; that there was merit in an averted crisis, and that in finding his nephew Sidney had, at last, done something quietly responsible, without fuss or fanfare. Perhaps the rest of his life should be like this? he thought. It would involve a concentration on things close to the heart; a dedicated care of friends and family; a quieter existence, one that depended on listening harder and loving better; never resting in complacency; acknowledging faults, doubts and insecurities; the balance between solitude and company, the wish to escape and the need to come home: a loving attention.

The Persistence of Love

I F EVER SIDNEY HAD a normal day ahead of him, Monday 18 October 1976 was most likely to be it. He was due to celebrate the early-morning communion to commemorate the life of St Luke; there was a Chapter meeting with the dean at nine o'clock and a reception for a visiting missionary at midday. Then there would be soup for lunch with some of Hildegard's home-made German bread. In the afternoon he had to take a trip out to Upwell to discuss a vacancy in the parish of St Peter's, with its fine thirteenth-century church, angel roof and Georgian galleries, and then he would be back in time for evensong, the supervision of Anna's homework, an early supper and a night of television: *Some Mothers Do 'Ave 'Em*, *Dave Allen* and *I, Claudius* (although he would probably have to fight Hildegard about the latter, as there was a documentary on the 1956 Hungarian uprising which he was sure she would prefer).

He had set his alarm for 6.15 a.m. but rose before it went off and took care to go about his ablutions as quietly as possible. Hildegard had seemed very tired over the last few weeks and he wanted her to get as much sleep as she could. It was still dark as he moved about the house, made a pot of tea, showered, shaved and got dressed. He didn't drink the tea himself, believing the old rule that the first food and drink to touch his lips should be the bread and wine of communion, but left a cup by his sleeping wife, hoping its aroma would gently wake her.

He let Byron out for his morning constitutional and left home just as the *Today* programme was starting. There had been a revaluation of the German mark, the prime minister was calling for a national discussion of the country's education system and there were demonstrations in Shanghai denouncing Chairman Mao's wife for nagging her husband to death. He would look forward to telling the family about *that* when he got home. He smiled as he imagined Hildegard's face and her lifted eyebrow.

There were some twenty people in the congregation, most of them regulars, and his doctor, Michael Robinson, was amongst them, together with a couple of newcomers who, he hoped, did not have troublesome issues that he was expected to solve. As his career in crime had developed, Sidney had become increasingly wary of strangers.

'Almighty God,' he began, 'you called Luke the physician, whose praise is in the gospel, to be an evangelist and physician of the soul: by the grace of the Spirit and through the wholesome medicine of the gospel, give your Church the same love and power to heal; through Jesus Christ your Son our Lord, who is alive and reigns with you, in the unity of the Holy Spirit, one God, now and for ever.'

They were in the Lady Chapel, his favourite part of the cathedral, and the sun rose as the service progressed. There was something particularly purifying, he thought, about this place and that light. It was humbling to witness the quiet faith of the Christians in his care, sitting with grace and in silence, spending time away from the troubles of the world in order to contemplate them all the more.

Having shared the peace and given his blessing, Sidney returned to Canonry House at a quarter to eight. There he found that neither his wife nor his daughter were up. He called to tell Anna the time and received a grumpily mumbled '*I know*', and then climbed up the stairs and returned to his bedroom. The lights were still off.

'Are you all right, darling?' he asked.

'Terrible headache,' said Hildegard.

'Have you had your tea? Can I get you anything? Have you had an aspirin?'

'I think it's a migraine. Very bad. Can you take Anna?'

'Of course. Would you like more tea? When is your first lesson?'

'Eleven.'

'Do you want me to cancel it for you?'

'It'll be all right.'

'I'll look after Anna.'

'Thank you.'

Sidney went downstairs and sorted out the orange juice, the toast and the cornflakes. He called his daughter once more and received an even grumpier answer. Was he going to have to drag her out of her room himself? He couldn't understand why it was like this *every day*. Hildegard had stuck a To Do list on the fridge: '*Anna's Grade V pieces, dry-cleaning, Boots, Cutlacks, Edis, Sugar Puffs, peanut butter, travel agent, Trudi letter.*'

Sidney wondered what she wanted to see a travel agent about. Had her sister asked her to return to Germany? Was their mother not well? Had he been told everything he needed to know?

Anna entered the kitchen. She hadn't brushed her hair or put on her school tie. Sidney asked where her satchel and blazer were. She couldn't say.

'Do you want me to look for them?'

'Where's Mum?'

'She's not feeling very well.'

'What's wrong?'

'Headache.'

'I've got a headache too.'

Anna poured out the cornflakes. Milk. Sugar. She sniffed loudly. Sidney decided not to ask where her handkerchief was.

'Are you taking me?'

'I will if you perk up a bit.'

'It's too early.' She began to munch at her cornflakes.

Sidney had got to that stage with his daughter when he had to extract information by using as few words as possible. 'Is it history today?'

'Maths. Science. First thing. I hate them.'

'But you like history. You do have it on a Monday, don't you?'

'It's all right.'

'Well,' said Sidney, 'I look forward to detailed discussions with you on the Dissolution of the Monasteries when you get home.'

'You'll be lucky.'

He left the kitchen and searched for the car keys on the hall table. 'In fact, I just can't wait,' he muttered, thinking that if this was the onset of teenage angst he was not sure he could survive the next few years of it.

Were all adolescents like this? At times Anna could still be sweet to him but then, even if nothing particularly dramatic or upsetting had happened, she would change into a sullen, self-obsessive with whom it was impossible to live without argument. She was going to be thirteen in December but she never seemed to inhabit her biological age, preferring to veer between three-year extremes either side. Sometimes she behaved like a charming, ten-year-old *Daddy's little girl*, but then there were moments when she could pass for an obviously chippy fifteen- or even sixteen-year-old. Sidney could never predict which daughter he was going to get.

They drove through the morning traffic out of Infirmary Lane and up Back Hill (why was it always impossible to turn right here during the rush hour?), passing the High Street, Market Square and Babie Care, the shop in which they had bought Anna's first clothes. The first hint of light that had illuminated the Lady Chapel had now been obliterated by cloud. Spits of rain fell on the windscreen. Sidney knew that if he said anything it would only annoy his daughter and so he turned on the radio. A reporter from Rome was saying that a group of bagpipers had celebrated the canonisation of a new Scottish saint, the blessed John Ogilvie, who had been hanged at Glasgow Cross in 1615. The next item told of a thirty-two-year-old Cambridge man who had been killed at a stock-car destruction derby at the weekend and there were calls for the sport to be banned.

Anna leant forward and switched to Radio One. Noel Edmonds was playing 'Disco Duck' by Rick Dees and His

Cast of Idiots. She turned it off. Was she going to be like her cousin Louis? Perhaps, one day, she would run away too.

'Thought you enjoyed that kind of thing?' Sidney asked as he pulled up some fifty yards from the school. He knew he was being provocative but thought a bit of teasing might encourage a response.

'You must be out of your mind. Are you picking me up?'

'Probably. One of us will. Have you got everything?'

'I don't know.'

'Please don't expect me to come all the way back with anything you've forgotten. Your mother will blame me for not having checked properly.'

'I won't. Thanks, Dad.' She hesitated before opening the car door. 'I'm sorry. I'm in a mood.'

'That's all right, Anna. I still love you.' She could be so disarming, but Sidney knew that he could not risk an attempt at an affectionate goodbye kiss. That would be embarrassing.

'Good,' she said.

'I don't always like you, but I still love you.'

'Ditto.'

Anna *almost* smiled, opened the car door, got out, slammed it shut and walked away without a look back. She had already seen her friend Sophie.

Sidney waited as the lollipop lady escorted the juniors across the road. She gave him a wave and he tooted his horn. Other drivers took this to be a gesture of impatience and hooted back at him. *Honestly*, Sidney thought, I am just being friendly.

He drove slowly back through town, trying to remember if they had enough aspirin in the house and if he should alert the school to the fact that Hildegard might not be in today, but he didn't want to speak for her (that never went down well). As he was held up by yet more traffic, he wondered if a staggered system of school and office opening times would ease the congestion. Someone in the council should think of that, he decided. Perhaps he might even come up with a proper suggestion himself? That would be something practical he could do for the community. Traffic calming. It was an unlikely additional career.

He arrived home just before nine and hoped that there might be time for a quick cup of coffee with Hildegard before he saw the dean and Chapter. He would just have to make sure that he didn't complain about Anna as that generally descended into an argument about who might be most to blame for her pre-teen behaviour. *I wonder where she gets it from.*

He unlocked the front door and Byron padded towards him hoping for food, a walk, company. The house was as he had left it. There was no sign that Hildegard had done anything at all. He wondered if she was still resting. It was unlike her, but then she wasn't often ill.

He walked up the stairs. Their bedroom was in darkness, but there was enough light to see through the gaps in the curtains. Hildegard was lying on her side, turned toward Sidney's space in the bed, her left arm reaching over to where he would have been, her right against her hip. He sat down and touched her shoulder, careful not to wake her from sleep but concerned to know whether she was all right.

'My darling . . .' he asked.

There was no response.

He turned on the bedside light.

Her tea remained untouched.

He moved the light down to the floor lest it was too bright and disturbed Hildegard's headache.

He touched his wife's hair and her face and felt her cold hand.

Now he could tell that she was not breathing. But he could not admit the dread that rushed in to him. It was the gap between the firing of the bullet and its arrival, the sound wave travelling faster than the impact. This was what he had always feared and yet never quite imagined: the heart-stop before the silence; the completion of a concert before the applause; the recognition of an ending.

He felt for a pulse in her wrist and neck. There was none. He lay down in the darkness and held his wife in silence. That left arm. Had she been reaching out for him to find that he wasn't there? Had she known that she was dying? Was her last moment of awareness one of finding him absent yet again? How much pain had she been in? At what point had she lost consciousness?

He remembered the times in their marriage that he had lain awake just like this, either unable to sleep or just before getting up, listening to Hildegard's breathing, matching her rhythm, wanting to breathe in synchronicity. Sometimes he had found it too loud and he had even accused her of snoring, only to be informed that *he* was the one that made all the noise at night. Once he was told he sounded like an elephant and Sidney had asked his wife if she had ever actually heard an elephant snore.

He readjusted his position and looked at her still, pale face, the grey-blonde hair that curled behind her left ear, the hole where her earring should be. A word came to him. *Limbo*. Perhaps that was where she was, halfway between this world and the next. It was as if he could still see her, in the distance, at the far end of a field but could no longer be sure if it was her. If she could tell him one more thing, say one more sentence, give him one final thought to remember her by, he wondered what it would be. Would it be in English or German, profound or light, said with her serious face, which meant she could not be contradicted, or that loving expression which told Sidney that she already knew he wouldn't take any notice of what she was saying?

Outside he heard traffic, birdsong – was that a blackbird? The cathedral clock struck the quarter-hour. They would have started their meeting at the Deanery. 'Typical Sidney,' one of them would be complaining, 'always late.' Another would blame it on 'one of his intrigues'. Then they would laugh. There had been so many.

But none of those intrigues were what this was.

He should get help, he knew, but then if other people came he would have to admit the truth. Witnesses would only tell him that this was not a dream.

He needed water but was not sure he could walk. He did not want to get up; to get up would be to lose this moment. To get up would let the world in.

He did not know how long it took him to get to the telephone. He managed to ask for the doctor. Yes, it was urgent.

He couldn't decide what to do while he waited; whether to walk or stand or sit. There didn't seem to be much point in anything. Once he had left the bedroom he didn't want to return. That would only prove to him what had happened,

275

that he hadn't dreamt it. There could be no miracle here, no empty room, no return to life. But he didn't want to be anywhere else.

Nothing that he did now could make any meaningful difference to anything that was about to happen.

It was going to be their fifteenth wedding anniversary. Last year it had been ivory. He looked at the keys on the piano and wondered if it would ever be played in the same way again.

He thought about when and how he would tell Anna. He could hardly wait until he picked her up from school that afternoon. But how could he spare her the worst of this?

The telephone rang and he did not answer it. What could he say? It was probably the dean's secretary wondering where he was. Perhaps it would have been easier to let her know straightaway. Then she could have told everyone for him.

He was just about to go back upstairs and see Hildegard once more (perhaps he had made a mistake, perhaps she was in a coma, perhaps he should have called an ambulance instead?) when the doorbell rang.

It was Michael Robinson. He said he was sorry. He asked Sidney if he was sure. He climbed the stairs. He entered the bedroom. He checked for vital signs of life.

There were none.

'When do you think this happened?'

'I was only out for half an hour.'

'Was she awake when you left her?'

Sidney explained. He then asked if Hildegard had been worried about anything. Was there anything she hadn't told him? Did the doctor know something he didn't?

'A migraine, you say? Was her sight all right?'

'I don't know. It was still dark in the room.'

'She didn't want any light?'

'She said it was too bright. Should I have guessed? Should I have done something more? What do you think, Michael?'

'It sounds like a stroke or an aneurysm. These things can come out of the blue.'

'Had there been symptoms? She didn't tell me anything.'

'Your wife said that she had been finding things exhausting and quite stressful, but I put that down to her time of life. She wasn't depressed. Her blood pressure was nothing to be alarmed about, but her thyroid was underactive and we organised some medication. You'll know about that.'

Sidney did.

'But these things happen and you can't prepare for them. One cannot call it natural causes. Perhaps it is more like fate or bad luck. It's random. Even if you had acted immediately, before Anna went to school, I'm not sure that we could have done very much. It was already too late. So please – and listen to me – don't blame yourself. Don't ever do that.'

'I'll try not to.'

'Don't. Does anyone else know?'

'Not yet.'

'Would you like my help?'

'I don't know what to do. I have to tell Anna first.'

'I'll sort out a medical certificate. You'll need that for the registry office.'

'Will there be a postmortem?'

'I don't think that'll be necessary. Why do you ask?'

'Don't they have them in cases of sudden death?'

'And in unusual or suspicious circumstances. But I am both glad and afraid to say that there is nothing unusual about this, Sidney. This is just life and death.'

They telephoned the undertaker and Nigel Martin promised to be there as soon as he could. He would be discreet. He had an unmarked ambulance.

The doctor asked if they should pray. Sidney was not sure he could do that. Michael said that he would speak the words for him. He always carried a pocket prayer book.

Go forth upon thy journey from this world, O Christian soul.

He waited with Sidney for the undertaker.

Nigel Martin had his wife with him. He thought that it was probably better if a woman made Hildegard ready for 'the move' unless Sidney wanted to do it himself.

Sidney did not think he could. He felt guilty but he was also unsure whether the person in the bedroom was that of his wife or merely an inanimate object, a vessel emptied of meaning. Even though her body remained there, implacably present, she had already left. The flesh and blood that he had loved and cherished was redefined as a corpse.

Mrs Martin found Hildegard's Chinese silk nightdress, her best gift from Sidney, and her hairbrush on the dressing table. She asked about the underwear drawer, the bathroom and where she could find soap and flannels. Sidney was not to worry. She was used to this kind of thing. It was probably easier if he left the room and let her do what had to be done.

Nigel told him about the Chapel of Rest. That would be the best place for Anna to see her mother, he said. They would make it nice for her. There would be candles. He just needed a couple of hours and then Hildegard would be ready.

It was time to go to his daughter. As a priest Sidney knew how to break bad news; to sit a person down, speak calmly, trying to reassure them that this tragedy of a death, either random or expected, was not the destruction of hope and happiness, but part of the natural order. If the bereaved collapsed in grief, he would hold them, speak quietly and allow time for sorrow. Then he would pray with them, offer practical help and a prompt return, fulfilling his duty and his obligations. He would come, he promised, at any time.

But on all those previous occasions he had been playing a part. He had been 'being a priest'. Now that it was his daughter, this was the real thing.

He got into the car once more. He remembered that this was a metaphor he sometimes used to explain to children the difference between the body and the soul. Imagine the body as a car, he would say, and the soul as the driver. When the driver no longer needs the car he gets out, leaving it empty, just as the soul leaves the body.

Anna was probably too old for the idea. It would just be one of Dad's stories. He wondered if she had ever heard it before.

It had turned into one of those dank grey days that marked the grip of autumn; a concentrated swarm of clouds passed behind the stark trees, hurrying the light. The garden birch tree creaked in the wind, a white polythene bag tangled in its branches.

At the school Sidney tried to explain what had happened to the headmistress and, even though the words didn't quite come out right, she seemed to understand everything he was saying. He imagined Michael Robinson had warned her.

'Take my room,' she said. 'Have it for as long as you need. I'll make sure you're not disturbed.'

Anna had to be removed from a history lesson. They were studying Henry VIII, the break with Rome and the Dissolution of the Monasteries.

'Have I done something wrong?'

'Not at all.'

'Then what are you doing here? Why have you come to see me?'

'It's your mother.'

'What?'

'I don't know how to tell you this, my darling.'

'What's happened, Dad?'

He took his daughter's hand. 'She's died.'

The words were out of his mouth. Now it was true all over again.

'I don't believe you.'

'I don't believe it either. She didn't wake up.'

'She did. You said she had a headache.'

'I know, but . . .'

'Have you been lying to me? Did you know before I went to school? Is that why you took me?'

'She said it was a headache.'

'Is that all? How can people die of a headache?'

'I'm not sure. The doctor said . . .'

280

Sidney was unable to maintain eye contact with his daughter. But then, every time he turned away, he couldn't help but notice the incongruity of the office in which they sat. They were surrounded by images of academic success and sporting achievement, with smiles, trophies, handshakes and congratulation.

There, and alone, Sidney and Anna had been abandoned to confront this terrible setback, hardly knowing what to say, terrified of upsetting each other still further.

'Why didn't you come and get me first?'

'I don't know, Anna. I had to send for the doctor. I'm sorry.'

'Can I see her? Can I come home now? Is that why you're here?'

'She's . . . she's . . .'

'Where is she?'

'I think she's . . .'

'Are you lying, Dad? Has someone killed her?'

'No, not at all. Nothing like that.'

'Then why has this happened?'

'I don't know.'

His daughter was almost a stranger, his own and yet not his own, growing away from him in her green school blazer and black skirt, her hair in need of a wash, the first breakout of spots on her chin, and with one of her shoelaces undone – her mother would have nagged her about that. What could he do to help her through the forthcoming adolescent world of anxiety and accusation?

'Is it your fault?' Anna asked.

'It's no one's fault.'

'Can we go now, Dad? Can we see her?'

'I'm not sure they'll be ready.'

'Who's "they"?'

'It doesn't matter.'

'Please Dad, I want to go there now.'

They left the school and everyone else in lessons, some of the pupils staring out of the window as if they had already been told, and drove back home.

To think that this morning Sidney had seen himself as the new controller of traffic-calming in this town. He looked at the other drivers, cars, people on bicycles and mopeds getting in the way, young mothers with prams on the pavement, dogs who weren't on proper leads drifting into the verges, and he was filled with intense fury. How could everyday life continue like this? Why were people still shopping, with their bags and trolleys, their impatient concerns and their pointless hurrying? Who were they all?

Sidney was so distracted he was not sure if he could remember how to drive. What were all the other cars doing on the road? They were all in the way.

He realised that he was going in the wrong direction. He had automatically taken the route to Canonry House. They had almost arrived by the time Anna reminded him. What was he doing?

He tried to remember how to get to the funeral parlour. He had been there often enough. *Up* Back Hill, *straight on* into Lynn Road, *right* into Nutholt Lane, *left* into New Barns Road, *left* into Deacons Lane just before the cemetery. It wasn't that hard.

He braked at a red light. At least he remembered to do that. But what was the point of traffic lights? Why were they holding him up? Was this a deliberate attempt to keep him from his wife?

They weren't quite ready. The undertaker sat Anna down and told her what to expect: the dark room, the casket (he didn't say coffin), the white silk lining, the candles. She would see her mother and yet, at the same time, the body was not as her mother had once been. Anna shouldn't be surprised or alarmed, because Hildegard was at peace: that was why they called it a Chapel of Rest; her vital spirit had passed on.

'Like a car without a driver?' she asked.

'That's right.'

'Can I see her, then?'

After twenty minutes she was shown into a small vaulted room at the back that smelt of bleach and air freshener. The coffin was raised and so, on entering the room, it wasn't immediately possible to see who was in it. This was, Sidney supposed, to give people time to adjust to the atmosphere, to delay the inevitable.

Hildegard was in the Chinese nightdress, her ash-blonde hair had been swept back and she wore a necklace of pearls that Sidney hadn't remembered providing. He had forgotten about earrings. He would have to go back home and get some. She looked like a dead bride.

At first Anna was scared to go near, frightened of the stillness. She was wearing her uniform. Somehow it didn't seem right, as if her mother's death was some kind of school project.

She leant over to see and her breathing changed. It was somewhere between a sigh and a great exhalation, an involuntary attempt to breathe life back into her mother.

My breath is your breath. You gave me life. Let me give it back to you.

She touched her mother's cheek. It was over made-up with a blusher Hildegard would never have used, covering the yellowing skin beneath. The undertaker had warned her about the cold but Anna shrank at the sensation. She stroked her mother's hand with her right hand. She started to cry but couldn't finish. Instead, she fainted.

Sidney just missed her as she fell to the floor.

When Anna came round she said she couldn't move. She wanted to stay there for ever, alone with her mother.

The undertaker brought her a glass of water. She wanted to wait until her mother started to breathe again, she said. If they stayed long enough, and if they prayed hard enough, surely they could force a miracle?

They remained for another hour until there was nothing left to do or say. Anna thought it was wrong to leave. Sidney promised his daughter she could return whenever she liked.

How long would her mother be there? He didn't know, he couldn't be sure, a week perhaps.

They drove home. Could Sidney get his daughter something to eat? No, she couldn't face anything. She felt sick. She went up to her room and closed the door.

Sidney put the kettle on. This was the start of all the things that he had to do alone since Hildegard had died: the first time he made a cup of tea for one, the first night he went to bed on his own, the first Christmas without her name on the cards or her place by his side. It was the beginning of imaginary rather than real conversations.

He knew he had to inform his family, Hildegard's sister Trudi (she would tell her mother in Leipzig), Geordie, Amanda, Leonard, Malcolm and Helena.

He phoned his sister first. She couldn't believe what he was saying.

'Please don't make me repeat it.'

'Hildegard's dead? But how?'

How many more times was he going to have to say this? Already he imagined social situations, services, receptions, parties.

I see you haven't brought your wife.

That's because she's dead.

Jennifer said that she would tell as many people as possible, even Amanda if he liked.

Yes, he did want that.

The only person he should ring, she said, was their father. He would need to hear the news from Sidney directly. Then she and the Church could do the rest, although he should also telephone Leonard, he had always been such a friend, and Geordie just in case.

'Just in case what?'

'You know.'

'No, Jennifer, I don't know.'

'Just in case anyone thinks there's anything odd about it.'

'Why would they think that?'

'She's so young.'

'People die young.'

'You know what I mean.'

285

'You think . . .'

'I don't think anything, Sidney. Other people do.'

'Are you saying that it's possible this might be treated as something suspicious?'

'You've been involved in a lot of difficult situations. You don't want people to think . . .'

'Oh, let them think it.'

Sidney put the phone down. As soon as he did so it rang again. It didn't stop ringing. He couldn't ignore it. The news was out.

Sophie's mother arrived. 'We tried phoning but we couldn't get through. The headmistress told us. So kind of her. Such a shock. We didn't even know Hildegard had been ill.'

'She hadn't. The doctor thinks it was an aneurysm.' And then, because Sophie's mother appeared not to know what that was, he explained. 'A brain haemorrhage. It's more common than people think.'

Was he now saying all this lest she think him a murderer?

'Do you want us to look after Anna for a night or two?' Sophie's mother asked. 'It's no trouble.'

'Do you think that's a good idea?'

'Sophie will go up and ask, won't you, Sophie?'

Sidney had forgotten that her daughter was by her side. Sophie shook his hand and looked him in the eye. She said she was sorry. He wondered if her parents had told her that was what she had to do. They could even have rehearsed it.

'You know the way.'

They remained in the hall. Sophie's mother was dressed with country practicality: a floral headscarf, Barbour gilet, jeans and flat rubber-soled shoes. The visit was an unexpected addition to the many chores of her day but it was one that she was sure to take in her stride.

'I know from when my father died that there are so many things you have to do. Register the death, tell people over and over again. You never know what it's like until it happens to you. It'll be hard for you to look after Anna at the same time. That's why you need us.'

She was probably right. Some time away from home would spare his daughter the grim repetition of funeral preparation and his own desperate melancholy.

Sophie's parents were kind, practical and rich. There were ponies, brothers, sisters, distractions (numerous pets and ballet lessons), and he was grateful for the offer even though he couldn't decide if he understood his daughter well enough to know whether this was something she would want to do or not. Under normal circumstances he would have asked Hildegard.

'I don't want her to feel abandoned.'

'We'll make her feel safe.'

'I don't know what's best.'

'I brought you a lasagne.'

Sidney had not noticed that she was holding some Tupperware. Where had that come from? There was a Tesco polythene bag too.

'You probably won't want anything but you only have to heat it up. There's a bottle of whisky as well. I know you probably shouldn't but Giles said it might help. Not that anything will. I'm so sorry. You are ready for the fact that no one will know what to say? It's normally you who provides the reassurance and now that it's our turn I think we'll all be guilty of letting you down.'

'I think I'll manage.'

'Will you tell someone if you can't?'

Her daughter came down the stairs with Anna. 'Can we go now?' she asked.

Finally alone, Sidney thought of his wife. It was impossible to concentrate on anything else: all the things they had said and not said, their cares and concerns, everything they had left unfinished.

He tried to think back to when they had first met – as if, by doing so, he could relive their lives. He remembered her first husband's funeral and the strange desolate calm he had felt in her presence afterwards. She was dressed in widow's black, her face partly obscured by a veil, and she wore no lipstick. It was as if all her feelings had been washed away. He had liked her guarded stillness, her mouth, her green eyes. Then, during the investigation into Stephen Staunton's death, they had spoken more and started to call each other by their Christian names. Hildegard had wept, Sidney had held her and he had done what he could as a priest and a friend. Then she sold her house and her piano and returned to Germany. He had thought that he would never see her again.

But something would not let them separate – he couldn't explain it, and Sidney had instinctively felt, not caring if it was true or not, that he would never be able to be himself if he remained far from her. So they had written and then he had gone to see her in West Germany. Afterwards,

Hildegard had come back to Cambridge, seen him going about his detective work (a stupid investigation at Corpus – one Fellow electrocuting another in the bath), and she had forgiven him for the distraction because she too had decided that they were linked in a way that could not be dissolved.

In 1961, after Sidney had been arrested in the DDR, he remembered how they had tried to get back to the West just as the Berlin Wall was going up, and how they had found themselves avoiding the checkpoints and barricades by half-swimming and half-wading through the River Spree. Hildegard had suddenly turned to him and asked: 'You do love me, don't you? I have to know if there's something worth living for.'

They had escaped through a park at night, found themselves in the English quarter and had gone to hear the Eric Dolphy Quintet. That was the day they had made love for the first time. It was all they could do to keep warm. It had been so inevitable they wondered why it had taken them so long.

When Sidney came back to Grantchester and told his friends that he was going to marry Hildegard, they had asked if this love was as secure as he thought it was. Did he want their advice? He had then told them all – yes, even Amanda – that this was secure, and he could not imagine ever being with anyone else. His love for Hildegard had an overwhelming sense of completeness that was like faith but more companionable. It was tender, honest, fragile, brave.

His friends had smiled and said that they hoped it was and they wished him well and he could still see the doubt in their eyes, but Sidney had no anxieties at all.

He remembered their autumn wedding in Grantchester, with the leaves of the trees mixing dark cherry and burnt orange, and Orlando Richards choosing the German music – '*Also heilig ist der Tag*', '*Bist du bei Mir*' – and Leonard Graham preaching and telling them (he, who knew nothing of such things at the time) that marriage was like a garden that needed to be tended, and Hildegard was the rose in that garden.

It was so long ago and, even though they had both been through the war, the beginning of their marriage had been a second innocence, when they had to learn both how to live with each other and how to love, differently and for each other. Sometimes Sidney had been scared of that love, he knew that now – frightened of its overwhelming intensity, fearing that if he lived entirely within it he would lose all sense of himself. And so, foolishly perhaps, he had been distracted by other things: by his work, his criminal investigations, his ambition, his love of novelty and his dread of boredom. How he regretted that now, the too many times he had absented himself from the only happiness he had ever known.

He could still feel the jolt of joy when Hildegard had told him that she was pregnant at last. He said that he owed her the world and she had replied – he could hear her saying it now, he could see her tearful eyes – 'I don't need the world, Sidney. I just need you.' He remembered Anna's birth and the drama when Abigail Redmond's baby John was snatched from the hospital at the same time and how he had almost missed the whole thing in order to sort out someone else's problems, and then had to wait, more fearfully than he had ever waited for anything in his life, by the side of a mother-in-law he had never quite known how to speak to, for the miracle of creation and his wife's words when he entered her hospital room: 'Meet Anna.'

Since then there had been trials and misunderstandings for which he had been so much to blame, vanities and self-indulgences. He thought of how much his wife had trusted him; how she had let him be free to go where sometimes he should not have gone, to find himself by being away from her, and how he had returned either wiser, chastened or filled with regret, knowing that surely, whatever happened, they would always love each other. He couldn't imagine it being otherwise.

But now here it was, in the midst of an alternative loneliness he had never dared to imagine. Hildegard, too, had been free to go and now she had gone: into an infinity of absence.

What was left of all that they had shared? What made their love abiding? Sidney sought out the old reasons, the comforts that he had always given others; the fact that love remains: in memory, children and in our very identity. Now he would have to go on living – pretending, perhaps, that his wife was still alive, that she would come back home through the front door at any minute, for it was impossible to imagine anything other than that, even if it drove him mad, because he would rather be insane than cope with the desolation of solitude.

In his bedroom that night he noticed that Hildegard's dressing gown was gone. The undertaker's wife hadn't removed that as well, had she? Perhaps it was in the laundry basket;

but no, it couldn't be: Anna must have taken it with her, just wanting the smell of her mother, the warmth of her skin, the tone of her voice.

In the subsequent days, people came round with soups, casseroles and simple suppers, anything Sidney or Anna could 'just put in the oven'. The precentor's wife was writing a recipe book, *A Hundred Ways with Mince*, and so she was quite in the swing of things, she said. All the troops were rallying round. Sidney only had to say what he wanted. Anything really, honestly, anything. It was no trouble.

Then bring me back my wife.

He remembered the *Book of Lamentations*: 'Is it nothing to you, all ye that pass by? Behold and see if there be any sorrow like unto my sorrow . . .'

But there was. There was Anna's grief too. How was he to assuage that? What could he say to persuade her that this was fate, chance and nobody's fault and there was nothing they could have done? How could he explain, in the language of faith, or in any language, that her mother had been taken too early, before she was ready, without her knowledge and with no time to prepare? Someone had said that it was 'an easy death' and that it was 'the best way to go', but not so soon. The fact that Hildegard was at peace, that she had died in her sleep, was insufficient consolation to those that remained and missed her and could find no way of ordering themselves without her, apart from attempting to live by her example, imagining that she was still with them.

She had stuck one of Anna's old school projects to the fridge, an acrostic poem. 'Describe me'.

Adventurous
Naughty
Nice
Artistic

Charming!
Happy
Amazing
Messy
Bouncy
Energetic
Radiant
Sparkling

Sidney had advised and preached before on the resilience of children but now that he had experienced such a loss himself it was hard not to think that everything he had ever said before had been a platitude. He would have to pray again, he knew, for guidance, help and humility, recognising that there was nothing he could do on his own. He needed the company of others: his friends, his colleagues, his daughter. Together they might eventually see this through, with patience, stoicism and an acknowledgement of the vanity of human wishes and the futility of earthly reward. Then life might yet have a purpose. But, for now, he wasn't sure he could do that. For now, he craved solitude and the necessary selfishness of grief.

He sat at his desk in his study, unable to work or concentrate, and gave himself over to the memory of his wife. He thought of everything she had meant to him and how much he could remember. They had known each other for twenty-two years, been married for nearly fourteen, and perhaps he could spend the next twenty-two remembering her, reliving their marriage but differently, as if he had behaved in a better way, acknowledging everything she had done for him, all her goodness and all her faults. He would not worship her, making her a much-missed saint, as Thomas Hardy had done to his wife ('Woman much missed, how you call to me, call to me'), but perhaps he would appreciate what he had been given in the first place: the fluke of their meeting and the depth of her love.

He imagined Hildegard standing in the doorway, smaller than usual because she had taken her shoes off, asking if he wanted a cup of tea or if, perhaps, he had already helped himself to something stronger?

He missed the way her voice dropped in tone when she spoke to him, as if their intimacy required a different register. He could still hear how she cut her laugh short, as if she had been caught enjoying herself when she should have been serious. He remembered her delight in Anna and her disbelief when either husband or daughter failed to behave in the way she had hoped, by being late, thoughtless, disrespectful, disobedient or unkind.

He missed her German; the way she sang Bach's aria '*Flösst, mein Heiland, flösst dein Namen*' as she crossed from room to room, getting out the decorations for the Christmas tree, the pewter moon and stars, the little hanging gingerbread house, the frosted lanterns. He could still hear her teaching Anna to count in German from an early age, singing her nursery rhymes and lullabies – '*Schlaf, Kindlein, schlaf*' – and he recalled the way the two of them would laugh at his attempts to join in when they sang, accusing him, so unfairly, of being tone deaf.

He remembered how, after the death of her first husband, he had first tried to show Hildegard his rudimentary German by repeating his two opening gambits, asking if she liked football (the question for men) and if she wanted to dance (the question for women). She had laughed at his pronunciation and his grammar but they had danced for a little moment in her front room all the same.

Had he known even then? he wondered. He was sure, now he said it to himself, that very first time; oh, at last, here you are, you are the person that I was meant to have found, thank God, thank *you*.

He thought of the long shadow of the war, of Hildegard's bravery in coming to England and staying, her forgiveness and tolerance in the succeeding years and her acceptance of those who were still anti-German, only showing her nationality during World Cup football and by refusing to watch *Dad's Army*, *Colditz* and *Where Eagles Dare* (even going to see *The Sound of Music* had been problematic). Her English became so fluent that people didn't realise she was originally from Leipzig, but she still had trouble with certain aspects of pronunciation, bringing the letter 'r' to the front of her mouth when she was tired, so that words like 'terrible' became 'te-ch-rible', and 'Thursday' sounded as 'Sssirstay'.

Sidney remembered how she only referred to him as '*mein Lieber*' when she was cross with him; and how, on their last wedding anniversary, they had been too tired to make love.

Although she hated being teased, Hildegard insisted that she *did* have a sense of humour. She thought that it *was* funny to tell her favourite joke about a balloon with claustrophobia at every children's party even though it could only be

understood in German: '*Ein Ballon sagt zum anderen: "Ich hab'*
Platzangst.'" He remembered the time she had laughed most,
when he had told her his own joke about the English couple
who adopted a German baby that said nothing until he was
five years old. The new parents were very worried but little
appeared to be wrong. Then, one day, the boy said: 'This
strudel is tepid.' His mother shouted out with excitement:
'Hans, you can speak! Why have you not spoken before?'
To which Hans replied: 'Because up until now everything
has been satisfactory.'

Sidney walked through the house and imagined his wife
calling him as she opened the front door. *Ich bin's.* It's only
me. He could still hear the sound of her keys landing on the
hall table and remembered how he would get up from his
desk and meet her as she came to find him. *Da bin ich wieder.*
Here I am. Sometimes he closed his eyes and held out his
arms as she approached so that he could simply feel the precision of her kiss on his lips – *bin wieder da* – before she took
off her hat, coat and gloves and sought out the next task.

The hall was empty of people. A letter from Germany
was waiting in the rack, the dog lead hung on a hook over
Hildegard's wellington boots, just by the walking stick that
she had bought in order to be 'a proper English country-
woman'.

Sidney followed his imaginary wife into the kitchen and
couldn't decide whether to make himself a cup of tea or
pour out a drink of something stronger but settled on the
speed of a glass of water as he remembered Hildegard singing as she cooked, with Anna shelling the peas or folding the
almond mixture for *Leipziger Lerche* into the brown mixing

bowl. He could see his wife turning to smile and asking him to lay the table, insisting on linen napkins even though it meant more washing and ironing. At breakfast she would always express surprise that he still ate his boiled eggs the wrong way round, with the big end at the top, because even though he would get the full flavour first, it meant there would only be white for the last spoonful and the meal would culminate in disappointment. If he ate them in the correct way, she insisted, with the little end at the top, then the experience would be one of continuous improvement. That was how a meal should be, she explained. It was like a piece of music, a three-part sonata; and she never did trust her husband to time eggs, roast meat so that it cooked through as it rested, or prepare red cabbage in the proper German way.

Finally she had given up on his foibles, just as he had decided not to contradict her when she told him, in one of her frequent battles to lose weight after the traditional Christmas excess of goose, *Stöllen*, *Zimsterne* and *Lebkuchen*, that potatoes were not fattening. It was just the butter that was the trouble, and black bread didn't really count towards calories either and dark chocolate was perfectly acceptable as a dessert for those on a diet. At the same time, Sidney was grateful, although he had never quite said it enough, that his wife never complained when they went to meals with parishioners and Hildegard was given the English cuisine she could not stand: eggs in aspic, devilled kidneys, cauliflower cheese, bloody rare beef and banana fritters.

He took his glass of water through to the living room and looked at the only picture they had of Hildegard's father, taken at a communist rally in 1932, the year before he was

shot dead. It was next to the mantel clock her mother had
sent them shortly after they were married and Hildegard's
first ever gift to him: a porcelain figurine of a girl feeding
chickens. There was a reel of white cotton on the floor by the
sofa with a pair of scissors and her little raffia sewing basket.
What had she been about to do, Sidney wondered, sew on a
button or patch a skirt, and what could have taken her away
from the task?

He placed the glass of water on a coaster and sat down at
the piano. He couldn't decide whether to play a note or not.
He looked down at the keys and wished he had learned.
Then perhaps he could have practised his grief. He could
hear Hildegard playing, swearing whenever she went wrong
– *Mist, verdammt, meine Güte* – before setting off on a long
stretch of a Bach partita or a Schubert impromptu and then
stopping again – *Das kann doch nicht so schwer sein* – wishing her
fingers could work faster and were more precise – hoping,
just once, that she could see a piece through to her satisfac-
tion. At the treble end of the piano was a half-squeezed tube
of handcream, a decorated lacquer box containing gold and
silver stars for her pupils' music, worn-down pencils, a
rubber, a sharpener and a metronome. He could hear her
calling out encouragement, sometimes playing along two
octaves higher, insisting on practice and repetition, breaking
the music down into sections and then building it up again,
like a swimmer emerging from a dive and heading out into
open sea.

He left the room and remembered his wife's tread on the
stairs as she came up to bed, carrying Horlicks or hot chocolate, placing it by his side and then making a final check on

Anna before the top light went out and she reached to hold his hand in hers. Then they would turn into their comfortable sleeping arrangement, she on her left side and he on his stomach (what she laughingly called his 'royal position' that took up more than half the space), and fall asleep.

Now Sidney sat on the bed in his daughter's room, surrounded by rag dolls, teddies and stuffed animals. On the wall were posters of horses and ponies, and a childhood painting of a clown. He remembered his daughter's favourite joke when she was a little girl. (What did the crocodile say when he was eating a clown? 'This tastes funny.') On the chest of drawers was the Black Forest weather house she had been given several Christmases ago, a photograph of her in the front row of the school netball team and the record player they had bought for her eleventh birthday. It had last played *Black and Blue* by the Rolling Stones. Her cousin Louis had given it to her. Next to it were copies of *Jackie* magazine, Anna's wild-flower press and pony books, recent homework with a drawing of a house and the rooms marked in French, and a pink comb and brush, a tug of blonde hair still attached. He remembered Hildegard patiently untangling it at the end of summer, before they went down to see his parents. The next time, he would have to do it.

Sidney looked at her favourite felt rabbit resting on the pillow and discovered her mother's dressing gown hidden beneath it.

He went through to the bathroom and saw the items the family shared: the Imperial Leather soap, the Johnson's baby shampoo that Anna complained about using because she was no longer a baby, the Colgate toothpaste and the three brushes in a mug: blue, green and pink. He opened the cupboards to look through cosmetics he had never bothered to find out about; foundation and concealer, Pond's cold cream, several types of lipstick, bottles of Shalimar, 4711 and a new perfume that he knew Hildegard loved: Diorella. There was a razor and cream for shaved legs, tampons, pills for an underactive thyroid and a box of blood-pressure tablets.

He hadn't discovered enough about Hildegard's health, her feelings about Rolfe, her fears about the future, Anna, their marriage, old age. He had thought he had understood his wife better than anyone but now he began to question whether he had known her at all. How much of her character remained elusive? Did she deliberately keep things from him or had he lacked curiosity?

He knew that she was fond of Rolfe, and he trusted what she told him, that it was nothing more than affectionate friendship. Sidney had those kinds of friendship himself, not least with Amanda, but why had Hildegard needed to see another man in the first place and what could he offer that Sidney could not? Even though he had wanted their love to be complete, perhaps it was not and he had failed her. But what more could he have done and how could he have made her happier?

Was she happy?

He thought so, content enough, in as much as any human being can ever be free from pain and anxiety. She had never really complained. She had not run off with Rolfe or fled to Germany, not that the simple act of staying was enough to justify her continuing affections – perhaps she was doing so only for Anna – but then Sidney remembered what

300

Hildegard had written on his birthday card earlier that year: 'if ever beauty I did see, which I desired and got, 'twas but a dream of thee'.

He opened the wardrobe in their bedroom and started to go through his wife's clothes, divided simply into winter and summer: everyday suits in navy, grey and cream; the hats for church and funerals; the all-purpose knee-length black dress with the square neckline and the three-quarter sleeves; her favourite blouses with the Peter Pan collars and the long pleated skirts that she once said she was too old to wear. He found the midnight-blue satin ballgown she had once worn for the Lord Mayor's Christmas party and then said she hated; and there amidst the wobbly hangers holding slips and shawls was the famous floral summer dress that Sidney had not liked enough and, when challenged, had made the disastrous observation that it looked as if his wife was wearing 'half the garden'.

There were dresses, tops, shirts and trousers he was sure that he had never seen before; a white blazer, a duck-egg-blue cotton smock, a pale-brown trench coat. Below, on a shoe rack, were the lace-up walking shoes Hildegard wore around town, burgundy mules, a pair of ankle-strap stilettos, tan leather slides, ballet flats and Dr Scholl's summer sandals. They were leaning against a hard-sided suitcase that looked new even though they had had it for years. Sidney sensed once more the regret that he hadn't taken his wife abroad more often, he hadn't earned enough, he hadn't appreciated her.

He remembered her getting up in the mornings, often before him, putting her clothes on in the dark and then coming back and changing them in the light because she had not been able to tell if her tights were blue or black and, besides, the outfit didn't work and it was safer to wear what she always wore. Perhaps there should be a uniform for piano teachers and clergy wives, she had once suggested, and Sidney had said there might as well be one, since the pressure to conform to the norms of polite society was still rife.

He sat on the bed and studied the chest of drawers that contained his wife's underwear, tights, gloves, scarves and jewellery. Underneath a framed print of Vermeer's *View of Delft* were framed photographs of their marriage, of Anna's first day at school, of a holiday on Rügen Island. They were propped up in front of her purse, yesterday's earrings, and a book that she was in the middle of reading: Heinrich Böll's *The Train Was on Time*. Inside, marking her place, was a post-card: '*Ich bin so froh, Du hattest Zeit mich zu besuchen. Mit lieben Grüßen, Dein Rolfe.*'

So glad you had the time to see me?

When had that been?

And '*Dein Rolfe*' – 'Your Rolfe'?

It had to be said that the man was persistent.

Had Sidney loved his wife enough? What was 'enough'? If love could be measured, he thought, surely it did not count as love? His affection should be indefinable, unfathomable, unaccountable, beyond measure. *How do I love thee? Let me count the ways . . .*

Now that it was gone there was nothing left to count.

He could *try*, he thought, to resume a normal life as priest and father – indeed he would have to – but he would only be occupying a part, like an actor unable to remember his lines.

That night, Sidney lay down on the right of the bed, keeping his wife's side empty, and then, when he could stand it no more, he turned over and onto it, lying across it, stomach down, as if smothering her absence, the obliteration of desire.

He thought he could hear her voice, telling him she was still with him, but it was only the wind.

Ich bin bei dir.

The next morning, he went to register the death at the Old School House in Market Street: Hildegard Annaliese Chambers, formerly Staunton, née Leber, born Leipzig 15 June 1923, died Ely 18 October 1976.

It was a day of bright, low sun, the kind of weather, he remembered, that they had had at their wedding. He looked at the last leaves on a sycamore tree outside the registry office and imagined they were either birds or dead souls, waiting to fall into limbo, their grip on the branch of life too frail to hold on for much longer.

When Anna returned home from school – she wanted to go, it would stop her thinking only of Hildegard – she asked her father why, if they thanked God after Louis had come back safely, they didn't blame him for taking her mother away. 'He' was either active in the world or he wasn't.

'It's hard to explain.'

'Do you understand it, Dad?'

'I think prayer is a way of trying to understand.'

'But what if there's no answer? How can God "explain" this? Mum wasn't old.'

'I think that's why people pray. It is a form of hope.'

'Even if they are deluded?'

'It's not only that. It's both a way of making sense of the world and a form of submitting; of saying that we cannot know everything. We have to acknowledge our weaknesses, our fallibilities, and understand that not everything revolves around us.'

'Then I'll try.'

'And what will you pray for?'

'For Mum. I'm going to write her a letter. The funeral director suggested it. Then we can put it in her coffin.'

'What are you going to say?'

'All the things I never said to her when she was alive. I'd like you not to read it, Dad. I'd like it to be just between us.'

'I understand.'

They began to make tea and toast. Anna liked crunchy peanut butter; Sidney preferred honey. He only just stopped himself from pulling down a third mug for his wife. They hadn't decided what to have for supper.

'What shall we do about your mother's wedding ring?' he asked.

'Did they take it off?'

'The undertakers did in case we wanted to keep it. Mothers often give them to their daughters. You can wear it on your right hand.'

'I'm too young.'

'You won't be young for ever.'

'You should have it, Dad.'

'Then I'll keep it for you.'

'Unless you'd like Mum to be buried with it?'

'I don't know, Anna. There are so many decisions to be made and there isn't enough time.'

'You never discussed this?'

'I didn't think your mother was going to die.'

'Ever?'

'If I thought about it too much I was worried it would happen.'

'That's a selfish way of thinking, isn't it?'

Anna said the words sadly but they still sounded more hostile than perhaps she had intended.

'I'm afraid so,' Sidney replied. 'But then I'm not sure that there is any other way. We can't always help our thoughts.'

'We can try to stop them. Bad thoughts. Not let them rise.'

'Or not act on them.'

'Did you ever ask Mum about Rolfe?'

'Yes, I did. But let's not discuss that now.' Sidney could not help himself. 'Did you?'

'You told me not to.'

'I don't remember doing that.'

'You did.'

'And did you obey?'

'I hate him, Dad. And I hated her for seeing him. I never knew why she needed him as a friend. And I hated you for seeming not to care.'

'I did care, Anna. I thought if I showed how much I minded then it would make everything worse.'

'Do you think Mum was punishing you for Amanda?'

'I don't know. I've done nothing wrong.'

'She wanted an Amanda of her own.'

'No, she had me.'

'But she didn't.'

'She did, Anna. And she liked Amanda.'

'Not all the time.'

'When did she say that?'

'She was annoyed. When you went to that art auction and Amanda bought that stupid painting.'

'She didn't tell me.'

'You were supposed to *know*, Dad. You were meant to guess. You think you are so sensitive to every situation and you couldn't even tell if your own wife was happy or not.'

'That's not fair, Anna. That's absolutely not fair.'

'I'm sorry, Dad. I didn't mean . . . I . . .'

Sidney started to cry. He knew he shouldn't. Not in front of his daughter. Not at a time like this.

'I'm sorry, Dad, I shouldn't have said that.'

'It doesn't matter.'

What was he doing? Why did he have to collapse like this rather than look after her? Who was the child now?

Anna held on to her father and told him he was going to be all right. It had to be. There was no other choice.

Then she ran out of hope. 'What are we going to do?'

'Love each other,' said Sidney. 'No matter what.'

Later that evening, the doorbell rang. Sidney did not want to answer but felt he had to. Everyone knew he was in. Where else would he go? In any case, it could only be another well-wisher, a parishioner bringing flowers, steak and kidney pudding or baked goods in Tupperware. He and Anna had so many reusable containers they could have opened a shop.

It was Vanessa Morgan offering her help.

'I didn't know you were back.'

'The dean telephoned. I know I may not be the right person.'

'I don't think anybody is. Come in.'

She held out her hand. Sidney shook it. What was this woman doing here?

'I'm sorry.'

'Thank you,' said Sidney. 'Everyone is. Would you like a cup of tea?'

'I'll make it.'

'It's no trouble.'

'I thought I could do things for you,' Miss Morgan went on, 'let people know about the funeral, for example; organise the reception afterwards if you want one. You can't be telling everyone about everything yourself. You need some protection.'

'From what?'

'Other people's kindness. After my mother died, I found their compassion so tiring, but I couldn't say anything because it would have seemed ungrateful. Unchristian even.'

'I think I know what you mean.'

'People want to talk about their losses too; everyone who came to me ended up talking about their own experience of death, what it meant to them and how it had affected them. My loss gave them permission to relive their bereavement. And, look, I'm doing the same to you now. I'm sorry.'

'Don't be,' said Sidney. 'It's helpful.'

'I'm not sure it is. I also wanted to make it up to you.'

'What do you mean?'

'For being horrible.'

'You weren't.'

'I was. I was arrogant. I think I must also have been jealous. I thought you had an easy charm and now I know that it wasn't that easy after all. You were performing.'

'You have to keep cheerful.'

'I had a bit of a breakdown, if I'm honest . . .'

'I think I knew.'

Why was this woman telling him now?

'But my faith helped me through as it should help you too, although there's no guarantee of that. You're either resilient or you're not. Sometimes you just have to give in to it all.'

'It's too much to think about.'

'You don't have to think about it.'

'I can't think of anything else.'

All Sidney wanted to do was lie face down on the bed he had shared with his wife and smother himself with her loss.

Hildegard's sister Trudi came for the funeral. She was on her own. Her husband had to look after their children in Berlin; her mother was too infirm to make the trip.

Sidney found it hard to cope with a woman who was an echo of his wife and yet, at the same time, not like Hildegard at all. She was more serious, careful with emotion, as if she didn't quite trust it not to reveal too much about herself, preferring instead to keep active enough to disguise any vulnerability.

She showed Anna how to make pumpernickel, proper German bread that was rich and dense and slightly sour, with an aroma of fennel and caraway seeds. As she did so, she told her niece stories from her mother's childhood:

their first party game (*Schokoladenessen*, in which Hildegard had definitely cheated), their grandmother standing in her best apron and teaching them *exactly* how to make *Leipziger Lerche*, their first boyfriends (not Günter, as Anna had thought, but Ulli, who was Jewish and had got out of the country just in time) and even Hildegard's first husband, Stephen Staunton.

Anna was surprised how casually this was mentioned. 'I only found out recently that Mum had been married before.'

'I don't think children have to know everything about their parents.'

'I think I should know *something*.'

'He was Irish. She wanted to leave Germany after the war and he took her away. He might as well have had a white horse. She was very excited and he was so charming. Dark hair. Strong, how do you say, jaw? Like a movie star. Your mother loved him as best she could, but he drank too much and he was unfaithful and then one of his lovers killed him.'

'*What?*'

'I assumed you knew that.'

There was a silence, filled only with the sound of their preparation. The two of them began to stir three different flours in a bowl, wholewheat, rye and strong white, before scooping out a third of it and then adding the bran, the caraway and the fennel seeds, salt and finely chopped shallot. Why did family truths come out like this, Anna wondered, and how much more was there to know?

Trudi added two different mixtures, one of yeast and one of molasses, into the bowl and asked Anna to fold everything together as best she could. 'Your parents were protecting you.'

'I don't like it when other people know more about my family than I do. What do you mean, "one of his lovers"? There were more than one?'

'I think so. But it was a long time ago. And it was how your father met your mother. So good things came in the end. Like you.'

'I'm not sure I'm a good thing.'

'You're the best thing. Believe me.'

'And I don't like secrets.'

'You don't have any of your own?'

'Yes. But I know what they are.'

Trudi fetched a damp tea towel to cover the bowl and left the bread mixture to rise for thirty minutes. If the conversation went on like this, they were going to have a good punch-down when the dough was ready.

'We all need secrets,' she said, 'although I'm not sure your mother believed in them. If I asked her anything directly she'd always tell me. She said it was why she never wanted to go back to the East. There, the difference between what you know and don't know makes you vulnerable. Power is knowledge. But my sister believed that if you lived openly, you had nothing to fear.'

'Do you think she loved Rolfe?'

'Are you asking me what I think you're asking?'

Anna put down her wooden spoon. 'And will you tell me the truth if I ask?'

Trudi started to clear away the packets, seeds and scales. 'It was friendship. Nothing more.'

'You're sure?'

'I would have known, Anna. I'm her sister. She felt sorry for him. She knew he adored her and she was flattered. It also amused her that Rolfe annoyed your father so much. It was a way of getting him to pay attention.'

'A game.'

'Perhaps. I do the same with my husband. It's nice for a woman to feel she's still attractive. It doesn't happen so often these days.'

'It's embarrassing.'

'I think you'll feel differently when you're my age. *Kinder, Küche, Kirche*. Your mother was very good at all of that.'

'Only one child.'

'But what a child!' said Trudi, kissing her niece on the forehead. She moved the bowl by the oven. 'We need to leave this in a warm place. Perhaps we could make a cake too? I thought about an *Eierlikör Torte*. Your father would like that but I'm not sure if you can get all the ingredients in England. Do you have any eggnog?'

'Women bring him cake all the time.'

'They're being kind.'

'Do you like Amanda?' Anna asked.

'I'm not sure. Do you?'

'She's always been very kind to me. She's my godmother. Sometimes she tries too hard to be my friend. I don't always like it but I feel sorry for her. Dad says she's made a mess of her life.'

'Your mother liked her.'

'She did?'

'Why would she not?'

'Perhaps she was jealous.'

'No, she always knew your father loved her best. She never doubted that, even when he was difficult to live with.'

'She told you he was?'

'She didn't need to tell me. I can see for myself. You only have to spend five minutes with Sidney to understand that he's not the saint everyone thinks he is.'

'I thought it was me.'

'We all know. We just let him think he's wonderful. He's not.'

'You don't think so?'

'He's a very good man. But we all have our flaws. And that's a good thing. Otherwise we'd be impossible.'

'I don't know, Aunt Trudi. My dad's not bad at being impossible.'

Sidney knew that he had to be brave in front of his daughter but everything he did or thought reminded him of his wife.

Cecilia Richards came from Cambridge with a cottage pie. Trudi said they were coping, they didn't need any more food, they could manage perfectly well, she and Miss Morgan were sorting everything out between them, but Cecilia insisted that Sidney would want to talk to someone who had also experienced sudden death.

She had lost her beloved over ten years ago – murdered by mistake, they had meant to kill someone else – and she had been left on her own with a young child: Charlie. He had been six years old at the time.

If Sidney wanted to talk to someone who had already been through it all, then Cecilia said that she would be happy to listen. People were very kind at first, she said, very sweet, but they couldn't ever understand and then they had to get back to their normal lives. They returned to that everyday place where the bereaved were no longer welcome. It wasn't their fault, she said, it wasn't anyone's, but somehow the grief-stricken were no longer allowed in. They could never be normal again.

Her husband, Orlando, had arranged all the music at Sidney and Hildegard's wedding. Now she offered suggestions, if Sidney wanted, for the funeral. Bach obviously – '*O Welt, ich muss dich lassen*', 'O world, I now must leave thee' – Mozart probably, or a bit of Brahms, such as 'How lovely are thy dwellings'. There was even a seventeenth-century German song by Paul Fleming: '*An Anna aus der Ferne*' – 'To Anna from afar'.

'I think that might be a bit much.'

'There's no such thing as too much grief, Sidney.'

'But we have to continue with our lives. Hildegard would have wanted that. Although sometimes I can hear her telling me off, complaining that we never gave her this much attention when she was alive.'

'I still talk to Orlando. I imagine him by my side.'

'How is Charlie?'

'Seventeen now. Taller than you. He's in his last year at school. He wants to be a cricketer but he still keeps up with his music. Do you remember how, at Orlando's funeral, someone had given him a set of comedy beards and moustaches and he couldn't stop putting them on, pretending to be different guests each time? He kept going up to people and interrupting their conversations. I told him to stop but now it's the only thing anyone remembers about the funeral; a little six-year-old boy and his moustaches. You have to let your children find their own way of grieving and then, amazingly, I can never quite believe how, they recover more quickly than you do; or at least they find a better way of not showing it.'

After her husband's death Cecilia said that she had been to see a bereavement counsellor who had told her to concentrate on three words: tears, talk and time. They had read the *Book of Lamentations* together. There was, she said, a liturgy of grief, and that repetition was a form of cure. Sidney shouldn't feel guilty if he wanted to go over everything that had happened again and again. She would be happy to listen at any time.

He asked if she wanted to stay for supper but Cecilia said no, she really had to be getting back, and she shouldn't intrude – what would his sister-in-law say?

'I don't think you need to worry about her.'

'It must be hard.'

'She's very different to Hildegard. I think we're having some ham and potatoes with red cabbage. Anna is staying the night with her friend Sophie. I might suggest we try some of your cottage pie instead.'

'And leave the ham? That's not going to go down well.'

'I can have it at lunchtime tomorrow. I've stopped minding what people think because I no longer seem to have any opinion on anything at all. But I'd like something hot. I feel so cold all the time. Do you think it's grief?'

And so, that evening, Trudi heated up the cottage pie and her brother-in-law checked as he started to eat to see if it contained baked beans. It had been the start of a stupid argument several years ago when he had offered to make Hildegard a Monday-night dinner and he had added baked beans to the filling (as his mother always did because it pleased them all and bulked out the meat for the five of them). But his wife said the base was too liquid and that it tasted 'all wrong'. Why couldn't Sidney follow the recipe she had left? Then he had lost his temper and said that if all his wife could find to complain about was the fact that he had added baked beans to a cottage pie there couldn't be much wrong with him and then she had shouted back that this was only the beginning of all the things that were wrong with their marriage, the tiniest tip of an enormous iceberg of Sidney's faults, and they had gone on, arguing and arguing, until Hildegard had suddenly burst out laughing at the ridiculousness of what they were both saying.

'Which other couple,' she had said, 'argues so much about baked beans?'

Now he missed even that. But he could not fall apart. He decided to seek out Geordie and have a drink with him, even if talking to his friend made him collapse all the more.

It was a bloody bugger of a thing, Geordie said, but Sidney noticed how tactfully he avoided talking about God or fate. He had thought Cathy might have been the first to go, what with the cancer and everything, but she was on the mend, she'd had another check-up, it was all clear, yet now this had happened it proved that you couldn't predict anything at all. Fate was like a dark cloud or a wolf in the road; there was always something waiting to get you if you ever relaxed and thought you had the business of life under control.

A wolf in the road? Sidney wondered if he had heard his friend correctly, and tried to picture death as a predator; not Father Time, but a beast with yellow eyes emerging suddenly out of a forest.

'Are you listening to me?' Geordie asked. 'It doesn't matter if you're not. I'll keep prattling. You just let me know if you want anything.'

'I don't know what I want. Or I do, but it's the one thing I can't have. I don't know whether I'll ever stop wanting her or if this feeling will ever go away.'

'It doesn't have to go away. You will have to learn to live with it. I don't know. I can't imagine. But I can get you involved in a case to distract you when you're ready. After the funeral, of course.'

'Do you have something in mind?'

'I've got plenty of things on the go. And with you around, Sidney, there's always the unexpected.'

'It's just that neither of us ever thought the unexpected would turn out to be this.'

Sidney let Anna choose the coffin: light oak veneer, brass handles, a nameplate.

As well as her letter, she put in her book of pressed wild flowers and a photograph from her fifth birthday with her mother clapping her hands and laughing as her daughter blew out the candles on the cake. They decided on the flowers together; a wreath of white lilies for the coffin, and a posy of violets, freesias and gypsophila for Anna to hold.

It was All Souls' Day. Sidney wanted to have the funeral in the Lady Chapel but the dean promised there would be too many people for that. Hildegard had been greatly loved. There were all her piano pupils, their parents, the cathedral congregation, the musical community, people from Germany. It had to be held in the nave.

Sidney didn't think they needed a car and asked for the coffin to rest in front of the altar, raised high, with standing candles on either side, already in place as the congregation arrived. They came just before eleven thirty in the morning, in dark suits and winter coats, protecting themselves against the wind and rain outside and the first autumn chill within.

Sidney sat on the end of the front row, with Anna by his side, then Trudi, his parents, his sister Jennifer, Johnny, Louis and Dan, his brother Matt with yet another new girlfriend (Roxy?), and then behind them were Geordie and Cathy, Amanda, Leonard and Simon, Helena Mitchell – Malcolm was taking part in the service – and Cecilia Richards. Sidney had not checked if Rolfe von Arnim was there and thought briefly about how he would greet him afterwards but told himself very firmly not to consider such a thing now. His job was to look after Anna. He took her left hand as she clutched the special posy of violets in her right.

The dean stood under the great Octagon and announced that people were here today to express their sorrow, proclaim their faith, and give thanks for all they had received through the life of this, their friend, the dearly departed, whom they had known and loved from the very first time they had met her.

It was the same welcome Sidney had given so many times on behalf of others and the words were harder to receive than they ever had been to say.

'O God, Lord of life and conqueror of death, our help in every time of trouble, comfort us who mourn, and give us grace, in the presence of death, to worship you, that we may have sure hope of eternal life and be enabled to put our whole trust in your goodness and mercy; through Jesus Christ our Lord. Amen.'

The opening sentences from the *Book of Lamentations* seemed irredeemably bleak, but Sidney knew that his wife would have wanted the darkness as much as the light, the old language, the tough heart of faith. He remembered Cecilia's words: tears, talk and time.

The choir sang the ninetieth psalm, 'Lord, thou hast been our dwelling place in all generations', with the resonant admonitory line: 'The days of our years are threescore years and ten; and if by reason of strength they be fourscore years, yet is their strength labour and sorrow; for it is soon cut off, and we fly away.'

Threescore years and ten. Hildegard had not even made it to fifty-four.

Jennifer read from 1 Corinthians 13, the choir sang '*O Welt, ich muss dich lassen*' and Purcell's 'Evening Hymn', and Malcolm took the prayers.

Leonard then gave the address, just as he had done at Sidney and Hildegard's wedding. He remembered first meeting Hildegard, the welcome she had given him, and recalled how difficult it had been for her in Cambridge after the war.

He did not shy away from mentioning the death of her first husband, the suffering and sorrow that had followed, and the miraculous grace that came after her union with Sidney. Their wedding had been almost fifteen years ago, it had taken place on a glorious autumn afternoon and he had quoted Blake at the time: 'I give you the end of a golden string. Only wind it into a ball. It will lead you in at heaven's gate. Built in Jerusalem's wall.'

He was convinced that Sidney and Hildegard still had that golden thread between them and that it could not be cut by death. Their love had made it unbreakable, and Anna was testament to that love. Anna was Hildegard's gift to the world. Her continuation. The pearl on the golden string.

He asked the congregation to thank God for all that he had given them through his love, and to pray now, especially, for Hildegard; for her loyalties, her affection and her example. He suggested that they remember her whenever they heard the music of Bach or thought about things that made them laugh with delight, for she was a woman who, despite suffering and tragedy, was determined to make the best of things, wasting neither time nor life. If she had been taken too early then at least she had achieved so much while she lived, through her music, her family – here Leonard asked people to pray particularly for Anna – and her service to others.

After long labour there was rest, after toil there was peace. It was a life well spent and her reward was everlasting.

There were more prayers and a final blessing and the service finished, just as Sidney and Hildegard's marriage service had ended, with 'Now Thank We All Our God' to the tune of '*Nun danket*'.

The committal took place in the burial ground outside the North Transept. The rain had eased slightly by the time the little family party emerged from the cathedral but the wind was still up. The undertakers removed the flowers from the top of the coffin and laid them by the side of the grave. Then they took up the cords with Sidney, Geordie, Leonard and Malcolm, and together they lowered the body into the grave.

The dean led the mourners:

'Hildegard has fallen asleep in the peace of Christ.
We commit her, with faith and hope in everlasting
life, to the loving mercy of our Father
And assist her with our prayers . . .'

Anna was given a special linen bag of soil. She threw the earth down onto the wooden coffin.

'Eternal rest, grant to her, O Lord,' said the dean.

To which the mourners all replied: 'And let perpetual light shine upon her.'

The dean continued: 'May her soul and the souls of the faithful departed through the mercy of God rest in peace.'

And then, at last, came the final 'Amen'.

It was over. Anna held on to her posy for a moment longer, then knelt down and dropped it into the darkness below.

The rain started up once more.

They held the wake at Canonry House. Amanda had provided champagne and canapés to celebrate Hildegard's life rather than mourn her death (she was solvent again, even rich, now that her inheritance had come through) and she was acting as the principal hostess, much to Miss Morgan's disapproval. This was made manifest by the determined way in which an alternative option of tea and sandwiches was offered.

Sidney could not worry about all this. His mother sat in a chair, her memory already fading, wearing a black dress that had once been useful for cocktail parties but now only did for funerals. Alec Chambers began conversations with strangers, trying his best to be interested in what they were saying but gave up around the fourth sentence, unable to concentrate on anything other than his daughter-in-law's death. Anna stuck with Sophie, disappearing upstairs, returning only to get more food and, it seemed from their behaviour, alcohol. Well, if they got drunk, Sidney thought, how could he blame them?

There were other conversations, repeated consolations: *all such a shock, who could have foretold it, so young, such a lovely woman, I wish I'd gone to one of her concerts, there was so much I still wanted to talk to her about, poor little Anna – although she's not so little now, is she – will you be all right do you think, is there anything I can do?*

The only person who didn't, couldn't and wouldn't speak to Sidney in a similar fashion was Rolfe von Arnim. But it was impossible to ignore him. He was wearing a trim dark suit, white shirt and a black tie and in his buttonhole was a pale-yellow rose and a cluster of red berries. He must have made it himself. It reminded Sidney of the sweet peas he had once given Hildegard and that made him angry all over again, and even more furious that he couldn't show it: not now, not on this day.

'I thought perhaps I shouldn't have come,' said Rolfe. 'I hope you don't mind. I wanted to say goodbye.'

'You are as welcome as anyone else.'

'I didn't think you'd want me.'

This is not about you, Sidney wanted to say, but retained his politeness. 'Hildegard was very fond of you.'

'She was such an inspiration.'

'She was to so many people.'

'But especially to me. As a musician.'

'*Und auch als Deutscher!*' Trudi interrupted, taking Rolfe by the arm and leading him far, far, away. '*Erzählen Sie mir doch bitte alles über meine Schwester. Ich habe sie in den letzen Jahren so wenig gesehen. Wir haben bestimmt sehr viel zu besprechen.*'

She had all of Hildegard's tact and directness. For the first time, Sidney thanked God she had come.

He went upstairs. He needed to go to the bathroom and then compose himself in his bedroom for a few moments – the crowd, the heat, the tension of the day. He was getting a headache, the first since his wife had died, and he thought then of the pain that had killed her, the swiftness of the attack. What if he were to die now too? He really wouldn't mind.

As he came back out onto the landing he could hear Miss Morgan arguing with Amanda in the kitchen: Hildegard's kitchen.

'You are not the hostess,' his volunteer housekeeper was saying, 'and you shouldn't pretend that you are.'

'I'm not pretending to be anything.'

'It's embarrassing. Your presence here, Mrs Richardson, is not helping matters.'

'Do you mean in the kitchen or with Sidney? I think I know what is helpful and what is not.'

There was a clatter of teacups, washing-up probably, and then Miss Morgan's not-so-subtle mutter: 'You have never been any good for him.'

'How dare you say that? Sidney is my best friend.'

'And how dare you dishonour his wife's memory by showing off like this? Shame on you.'

Amanda began to leave but Anna stopped her in the doorway. 'Don't.'

Then she turned to Miss Morgan. 'I know you are trying to help but please don't speak to my godmother like that. She is my friend too.'

'I'm sorry,' Miss Morgan replied. 'I didn't mean it. I was defending your mother.'

'She doesn't need defending. Everyone loved her.'

Sidney leant against the wall to steady himself. He closed his eyes and wondered if he might faint. Then he could fall down the stairs. Perhaps he might even kill himself. That, too, would be a good thing.

He heard his daughter coming up the stairs and felt her arm supporting him. 'What's wrong, Dad?'

He stopped, uncertain for a moment where he was or what he had done, guilty about his thoughts, his momentary desire for death.

'You sound just like her,' he said.

After everyone had gone home, Sidney and Anna returned to 'normal life', whatever that meant: school and the cathedral, home, work and holidays. Sidney thought of his soon-to-be teenage daughter and his responsibility over the next years as she tried to work out whether the woman she was becoming was the woman she actually wanted to be.

Anna tried her best to hide her grief in front of her father but it manifested itself in other ways, in an increasing lack of confidence, sometimes in silence and withdrawal, at other times in defensive attack. It was a quiet resentment that, although combative, was also fragile, as if she was pushing at the limits both of Sidney's patience and her own self-confidence.

I don't want any supper. My bedroom's tidy enough. I don't need to put anything away. There isn't any washing-up in there. I like taking my socks off. I'll pick them up later. I don't have to do my geography. It's not due until next Tuesday. Why are you always having a go at me?

There was the vegetarianism and the failure to recognise the connection between food intake and skin condition (a diet that seemed to consist entirely of tomato soup, peanut butter, white bread and Sugar Puffs was hardly going to help). Then there was the way Anna let her hair fall over face, her refusal to tuck in her school blouse, her strange attitude to personal hygiene – especially teeth cleaning – and her belief that walking around in boots with untied shoelaces was fashionable.

How had his little girl, once so eager to gather wild flowers, paint and draw and dance and roll down hills, turned into this?

In the past he had been expressly told by his wife not to comment on or react to any of his daughter's provocations but to let her 'find her own way'. It was important to know Anna's secrets but not to let on that they knew, to allow her the privacy of secret rebellion. That was all very well, but how was he going to manage this on his own? He could hardly bear to talk to his daughter about sex and boyfriends and he wondered who might do that. Sophie's mother? Her doctor? His sister? Jennifer was the safest option, but she didn't have Hildegard's ability to combine rigorous discipline with a sudden ability to let go, to throw it all away and abandon herself to the joy of the present moment.

He realised how much his wife had done and how she had protected him from the grind of everyday life; although how had she been able to do all this and teach and play the piano was something of a miracle, especially when Sidney had spent so much time away from her. She had once referred to his parenting as 'the night shift'.

The greatest mystery was why God had allowed her to die; and how could Sidney live without the presence of someone he was used to speaking to every day? There was no piano, no singing, no conversation, no laughter, no admonition, no argument.

Even the silence was different. It was no longer companionable, bordered by the possibility of interruption, but a void without meaning. He was used to the silence of prayer, but that wasn't the same thing at all. It included the meditative, a sense of apprehension, a spirit of waiting, but there was no point waiting for a dead wife.

Now he resented every minute that he had left her or wanted to be on his own or thought that he had better things to do. Why couldn't he have listened to her and why could he not remember more? Perhaps he could go away somewhere and dwell in her memory, letting the moments come to him, recovering his past and healing his future?

He wondered, even, if he should give up being a priest. He remembered a bombed-out chapel in Italy, in wartime, when he had thought that he could not bear any more suffering. He had reached the limit of what a human soul could take and he had stopped everything and thrown himself before the ruined altar and asked for mercy. Then faith had somehow, he didn't know how, returned to his soul, filling him with grace, giving him light and hope. Now he felt one great emptying, as if even the blood in his body was evaporating, his bones collapsing. How much longer would he be able to go on walking or stand upright? There was nothing to support or sustain him any more apart from his daughter. That, at least, was one thing he still knew he could not give up on. He might be able to give up on his faith, but he couldn't abandon her.

He went to see the dean and they sat drinking whisky until Sidney wanted to close his eyes and fall asleep. Felix Carpenter spoke slowly and kindly (they, too, had their silences) and told him that sometimes you only see the light when you look up from the bottom of the well.

'I don't know if I can do that, Felix. Sometimes my head is so heavy I can hardly lift it. I know that sounds pathetic.'

'If it is what you feel, how can it be pathetic?'

Sidney could not give up on faith because, like the light, it always came back from the night. It refused to give up on him.

'Remember the vows you took at your ordination,' said Felix. 'You have been called and chosen and invested in the tradition of the laying-on of hands and the invocation of the Holy Ghost for the office and work of a priest in the Church of God. You have to persist.'

Sidney had once said the same thing to Leonard.

'Our life is a testing ground, Sidney; we all walk in the valley of the shadow of death. Now you have been tested and asked to come back out into the light.'

'I think I was prepared for anything but this.'

'We are all cut flowers,' said the dean.

Amanda drove up from London and took him down to Grantchester. She wanted to return to the place that he had always gone for respite when he was a vicar; a hillside view just off the Roman Road for Wandlebury Ring and the Iron Age forts of the Gog Magog Hills.

That's what you sometimes had to do when you were unhappy, she said; go back to the place in your past when you were happiest.

It was Armistice Day. Sidney had kept the eleven o'clock silence that morning and remembered those who had lost their lives in war, dying far younger than either he or Hildegard. It made him feel guilty that he had not been more grateful for the joys he had known rather than sorrowful for the love he had lost.

They left Byron at home, since he was too old for long walks (he would surely be the next to go), and parked in a lay-by off the main road, allowing room for movement through a five-bar gate. They then made their way up a familiar muddy track scattered with gatherings of water that would freeze that night. Fieldfares and redwings circled in the sky. Already there was a mist in the lower field. It would be dark by a quarter past four. They wouldn't have long.

They talked about all that had happened and how, when they had first come to this place, they couldn't possibly have imagined that their lives would turn out this way. Amanda had broken off her engagement to Guy Hopkins, Sidney had hardly met Hildegard, and now here they were, both widowed and still in their fifties.

'I'm sorry about the wake,' Amanda said.

'What do you mean?'

'The argument in the kitchen with Miss Morgan.'

'Oh, that doesn't matter.'

'It reminded me of Mrs Maguire all over again. She's very proprietorial.'

'It's good to have someone on hand.'

'But you don't even like her!'

'I am grateful for her support.'

'Anna was very kind. You had a funny turn. Was it the stress of the day?'

'Probably. I don't know, Amanda. The day passed in a daze. I could have fainted at any moment.'

'I was worried that you were going to fall down the stairs.'

'I think I wanted to.'

They walked on, the only sound coming from the voles, shrews and mice in the hedgerows and a squadron of jackdaws crying out in greeting and alarm, wheeling above them.

It was the kind of companionable silence that Sidney had almost forgotten, and then he said, idly, without really thinking what he was saying (perhaps it was just for something to say): 'It's odd, isn't it?'

'What?'

'They have them in comedies . . .'

'What?'

'Falling downstairs, the pratfall, the big farcical moment, and yet in real life people can die as a result. How do actors signal that it's funny?'

'I suppose it depends what comes before and after.'

'Like life.'

'No sermons, Sidney.'

'At the moment, Amanda, I don't know if I can ever preach again.'

'Don't say that.'

They approached a couple of male pheasants, past their moult and in feathered prime, pecking at the remains of some long-scattered seed and then abruptly taking off. Guns from a shooting party sounded in the distance. It was hard to tell if the birds, prey only to the perils of chance, were flying into their path or not.

'Have they given you some time off?' Amanda asked.

'As long as I need. They don't really mean that, of course.'

'And what will you do?'

'I don't know. The important thing is to spend some time with Anna.'

'If you need my help . . .'

'It probably has to be the two of us.'

'I meant money. If you want to go away. It must be terrible.'

'It is.'

Sidney did not know what more he could say. He felt guilty now about being out and about with another woman, a guilt he would never have felt when his wife was alive.

'I'm not sure whether I should tell you this . . .' Amanda began.

'You've started.'

'Hildegard once asked me to look after you.'

'Why? When?'

'She said that she never worried too much because if anything ever happened to her, you would always have me. I told her that it was different, that we were different, but she said it didn't matter. She knew that you would be all right.'

'But I'm not all right.'

'That's what I told her.'

'What did you say?'

'That you would be lost without her.'

'Well, here I am: lost.'

A three-quarter moon had appeared in the sky. Soon it would be dark. They turned and headed back to the car and then, just before they reached the lay-by, Amanda said she had an idea. Why didn't Sidney and Anna take a short trip to Germany, father and daughter, just the two of them? They could go to Leipzig, perhaps, and Anna could see where her mother had been brought up, imagine the kind of life she had led and visit her grandmother. If he got on with it, they might even be able to see the Christmas markets. She was sure Anna would like that.

'I don't know. It would be quite an undertaking.'

'When else would you do it? Take her away from Ely. Get her out of the house and its memories.'

'I don't know if she would want to come.'

'She will if you make it all about her and her mother.'

Sidney thought about those times when he had visited Hildegard before they had married: in Berlin, in Hamburg, to see St Michael's Church and the Trostbrücke, and Koblenz where they had taken a boat to Boppard and cruised through the Rhine Gorge to Rüdesheim. He remembered the Christmas markets in both East and West and how, when he and Hildegard had first started out in their marriage, and had so little money, they had given each other presents by rewrapping possessions they already had but had forgotten about.

Would Germany still be Germany without her? He couldn't imagine it.

Amanda repeated that she would pay. 'But let Anna decide.'

'I'm sometimes amazed she's my daughter. I can't understand how we can exist together, how we talk or what we do or how I've had anything to do with her at all. Sometimes she's an indelible part of me, at other times she's a stranger. I don't know what to make of her; and I am pretty sure she doesn't know what to make of me either. When I'm at my lowest I think she would have preferred it if I was the one that had died.'

'That's nonsense.'

'I don't know. She was probably expecting it more than the death of her mother.'

'She wouldn't have wanted either of you to die. You're being ridiculous, Sidney.'

'I just don't know her, Amanda.'

'Then that's why you need to go to Germany.'

Father and daughter flew to West Berlin and then, after over an hour at the border checking visas and passports (Sidney hoped that there wouldn't be any paperwork that reminded the authorities of his brief arrest after a misunderstanding in

1961; he had never told Anna about it – perhaps now was the time?), they took the train to Leipzig and booked into two single rooms at the state-owned Hotel Deutschland on Augustusplatz.

Anna was unusually quiet once they had crossed into the GDR, taking in the change from West to East, the increasing numbers of soldiers and patrols, the political banners hanging from the public buildings and the murals glorifying the achievements of the workers under socialism. *FÜR VOR-BILDLICHE LEISTUNGEN: Beste Einheit.*

She was surprised by the industrial nature of the landscape, the chimneys that churned fumes up into a sky already filled with thick mist, heavy rain and fine dust from the carbo-chemical factories lining the railway track. In the distance, cranes lifted steel girders and prefabricated panels for functional apartment blocks that now replaced some of the finest architecture in Europe.

Sidney was determined that the trip should suit his daughter rather than himself and they confined their ecclesiastical tourism to two churches: St Thomas's, where Bach had been cantor, and St Nicholas's, which had a lively pastor prepared to share services with Catholics, knowing that the only chance of Christian survival in an atheist state was to unite.

They began with a visit to Hildegard's mother in her worker's apartment in Konradstraße. She was now in her late eighties and was distressed that she had lost a daughter before her time – why hadn't God taken her instead? She would have been happy to go in Hildegard's place, she was ready enough – but she was glad to see Anna. She was so like Hildegard.

332

'*Wie die Mutter so die Tochter.*'

Sibilla Leber cradled her granddaughter's face: '*Du siehst wie ich aus! Oh, um wieder jung zu sein . . .*'

She reiterated her socialist principles and hoped Anna would come to Leipzig to perfect her German and study at the university. It was the best place to build a well-developed personality, with excellent mental, physical and moral qualities and a class outlook rooted in the Marxist-Leninist world view. Only in the East could her granddaughter imbue herself with collective thoughts and actively contribute to the shaping of socialism. It was important, she said, to continue the family values of *Glaube, Pflicht, Familie, Freundschaft und Freiheit vor allem*: faith, duty, family, friendship and freedom above all.

Was Anna a good Christian?

Anna said that she hoped she was.

And a good socialist?

She wasn't so sure about that.

'*Je stärker der Sozialismus, desto sicherer der Frieden,*' Sibilla Leber concluded. There was little point debating the matter.

They spent the next few days seeing Hildegard's childhood home in Gustav-Mahlerstraße and her school in Manetstraße. Anna sat on a bench in the park by the Lutherkirche and rode on the carousel at the small fair where her mother had played as a child. At one point they passed Runde Ecke, the Stasi headquarters, but Sidney decided not yet to tell his daughter how he had been imprisoned there. Who knows, he thought, the *Volkspolizei* could even be following them.

Instead they walked round the modern university and then, just outside the Rathaus, they found the spot where Hildegard's father had been shot by the Nazis. There was a memorial to him on the wall, accompanied by an inverted red triangle.

Hans Leber
Märtyrer: Held
7.4.1933
Es lebe der Kommunismus!

'Long live communism,' Anna translated. 'To think Mum carried so much of that past in her memory. She never even talked about it.'

'It was often hard to tell what went on in your mother's head.'

'But you knew, didn't you, Dad?'

'Not all the time. She liked to keep some things back. I think she hoped that there was a part of her I'd always be scared of.'

'And were you?'

'I was terrified.'

On their last evening, as they were walking through the Christmas market, and just as Sidney was about to launch into a bemused discussion of the non-Christian nature of the decorations on sale (folk figures, snowmen and festive workers), Anna asked: 'Do you think you'll ever marry again, Dad?'

'I don't think so.'

'Not even Amanda? One day you might.'

Sidney snapped into concentration. 'Amanda is divorced. I can't marry a divorcee.'

'What if you gave up being a priest?'

'I can't do that.'

'But if you loved her, you could. Leonard stopped.'

'He's different.'

'But the principle is the same.'

Anna had begun to pursue subjects with the same determination as her mother. Her father didn't know whether to be proud or annoyed.

'I really don't think that situation will arise,' he continued. 'Is there anything you want to take home with you?' He picked up some little wooden figures of children going to school in their best winter coats and bobble hats. 'These are nice, don't you think?'

His daughter said nothing but waited until he looked at her.

'I have no plans to marry again, Anna.'

'Then promise me that you won't.'

'I don't think that's fair.'

'Why not?'

'What if you get married yourself, Anna, and I live to be a hundred and I'm left on my own? You don't want to be looking after me when you've got a husband and children.'

'I will. I'll look after you for ever, Dad.'

Why this new kindness? Sidney wondered. This is what his daughter could do to him. In the midst of her infuriating refusal to leave a subject alone, she could open his heart and let it bleed with love.

'That's very kind. And I will love you for ever, too.'

'As much as you loved Mum?'

And there she was, back on the attack again. Why couldn't she just let it go?

'Yes,' said Sidney, 'as much as I loved your mother.'

'And no one else?'

'No one else.'

'You promise?'

'I promise that I will never love anyone as I loved Hildegard.'

'That's not enough.'

'It is, Anna. I can't predict what is going to happen to either of us. We know that nothing will ever be the same again. But don't hold me to ransom. I loved your mother more than anyone. And then you came along. And I loved the two of you more than anyone. That is all I can do and all I will ever do.'

'You can promise me that?'

'Yes, I can easily promise you that. Now, what about some supper?'

He took his daughter into an arcade and downstairs into a basement restaurant, hoping that a difference in location would lead to a change of subject.

'You know what they say? "If you haven't been to Auerbach's Keller then you haven't been to Leipzig." I just hope the food's all right.'

The restaurant was filled with locals drinking wine and Nordhäuser Doppelkorn as waiters dressed in red waistcoats explained what was off and what was on the menu. Anna's vegetarianism was surely going to cause a few problems in a land of stout meat-eating, but she finally found her way towards a cream of mushroom soup followed by a vegetable stew with peas, carrots and dumplings. Sidney conformed to local expectations with jellied meat followed by medallions of pork, beef and lamb served up with savoy cabbage.

He noticed that the restaurant also offered *Leipziger Lerche* and wondered if his daughter would mention it. When the waitress came – brusque and determined not to be overawed by bourgeois Westerners – Anna ordered in German and asked for a dollop of cream. Sidney said he would have the same and they wondered out loud if they could be 'as good as Mum's'.

'They might even be better,' he added.

'Don't say that!'

'She can't hear us.'

'Perhaps she can? It's funny. I've never seen the words written down. I always thought they were spelled with an "s". Mum always used to say "Lersche", the same way people here pronounce the town "Leipshig".'

'It's the Saxon accent. Your mother prided herself on her Hochdeutsch but there were a few words that always gave away where she came from. She never forgot her roots.'

'Then I'm glad we've tried to find them.'

When the cakes arrived, warm on a plate and accompanied by extraordinarily expensive coffee (the country was in the middle of a shortage), Anna was surprised to discover a cherry at the bottom of each one.

'That's weird.'

'Your mother always preferred apricots. You know that when they were first made they were filled with meat? In fact, they were made with larks and roasted with herbs and eggs.'

'The birds?'

'Hildegard said there used to be thousands of larks in Leipzig but the practice of killing them was outlawed in the nineteenth century. The cherry is supposed to represent the heart of the bird, but your mother couldn't bear to think of that. She loved they way they sang in high summer. So she used apricots instead.'

'She never told me.'

'I think she imagined that, with you being a vegetarian, it might put you off.'

'No, it makes me approve of them all the more. These are good. I like the glazed topping but I still prefer Mum's.'

'She'd be glad. To be better than a Leipzig baker . . .'

'I do like to think she can hear us, Dad.'

'Then I'm sure she'd approve of our conversation.'

'I find it comforting to think of her watching over us.'

She finished her plate and smiled at her father. It was the first sign of cheerfulness since her mother's death. Sidney didn't know what to do or say. He realised that he could not predict his daughter's behaviour at all.

'Thank you for bringing me here,' she said. 'I feel I know her better now.'

When they returned home, Sidney noticed that one of the letters in the Christmas post had come from 10 Downing Street. What on earth could the prime minister want – apart from to wish him a happy Christmas? Surely James Callaghan couldn't have written to every clergyman in the country? He wasn't that desperate for votes.

He opened the envelope and discovered that he had been offered a new job. The Queen would be honoured, the letter

338

said, if Sidney were to accept a position as the next Bishop of Peterborough.

Was this supposed to be some kind of silver lining in his cloud of despair? Why him? And why now?

He went to see the dean. It was five o'clock in the afternoon and just after evensong. The anthem had been 'If ye love me, keep my commandments'.

'Did you know about this?' Sidney asked.

'The archbishop did mention it.'

'And are you responsible?'

'I may have put in a word.'

'Why?'

'We all think you'd make a fine bishop, Sidney. And, who knows, you might even enjoy it.'

'But all that responsibility! I'm not sure I'm up to it.'

'If you thought you were born for the role you probably wouldn't be very good at doing it.'

'It means being in the public eye all the time.'

'I thought you didn't mind a bit of attention? Keeping a low profile, Sidney, has never been one of your strong points.'

'But this is different. Being a bishop is like being in some kind of Gilbert and Sullivan operetta.'

'And you don't think you're in one already?'

'Seriously, Felix. I've seen what happens to clergy who climb the greasy pole. They are so used to preaching and making speeches that they become pompous without noticing. Their voices get louder; as does their laughter. They seek to dominate rooms. They exist solely on a diet of Coronation chicken and buffet suppers. I can't believe that God is calling me to do this.'

'You've always thought that you were a better detective than a priest. Now's your chance to prove the opposite.'

'I'd have to give up on the detection.'

'You would. And that might be a good thing. We all think you've done your bit. Think of the episcopate as a replacement for all that drama.'

'As I think I've made clear, Felix, I don't need anything dramatic.'

'I rather think you do, Sidney. Remember that for all our faith and ceremony we are only a hop, skip and a jump away from the theatre. You'd have a staff, cope and mitre, even a rather impressive amethyst ring.'

'I'm not convinced.'

'And there'd be plenty of support: a chaplain, a secretary, a chauffeur. The Bishop's Palace is rather fine . . .'

'I sometimes think that the higher up the Church of England you go the further you get from Jesus . . .'

'. . . Victorian Gothic, but some of the old abbot's house from the thirteenth century survives, if I recall correctly: a lovely undercroft, decorated columns, a good garden. It even has its own "heaven chamber" with rather fine vaulting. You could be there in time for the Queen's Silver Jubilee celebrations. They have great plans, I gather. Lunch in the Bishop's Palace, perhaps. That would be nice for Anna.'

'She'd miss her friends.'

'You could keep her at school in Ely for the time being. And you'd have more money – seven or eight thousand a year.'

'Anyone would think you were trying to get rid of me.'

'Nonsense. I only want you to make use of your talents. A man needs to be stretched.'

'I'd have to ask Anna.'

'She won't be keen, but children are resilient.'

'She's got her O levels soon enough. I don't like to think of her moving school.'

'She could board.'

'I don't want to be apart from her.'

'But maybe she needs to be apart from you. Find her own way in life.'

'I know. Eventually.'

'You have to let them go, Sidney.'

'It's too soon.'

'It's always too soon.'

'Do you think people would expect me to marry again?'

'Not soon. And probably not a divorcee.'

'I wasn't thinking of that. I was thinking how impossible it would be to live with anyone other than Hildegard.'

Without asking, the dean poured out a couple of stiff whiskies. 'You know, Sidney, when I was seeing the archbishop at Lambeth to talk about all of this, I had to wait outside his study for a little while. He was seeing some Orthodox patriarch. So I took some time to look at the paintings of the previous incumbents in the Great Hall. There are whole corridors of them leading to the guard room and the chapel.

'I particularly liked the one of Tait. His portrait is almost full length, and it's the saddest I have ever seen. He was the first Scottish archbishop. It was 1868. Earlier in his life, when he moved from Carlisle to be Bishop of London, they asked him to do so in the same year that he lost all five of his daughters to scarlet fever: five children in five weeks. And yet he thanked God for the blessings they had brought him over the previous ten years and for all the sweet memories of their little lives. His face has such pain; but it also shows compassion.

'I think that if I ever felt bereft, or that life was impossible, he's the man I'd most like to talk to. I know he would understand without ever having to say very much. And yet he must have wondered if he could do the job or if life would be the same after all that suffering. He lost his wife and son too. Apart from his sister, he was quite alone when he died; and yet he was a great archbishop, a bringer of people together, a pacifier. When he went back to his old school for a prize-giving or some such ceremony, he told the boys: "I hope and believe that you are going forth into life, not to seek the applause which depends on the fleeting breath of your fellow-men, nor that success which ends only in this life, but that you will remember that another Eye besides that of man is upon you, and that a higher approbation is to be won than that of your fellow-creatures."'

'We have to be more than ourselves.'

'Will you think about it, Sidney? Promise me that.'

'I'll try. And will you pray for me, Felix?'

'I do so every day.'

Sidney walked back to Canonry House wondering what on earth he was going to do, how he would talk to Anna and in what way their lives might change. There was a heaviness in the air, and yet, at the same time, the atmosphere was brittle and inconsistent. Soon it would rain.

He remembered Anna's birth. How quickly she had grown up and how much he had missed. Would he neglect her even more if he became a bishop, or would he be able to devote more time to being both a priest and a father? He certainly couldn't do any more detective work. He would have to give that up anyway. It was ridiculous to keep on doing it and, in any case, Geordie would be retiring in a few more years and he couldn't work with anyone other than him. No one else would have the patience.

He would probably miss the drama, the search for justice and the need for solutions. The world of faith and doubt was more continually ambiguous; the quest for meaning more intellectually complex. He would also have to devote himself more wholeheartedly to a life of prayer and responsibility, both in the Church and in the home, and then he could use all that he had learned to comfort the afflicted, support the weak and further the common good.

The dean's words about Archbishop Tait had moved him very much. He should try now, once more, to lead as exemplary a life as he could, eschewing the heroic vanity of his criminal investigations. Other people could do that. That's what policemen were for. Let them do their jobs and Sidney could do his.

Well, at least it was one thing decided, he thought to himself, glad that he had avoided the forthcoming shower. No more investigation. He wouldn't have to worry about that kind of distraction. He would tell his daughter that he had given up on all that running round the country trying to solve impossible crimes. Now he would have more time for her. And then, after he had told her this, they would discuss

343

her schooling and her future. Only after he had done that would he raise the possibility of becoming a bishop.

He wondered if Anna might even like the idea, perhaps even be proud of him, but then he thought he could hear Hildegard's voice in his head counselling caution and humility.

'Be careful, *mein Lieber.*'

He was getting ahead of himself. He needed to rethink everything from Anna's point of view and present it as such.

He turned the corner into Infirmary Lane with a renewed sense of purpose. This was something to get on with, he decided. He would emerge from the shadow of his wife's death with a new sense of direction and he would lead a different life.

'No more criminal investigation,' he repeated to himself. 'That's enough.'

He saw a figure outside his front door, a man who had forgotten his umbrella, waiting with his mackintosh half over his head as the rain started. It was Geordie. 'Something's come up,' he said.

'What is it?'

'I need your help.'

'Haven't you got anyone else?'

'No, Sidney. You're the only man who can sort this out.'

'What is it?'

'Have you got time for a quick pint?'

A Note on the Author

James Runcie is an award-winning film-maker and the author of nine previous novels. *Sidney Chambers and The Persistence of Love* is the sixth book in 'The Grantchester Mysteries' series, which began in 2012 with *Sidney Chambers and The Shadow of Death*. In October 2014, ITV launched *Grantchester*, a prime-time series starring James Norton as Sidney Chambers. The second season aired in spring 2016, and the third in spring 2017. James Runcie is the Commissioning Editor for Arts at BBC Radio 4. He lives in London and Edinburgh.

www.jamesruncie.com
www.grantchestermysteries.com
@james_runcie

A Note on the Type

The text of this book is set in Baskerville, a typeface named after John Baskerville of Birmingham (1706–1775). The original punches cut by him still survive. His widow sold them to Beaumarchais, from where they passed through several French foundries to Deberney & Peignot in Paris, before finding their way to Cambridge University Press.

Baskerville was the first of the 'transitional romans' between the softer and rounder calligraphic Old Face and the 'Modern' sharp-tooled Bodoni. It does not look very different to the Old Faces, but the thick and thin strokes are more crisply defined and the serifs on lower-case letters are closer to the horizontal with the stress nearer the vertical. The R in some sizes has the eighteenth-century curled tail, the lower case w has no middle serif and the lower case g has an open tail and a curled ear.